To Barbara,
From
[signature]
May 2015

THE THIRTEENTH CHILD

David Dean

Genius
Book Publishing

Encino, California

D1452481

Published By:
Genius Book Publishing
PO Box 17752
Encino, CA 91416
www.GeniusBookPublishing.com

Follow us on Twitter: @GeniusBooks
Like us on Facebook: GeniusPublishing

ISBN: 978-0692212387

Second Edition

ACKNOWLEDGMENTS

With the birth of a novel, the author, at some point, gratefully becomes a small cog in the machinery of creation. If he is truly fortunate, he awakes one day to discover how many people had faith in his efforts and loyally contributed their own. I am one of the fortunate.

"The Thirteenth Child" was saved from an early grave (no pun intended) by the intervention of my publisher, the dedicated, hardworking, and I like to think, keenly astute, Steven W. Booth. This intervention may not have happened had his equally perspicacious wife, Leya, not recognized the potential of my novel as she labored at proofreading it in its earliest incarnation. Their continued faith is demonstrated in this much improved second edition. To both of these folks I remain terribly grateful.

Developmental editor Chris Westphal weighed in and taught me that there is some brutality required in the creative process, and that the reader, not the writer, is the most important person in the relationship of book, author, and audience. He also suggested the title of the book which I instantly adopted as my own. My original title was more of a short story.

Finally, I must pay homage to my own family who has been my very earliest supporters and critics. Tanya, Bridgid, and Julian have suffered through numerous readings and been both kind, and demanding, seldom settling for my "best" efforts, in spite of the fact that I am their dear and beloved father.

And, of course, there is Robin, my wife and companion of many, many years, the patron saint of all that is worthy in me, and the forgiving lover of all that isn't. Her faith has never wavered and I hope it never does.

THE
THIRTEENTH
CHILD

CHAPTER ONE

Megan Guthrie watched from the swing as the older girls, all giggles and whispers, swirled across the schoolyard like a flock of starlings. The few boys left in the playground slashed away at one another with sticks, shouting and laughing, the entire group drifting toward the lit widows of their homes. As the autumn darkness crept forth from the nearby woods, the arc of Megan's swing deteriorated with lack of attention, coming slowly to a standstill.

Hopping down from the rubber seat, she watched as the others broke into ever smaller groups, some girls now walking with boys as they headed for their respective houses. Megan had no idea why those girls should be interested in boys, who were always pushing and yelling.

Noticing the dust on her pink sneakers she knelt to brush them off so that she could see the white kittens imprinted on them, smiling at the bows on their heads. When she straightened up she saw a boy watching her from the wood line. Her mouth puckered in discomfort at being scrutinized, even as she stared back across the intervening distance.

In the graying twilight, she could see that he was a teenager, which did not so much surprise her, as she had overheard remarks from older kids in the playground about teenagers and their fondness for the woods. These types of remarks were always accompanied by the kind of laughter that made Megan feel stupid.

She did find it surprising that the boy was wearing a shirt much too small for him—a green tee shirt that was torn and stained. The rest of him was obscured by the vines and shrubs that grew in profusion right up to the short, chain-linked fence he stood behind. As evening settled over them, his partially exposed torso and face glowed whitely.

Raising a hand into the air, he held it there. Megan waved shyly back, then folding her hands together looked down at her shoes. She could no longer hear the other children and longed to turn and see where they might be, but the boy's hand arrested her like a warning—a hand that was much larger than her own father's, with fingers as long and thin as a crab's legs. Even the crickets that had been so loud moments before were now silent. Megan's small nose wrinkled at the cloying odor that crept across the damp grass like a fog. She studied the kitties in her discomfort, but they appeared very far away now.

Looking up once more, Megan found the boy on her side of the fence and scant yards away. She gasped, but he held up an impossibly long finger as if to silence her.

His large face was clearer to her now, and he was smiling, a panting half-smile that reminded her of her dog, Barclay, a big, happy Labrador retriever, always pleased to be in her company. Still he remained silent, as did the world around them; the musk that traveled with him cloaking Megan in a warm drowsiness.

She had never seen a boy, or anyone else for that matter, with such long arms and legs and she thought he looked like a large white spider, or perhaps a grasshopper. The blackened jeans he wore came half way down his stringy calves.

Then he was with her, and his face, its great eyes glistening with a color that reminded her of dragonfly wings, appeared before her own. The long thin arms, which he carried before him in the manner of a praying mantis, unfolded slowly toward her, the fingers spreading open like the clam rakes she had seen the local fishermen use. It was then she became afraid, a tiny moan escaping her lips.

❧

Preston Howard awoke and sat abruptly upright, his head throbbing with every pulse of his heart. Clasping one side of his skull with one hand, the other fluttered through the dry leaves in search of the bottle he knew must lie close. Seizing it at last, he grunted in satisfaction, sweeping off the cap with a practiced motion while bringing the bottle to his parched lips.

The whiskey spread through his guts in a warm, welcome gush and, like a vapor, rose up his spine to arrive at his clouded brain. Once there it swept away the pressure and confusion, and he found the world around him taking on bearable color, recognizable definition. It was much darker than when he had sat down to rest and refresh himself.

Squinting through his smarting, bloodshot eyes, he was able to conclude that he rested at the very edge of the elementary schoolyard.

Sweeping a hand through his long, unclean hair, he tossed the now-empty bottle onto the grass. As he struggled to regain his feet he noticed a boy, revealed as a silhouette cut as sharply as if with scissors—a black crepe figure some twenty yards distant.

The sun, sinking below the horizon, streaked the blue of the sky with fingers of crimson, its failing light clothing the field in shades of gray. Standing perfectly still, the boy appeared to be watching something intently. .

He leaned forward—was that a little girl standing there? The whole scene had an unearthly stillness about it, a sketching of something terrible about to happen.

Struggling to raise himself up, Preston felt suddenly alarmed. Using the tree he had passed out beneath, he pushed himself upwards by his long skinny legs, his worn tweed jacket sliding roughly up the bark. A flock of crows, hidden in the treetops, clucked and chuckled darkly to one another, then went silent once more.

As Preston gained his considerable height, the boy who had somehow closed the distance between the girl and himself with eye-blurring speed stopped, frozen in the act of reaching out for the child, and turned his great head to look at Preston. The boy was now staring at *him* and Preston froze too, his thick, dry tongue sticking to the roof of his mouth.

"Hey," he managed to gasp. "What are you doing there?" He flapped a hand helplessly at the two of them.

Even at a distance, the boy's utter stillness was uncanny and unnerving, especially now that Preston understood himself to be the target of his patient scrutiny. No child could be *that* still, he thought.

The girl dropped to the earth like a marionette whose strings had been cut and lay still, the boy poised over her body.

Pushing off from the tree, Preston stumbled a few feet in her direction, beads of sweat forming along his receding hairline. "Little girl," he slurred, "Are you hurt?"

The strange boy suddenly closed the distance that separated himself and Preston, arriving before him like a wind, his face mere inches from Preston's own. Preston caught a whiff of a cloying, musky odor and felt himself back-pedaling until once more his back was against the tree.

Appearing no more than fourteen, the boy was indifferent to Preston's startled scrutiny, studying the older man in his turn without the least appearance of self-consciousness. Beneath the patina of filth, Preston could see that the child's flesh was a sickly white, his hair a muddy brown, thick and wavy, strewn with leaves, twigs, and other debris from the forest floor.

It was the eyes, though, that arrested Preston's attention; the remarkable eyes, overly large and almond-shaped, quickening with any sudden movement made on Preston's behalf—canine, or feline, Preston couldn't decide, but hardly human. The mouth did nothing to dispel this animal impression, as it was impossibly wide, frog-like, the lower jaw hanging open in a parody of a smile.

The boy began to gently pant and Preston recoiled from his foul breath.

Though he tried to contain his horror at the child's unnaturally long limbs and digits, he was certain that his disgust must be evident. Yet, the boy appeared unaffected, composed; almost cheerful.

What kind of child was this? Had the mother and father of this boy kept him hidden away, he wondered? It seemed incredible that he had ever run amongst the children of Wessex County.

"Who are you, boy?" he asked. "Who are your parents?"

The boy appeared to consider these questions while plucking something that wriggled from the tangle of his hair. After studying his capture for a moment, he plopped it into his mouth, chewing it thoughtfully before allowing the crushed remains to slide off the end of a long, pointed, blood-red tongue.

Wincing at this casual and nauseating act, Preston managed to say, "Where do you live then? Do you live nearby?"

The boy examined his horny nails before sucking on the one that had pierced the devoured insect. After a moment, he lisped, "Nearby."

Preston observed the long, furred hand and felt faint. The feet were similarly covered in stiff hairs, and were too long and narrow. "Nearby?" he asked, "Where, nearby? Have you recently moved here?"

Ignoring the first half of his question, the boy answered the second. "I have always lived here," he said through his teeming, overly-long teeth. "I live here, yet."

"*Yet...*" Preston repeated. "I have never seen you before."

"I have just awakened," he replied.

Preston was unable to detect guile or sarcasm. In the near distance, the sun sank redly into the Delaware Bay.

"Why are you here anyway?"

"I like the children," the boy answered. "I come to play with them."

Preston's thoughts returned to the little girl lying in the damp grass, even as he felt his head growing heavy. It seemed the musky odor of the boy had grown stronger in the last few moments, though the smell seemed less repellant than before.

A sudden and distant memory of his days as a literature professor occurred to him, even as he slid drunkenly back down the trunk of the tree, his narrow rump settling on the soft, damp earth. "Gabriel," he said aloud to the darkening gloom, remembering the famous story by H. H. Munro about a gentleman who finds an unsettling, feral boy living on his estate. "That's who you are—Gabriel-Earnest!"

The boy's eyes remained fixed upon him, but Preston no longer felt afraid—he felt incapable of any fear at all. "Have you read the story?" he asked, then giggled. "Of course you haven't... who reads anything good anymore?"

His head, sinking onto his chest, suddenly popped up once more before settling by degrees a final time. After a few moments he began to snore as the boy continued his uncanny scrutiny.

"Gabriel," the boy said at last, as if trying the word out. Then, in the few remaining moments before the world was plunged into blackness, he turned with astounding swiftness, bounding like a deer across the playground. Slowing only long enough to scoop the still-unconscious girl into his arms, he carried her over the fence and into the woods. Not a branch was disturbed by his silent passage. He was gone.

After a few moments, Preston's head snapped up once more, his eyes flying open. Scrambling to his feet at the thought of the little girl, he cried, "Hey... I..." But there was no one to be seen in the heavy dusk.

Turning round and round in the gloom, staring wildly, he feared his mind was, at last, coming loose from the drink. But as true darkness fell, he too fled towards home and away from the silent schoolyard.

CHAPTER TWO

Hearing the insistent summons through layers of exhaustion, Nicholas Catesby remained sunk into his mattress like a man dropped from a great height. After a while he heard someone say tiredly, "Oh God," then realized that it was himself.

Shrilling into life once more, the sound of the cell phone sent his large hand slapping and pawing across the surface of the nightstand, seeking the source of his torment.

His thick fingers closing upon their prey at last, Nick sat up in a single motion, bringing the phone to his ear, and mumbling, "Chief Catesby." The pause on the other end allowed the unmistakable crackle of police radio traffic to bleed over into the connection.

He heard a woman say in the background, "Ten-four; I'm getting him on the line now." Then suddenly she was in his ear,

"Chief," a raspy female voice questioned, "Are you there?" His bedside clock glowed 4:40 AM.

Nick thought Diana sounded frightened and tired and he could tell from long experience that she had made herself hoarse making lots of phone calls. None of this was good.

"I'm here," he answered. "What have you got?" He flicked on his bedside lamp, wincing at the sudden light. Reaching out to his wife's side of the bed, he found only cool sheets awaiting his touch. After nearly a year it still surprised him.

"Brace yourself," Diana said. Nick sat up straighter, finding himself doing exactly as she commanded. As she was not an alarmist, he was greatly alarmed. "We've got a missing child."

Nick felt the pronouncement like a physical blow. "You're fuckin' kidding me, D," he choked out. "Who is it?" He felt like he was waking up to a nightmare.

It was the anniversary of little Seth Busby's disappearance seven years before; he had posters plastered all over town. He did it every year leading up to the anniversary in the hopes of someone remembering something after all these years. Every year he was disappointed. He was scheduled to meet with the child's parents today, prior to making yet another televised plea for information. My God, he groaned inwardly, is this some kind of terrible, cruel joke?

"It's a fourth grader from the public school. Her name is Megan Guthrie. Her family lives right next to the school as a matter of fact."

"How long has she been missing?" Nick asked.

There was a slight pause, "Since yesterday evening, around sundown, between six-thirty or seven."

Nick glanced once more at the clock, making hasty calculations, then said, "D, that's over ten hours ago. Why wasn't I called before now?"

There was another pause. "Chief, I was told by the captain not to bother you until he gave the word. He said he didn't want to worry you." She didn't sound like she believed Weller's excuse, and neither did Nick.

"That was very considerate of him," he drawled. "Is there any reason to believe this is a kidnapping?"

"I don't know, Chief, but I don't think so from what I've picked up so far. It sounds like she just wandered away from the other kids when they were on their way home from the school playground."

"I see," he replied, thinking hard. "Am I to take it that little—or no—progress has been made up till now, and that since Captain Weller has not made himself a hero that I'm being called in to shoulder the blame?"

There was no answer to this from the other end and Nick felt ashamed for putting a dispatcher into the middle of a personal issue. "I'm sorry, D. Ignore what I just said… I'm not completely awake yet. Guess I'm a little cranky… sorry."

"That's okay, Chief," Diana responded. "I've worked here for a while, you know… I understand."

Nick swung his legs over the edge of the rumpled bed and strode toward the bathroom. "I know you do, D. That's why you're the best. I'll be there in a few minutes," he promised.

"Tell the Cap to get everyone together: detectives; the day-shift patrol sergeant, school resource officer, and ask for a K-9 team from the sheriff's office. Also make sure the Prosecutor's Office has been notified as well and see…"

"They're all here, Boss," she interrupted him. "They're all in the squad room waiting on you."

Nick stopped short. "I see," he managed, imagining a room full of impatient officers awaiting their tardy chief and feeling the flush of humiliation warming his throat. "Well, I'll be there as quickly as I can." He decided to forego the shower and shave.

☙

The sun was just reddening the horizon as Nick hurried down the deserted sidewalk. His home was only two blocks from the police department. The morning was cool, with just a touch of crispness in the freshening breeze. The autumn was not yet old, and winter still seemed far away as Nick strode beneath the posters of Seth Busby that fluttered and snapped along his way.

Even in the grey light of coming dawn, he recognized the boy's face as it had been seven years before, while the age-enhanced version was the face of a stranger—a reproach for his failure to bring the boy back to his still-grieving family.

A chill ran through him as the breeze ruffled his thick, dark hair, hair that was just beginning to show some gray. Zipping up his jacket, he crossed the street to the police department.

Giving Diana a nod through the bulletproof glass of the lobby window, he even managed a tight smile as she nodded back and buzzed him through. The hum of subdued conversation reached him from the squad room. Just before entering, he took a deep breath and then slowly let it out. It was going to be a long day. He pushed through the door.

At a glance he could see that, indeed, everyone had been gathered. "Good morning," he said to the entire assemblage, which was answered with a mumbled chorus of the same.

Besides his four detectives, the on-duty and on-coming shift sergeants, a couple of dispirited-looking investigators from the prosecutor's office, and the sheriff's K-9 team, he recognized the ever-affable Jack Kimbo from the regional F.B.I. Office.

Smiling even at the ungodly hour of dawn, Jack raised a coffee cup in greeting and pointed to it. Nick grinned back. He was very glad to see the rumpled Kimbo. They had known each other for years and he had never failed to be a reliable source of expertise and support on the cases that they had worked together. They had first met on the Busby case, and it was obvious by his presence that kidnapping had not been ruled out in this one either.

Nodding back, Jack swept the coffee pot up and began to fill the cup. Without asking, he added two creamers, but no sugar, handing it to Nick. "I still remember how you like it, big boy," he said, peering over the rims of his glasses.

"Thanks, Jack, you're sweet," Nick replied without the trace of a smile. Then, "It's good to see you." He turned to the room at large and spotted his second-in-command, Captain Shadrick Weller.

The Captain appeared to be hunkered down in the midst of his supporters, made up mostly of the small detective bureau, as well as the most nakedly ambitious of the patrol division. He caught Weller peering at him from beneath his shaggy eyebrows. "Chief," Weller said curtly. The rest of his entourage found other places to look.

Nick shook his head to clear it, took a deep breath, and drew himself up to his full six foot height. "Gentlemen," he boomed, as all eyes turned towards him, "will someone please tell me what the fuck is going on?"

Sitting up straighter, Shadrick paused. As usual, he was unhappy with being treated like a subordinate. Or perhaps he just didn't have a good answer, and wanted to cover. Nick would probably never know. "We searched her house, of course. You know the drill, Chief; just in case she had snuck in and was hiding. Patrol took statements from the neighbors, but no one saw her leave the school grounds. Then we got a scent item from the mom—the little girl's pillowcase—and brought in the dogs. It's the only lead we've got. The dogs tracked her up to the schoolyard fence, but wouldn't go any further."

Nick arched an eyebrow.

"Don't ask me!" Shadrick threw up his hands. "They started whining and pissing and turned tail for home. There was a funny smell might have put them off."

"Funny smell?" Nick asked. His stomach started to tighten.

Weller ignored him. "In any case, the Fire Chief is organizing volunteers over at the fire house." He pointed out the window at the brightening dawn. "They're ready to go as soon as you finish your coffee, Chief." Nick felt his face harden at the obvious dig. A small smile appeared on Weller's mouth. He had scored a point. "Maybe the goddamn dogs will do better then."

Shadrick Weller came from one of the "original" families in town. The Wellers had arrived from Long Island with a charter from William and Mary to purchase one of the first tracts of land in what would later become Wessex Township, New Jersey. The county museum proudly displayed the deed his namesake ancestor had received from the crown in 1695.

Nick's family, by comparison, was a relative newcomer, having only migrated up from Maryland in 1745. Preposterous as it was, Shadrick had the ability to make lineage appear to be an important issue—only the "originals" should hold the seats of power, and that included the position of Chief of Police. It was hard to believe that once upon a time they had been partners.

"A couple of my guys will be working with your detectives," Jack spoke at his elbow. "We don't have any evidence that this is a kidnapping, yet, but her getting over that fence worries me. It doesn't make sense, unless she was taken, or lured somehow. The office crew is combing records for local pedophiles in the meantime… just in case."

Nick nodded thoughtfully. His eyes searched each of the faces in the room, finally meeting Shadrick Weller's, but only for the briefest of moments. Weller looked away.

Nick drained his coffee and reached for his uniform jacket. "All right, gentlemen. We've pissed away enough time. Let's go find that little girl."

☙

Nick and Jack walked several yards behind the Sheriff's K-9 handlers watching the dogs work. After picking up the scent from the unwashed pillowcase Megan's mother had provided they took off across the schoolyard, straining at their long leashes.

"They're definitely on it," one of the Sheriff's deputies remarked. "They've got a good scent trail."

The two bloodhounds lumbered forward, snuffling the earth, as a German shepherd, brought along as back-up, followed curiously.

Nearing the sagging chain link fence bordering the schoolyard, they broke into a run, the sheriff's officers trotting behind them. Reaching it, they stopped suddenly, turning in tight circles and blowing loudly through their dripping nostrils. Nick noticed the handlers glancing uneasily at one another.

"They find something?" He called out. "What is it?"

The older of the two answered, "I... no, I don't think so. I think they're freaking out again."

Suddenly one, then the other, pissed where they stood and began to whine. A low growl rumbled up from the shepherd's throat though he had been kept back several yards.

"What the fuck?" Jack whispered.

The hounds began to pull in the opposite direction, and as Nick caught up he could see that they had begun to shiver. "What's wrong them?" he demanded.

The dogs slunk towards the waiting K-9 vehicles, clearly eager to be away from there. "For Christ's sake," Nick breathed.

The handler looked up at him. "I don't understand it, Chief. I really don't. They did the same thing last night."

Nick strode past to the low fencing sagging beneath the weight of vines and briars. "What's that smell?" he called over his shoulder as a faint musty odor drifted to him from the shadowed woods beyond. He turned to ask Weller a question, but the

Captain was standing back, watching. Nick turned to Jack. "Is that the smell you encountered before."

Jack and the senior handler, a man named Miller, came up to either side of him. "Yes, sir. The same damned smell," reported Miller.

"Yeah… what is that?" asked Jack.

Miller frowned. "Skunk, maybe?" Then his face brightened somewhat. "Maybe that's what's wrong with the girls," he hooked a thumb at the two disgraced hounds being led off the field. "Maybe a skunk's come through here recently. They spray everything within sight when they got little ones hid nearby."

Nick favored him with a doubtful look. "That's no skunk," he said. "I don't know what it is, but it's no skunk."

The handler turned away to follow his partner, adding, "Sorry, chief… really. Never seen the girls act like this before."

Jack chuckled, "Damn if it doesn't make me feel a little light-headed."

Nick turned to the agent, a thoughtful expression on his face. "You know, I feel a little dizzy myself. Meth lab…?" he ventured, glancing into the woods.

"No," Jack assured him. "It's not that… but something. Shall we see?"

Nick nodded in agreement and turned to the searchers waiting in the parking lot. Seeing that the useless dogs had been secured, he gave a whistle and wave of his hand and the line of officers and volunteers began to move forward. When they reached the fence line, Nick helped the more portly Jack over it, joining him on the other side.

"Jack," he said in a low tone as they began to push on into the tangled forest, "You and I have seen dogs do that before… remember? Seven years ago when we set out to find Seth Busby. Different dogs, same reaction."

The agent glanced over at him. "Yeah," he whispered, "I remember. I was hoping you wouldn't—things didn't turn out so well that time."

"The smell too, Jack. I had almost forgotten it. That was there, too."

"Yeah," Jack agreed.

Both men pushed deeper into the undergrowth.

℘

As the light bled out of the bright October sky, shadows crept eastward through the dense maritime forest, coalescing into a damp grey uncertainty. Nick sent word for the team leaders to get a head count of their people and bring them out. With the coming of night there was little more that could be done, and he couldn't risk any of the searchers getting lost or hurt. Besides, he would need them rested for the following morning.

Trudging silently back toward the schoolyard, Jack slapped him on the shoulder, saying, "Tomorrow, my friend, tomorrow."

They broke out into the schoolyard once more. Nick saw two figures detaching themselves from a clutch of on-lookers in the parking lot. It was a man and a woman. The man began trotting toward him while the woman stumbled along behind. Nick recognized Megan's parents.

"Oh God," he breathed. "This isn't going to be easy."

"Why are you stopping?" the man began to shout as he drew near. He had heard the command to shut down for the night at the command post in the school lot. "Megan's still out there!" A helicopter flew with a clatter over their heads.

Nick looked the desperate father in the eye and said, "It's getting too dark for us to find anyone, Mister Guthrie. I know you don't want to hear that right now, but I do have to think of the safety of the searchers, too." He nodded at the police officers and volunteer firemen emerging from the woods and edging closer, drawn by the commotion. "We're going to start again at first light…"

Jack intervened, pointing skyward, "We still have aerial assets… helicopters with night scopes looking for her, sir. They'll keep working the area for a while…"

"That's my little girl out there in the woods," Guthrie screamed, spraying both men with spittle, his square unshaven face contorted with rage and fear. "Don't you leave her out there like did the other one, goddamnit—like you did, Seth Busby!" He squared off with Nick. "Don't even think about giving up on my Megan!"

Silence fell over the gathering crowd and every eye turned from meeting Nick's own.

"I'll find her," Nick promised. "I'll never stop looking and I'll find her."

Megan's father turned away, replying hoarsely, "Bring her home, Chief. Please bring her home to us."

His wife, still standing where she had been left, stared at the darkening woods beyond the fence, her faded blue eyes streaming. In her hands she twisted a damp handkerchief, bringing it to her mouth like a stopper. But the wail escaped her lips even so, floating over the heads of the men and women gathered there, the sound as lonely and lost as her little girl. Nearby, her husband's sobs drifted to them as a soft undercurrent of sorrow to his wife's keening cry.

Breaking the spell, a woman with the rescue squad rushed to her side, slipping an arm over her shoulders and murmuring meaningless words of comfort. The rest quietly stowed away their gear before turning for home, and their still-intact families.

CHAPTER THREE

The following morning, and surprisingly early for him, Preston shakily joined his daughter for breakfast. It was just past seven and the sun was beginning to dispel the darkness that lingered longer each day. He found Fanny in her flannel pajamas and Indian blanket housecoat shuffling about the kitchen. Preston had always known her to be easily chilled, and he put this down to her thinness.

For his part, Preston wore a pair of worn and faded green sweat pants that he never remembered owning and would never have stooped to buy in his heyday. Over his freshly laundered undershirt he had wrapped himself in a blanket that Fanny always left folded at the foot of his bed, even in summer. There was a distinct chill in the morning air, he noted, as he slid cautiously along the hardwood floor in his threadbare socks.

Reaching the table, he sat down without speaking, and Fanny placed a mug of black coffee in front of him. Preston waited until she had turned back to the stove to bend down and slurp the hot liquid as quietly as he was able; he could not yet trust his hands. It was apparent from his daughter's silence that he had done something very wrong the day before, but could he not recall what it might have been. As it had obviously affected his only child, he could only surmise that he might have misbehaved at the library. Fanny's first spoken words of the morning confirmed this.

"You're not to go into the library today, Dad. I mean it. You're going to get me fired before all is said and done."

Looking up from beneath his spiky, gray brows, he found her regarding him with folded arms. She looked the very image of her lovely mother, he thought, though with a far more resolute demeanor than his wife could have ever evinced. He noted with some pride that his only child was a winsome-looking wench, even if she was his own flesh and blood. She had her mother's chestnut-colored and abundant hair which she wore scooped up into a ponytail. She was also thin like her mother—too thin, he thought, and some of that was him.

Her eyes were large, the color of café au lait, with long, arched eyebrows. Her skin was clear and just a little too pale, her nose just a little too long. But her mouth was wide and generous, trembling to life in unguarded moments.

He foggily recalled some sort of disagreement with another patron—a man with highly questionable taste in literature. Was that yesterday… or the day before? The vague memory made the pulse in his head throb; each beat pumping a painful pressure into his egg-fragile skull. "Aspirin," he pled, before shading his burnt eyes from the invading rays of the brilliant autumn sun. She had him at his low ebb, he thought. How perfectly female.

"There's two right in front of you," she pointed out, while at the same moment sliding a plate with dry toast across the table to him. She set her own plate down with a clatter and Preston winced. Gobbling down the two white tablets, he sucked up another mouthful of the steaming, black liquid.

"Are we out of marmalade?" he asked, regarding the wheat toast balefully, "or is that part of my punishment as well? It wouldn't take much to weaken an old man like me, would it?" His mouth felt coated with something greasy and black. "Keep thinning down my feed long enough and before you know it I won't be able to climb out of bed. Now wouldn't that just be dandy for everybody?" He took a bite of a dry slice and chewed with his mouth open for effect.

Fanny put two spoonfuls of creamer into her own coffee, took a sip, and then began to spread orange marmalade onto her own toast from a small ceramic pot in the center of the table. Preston watched this with embarrassment and dismay.

"Pop, I'm not going to ladle it on for you. Hungover or not, you're a big boy and I'm not your mother... or mine for that matter."

He had forgotten that this was where she kept his preferred spread. Looking down, Preston muttered something indistinct, then added, "It's a public building, isn't it?"

Fanny took a small bite of her own toast before saying, "Yes, Pop, it's a public building, and a public library that I just happen to work at and that just happens to provide us both with the only income we have. Mrs. Cohansey had a 'talk' with me yesterday after you had to be escorted out again. Do you know what she wanted to speak with me about, Pop? Can you guess?"

Preston avoided both his daughter's gaze and question, saying, "You can't be fired for something I do. Just let them try something like that... we'd *own* the damned library. We'd *own* this entire Godforsaken county," he declared.

Fanny's expression remained unchanged and unmoved. "Dad, do you remember when I got my first job in my major...

the one your old boss was kind enough to give me after I graduated? Do you remember what happened?"

Preston still wouldn't look at her, slopping the marmalade onto his bread. He brought the slice to his lips with hands that now contained only the slightest of tremors thanks to the aspirin and coffee. "Pity work," he said around a mouthful of rinds and syrup, "Wergild—just trying to ease a guilty conscience."

"You said then that they couldn't fire me because of your behavior and you never stopped testing that theory. You spent more time in the college library the nine months I worked there than you ever did as a tenured professor. The president was kind enough to give me a job and allow you to continue to use the facility in spite of everything that had happened. Maybe he did pity us. If you ask me, we were pretty pitiful."

Folding her arms, she studied the man who had destroyed her mother, and his own career, with his unrepentant alcoholism: a preening and self-absorbed intellectual who had laughingly refused the least counsel by his fellow professors. Even the repeated warnings of a beleaguered college president had gone unheeded: Too many missed classes, too few students registering as a result of his abrasive reputation. Papers left ungraded, or so savagely reviewed, that few cared to volunteer for the experience.

Fanny looked down upon the author of his own family's destruction, the man who, in a state of drunkenness, had revealed to his teenaged daughter that he had named her after Fanny Hill, the heroine of a classic pornographic novel of the eighteenth century.

The final straw had been at his long-overdue disciplinary hearing, to which he had arrived half an hour late and stinking drunk, proceeding to chastise the college president for his intellectual flabbiness. He had been dismissed, becoming not only unemployed and unemployable in academia, but a pariah, shunned and looked down upon, an intolerable fate for a man such as he.

Her mother had died of cancer a few years later, though Fanny secretly believed that it was somehow self-inflicted, that she had just given up. A simple, plain woman, she had been slowly crushed by her husband's appetite for self-destruction.

"You weren't fired because of me," Preston snapped, "It was because of budget tightening. It happens everywhere, all the time—nothing to do with me."

"That's right, Pop... nothing to do with you. I just happened to be the one they let go. And you're right too about the budget cuts, happens all the time, everywhere, especially when you're not senior staff... like me... now... at the library."

Preston opened his mouth to protest, but she cut him off. "Pop, I've put up with a lot over the years because you're my dad and you don't have anyone else... and for some reason that isn't very clear right at this moment, I still love you. You don't deserve it, and you don't do much to earn it. But I'm at the end of my rope with you now. 'We' can't afford for me to lose this job, and I'm not going to... period."

Taking a deep breath, Fanny added, "You cause one more scene at the library and I'll put you out on the street. Do you understand me? You can go live at that hobo camp off the railroad tracks... no one there will give a damn *what* you do. Or what you have to say, for that matter—you wouldn't like that."

Preston looked up at her from beneath his brows. He had met some of those men in his travels. He knew how far he had yet to fall and felt a shiver of fear at the prospect.

"Do we have an understanding?" Fanny persisted.

"Yes," he agreed.

They regarded one another across the table. He knew she had given up a lot for him... possibly a husband and children of her own. More than she should have.

Snatching at the newspaper, Preston began to study it with feigned interest. After several long moments of silence, he heard

Fanny rise from her chair and begin to clear the table. When the water began to splash into the deep porcelain sink he chanced a look—she was involved in the wash-up and had finished with him. Throwing the paper up once more as a screen, he found that he was looking at a headline that read, "Child Missing From Wessex Township." The image of the strange boy's face only inches from his own suddenly returned to him, and he shuddered at the memory. He had nearly succeeded in convincing himself that what he had seen in the schoolyard had been a hallucination.

Tossing the paper onto the table top as Fanny went to her room to prepare for work, he called after her, "I may have seen something important the other night, Fanny. So I'm going over to the police department today and give them the benefit of my observations; see if I can't get this missing child business cleared up for them!

"That police chief of theirs seems like an idiot, from what I've seen of him. Why's he been mooning around the library recently, anyway? *He's* no reader, by god!

"Anyway, I'm sure he could use a little help, and since I'm on sabbatical from the *public* library, I may as well offer my services."

Fanny, having turned on the shower in the master bathroom, heard none of this.

ℭ

Nick stared at the phone with a hollowed-out gaze, its ringing a shrill alarm to his already frayed nerves. Between every ring, the silence returned to his large, cluttered office like the aftermath of thunder, seeming to darken the room with its quiet possibilities. He had hardly slept a wink thinking of the Guthrie's terror and grief, of Megan's long, long night someplace without them. He had prayed for the first time in many, many years… prayed that she was still alive…still unharmed.

The phone rang once more and Nick reached out, lifting the receiver. A relief dispatcher, brought in to help handle the volume of calls generated by the Guthrie search, said, "Chief, I'm sorry to bother you, but there's a man in the lobby down here who's making a real fuss about seeing you. He says he knows all about the missing child and will not be…" She paused to get her words right, "… he says he will not be fobbed off on some lackey." She took a breath; then added, "The sarge says you'll know him when you see him. He's an old drunk around town."

Sighing, Nick massaged his forehead with his free hand. Situations like this always brought the cranks out of the woodwork. By rights, he should have Mister Howard thrown out of the building, as he felt certain that this was the identity of his high-handed visitor… the language was a dead giveaway.

Then he thought of the lovely woman at the library who had begun to increasingly haunt his thoughts, and hesitated. He could not bring himself to deal with Fanny's father in quite such a fashion. Besides, he rationalized, what else was he really doing? What did he have to go on that he could afford to discard any potential source of information without first properly investigating it? Also, it was undeniable that Preston Howard roamed through the area like a wraith, both day and night. Who knew what he may have seen.

"Ask the sarge to bring him around to the interview room and I'll meet him there. Thanks." Placing the receiver back in the cradle, he rose from his chair. The splendid autumn sky outside his windows looked as brittle and clear as crystal, the pinkish streaks burnt away by a white sun that seemed far too distant. He thought of Megan Guthrie and wondered if she were witnessing the same dawning, then shuddered.

He hoped the old man wasn't too drunk at this hour of the morning.

℞

The room in which Preston had been left to wait was small with but a single door. He noted a camera mounted high up in the corner of the ceiling, its lens pointing directly at the plastic chair he had been none-too-courteously instructed to occupy. Attached to the cinder-block wall next to his left arm was a metal pipe similar to a towel rack but sporting a single handcuff dangling from a steel cable about a foot long. With a smile at the camera he rose and quite deliberately took the chair opposite. Preston noted with unease several puzzling smears marring the institutional green of the wall above the bar. He calculated that they were at about head level with a sitting man. Feeling his palms grow damp, he shifted in his seat.

If Chief High-and-Mighty did not show up within the next two minutes he was leaving, he promised himself. He glanced up to check the time on the wall clock in order to begin his countdown and was disappointed to find none. As he no longer owned a watch, he recognized at once the designed limbo of the near-featureless room.

Dropping his gaze to the worn, curling linoleum, he began to wonder why he had bothered to come in the first place. What business was it of his when people misplaced their children? What did he really care?

The liquor store was due to open soon, he reminded himself, unconsciously running the fingers of one hand across his dry lips. He would come back later, after a little fortification, he decided—his memory worked better with a little lubrication in any case. He rose to his feet just as the door was thrown open, his escape blocked by the large frame of Chief Catesby.

Involuntarily, he took a step back, bumping his head against the wall. He grimaced in pain. At the same time, he derived some satisfaction in seeing the policeman look confused for a moment at not finding him in the "suspect's" chair. The grey-blue eyes slid quickly to him, however, and Preston felt the official scrutiny like the promise of violence.

Straightening up, he refrained from rubbing the back of his head. "I didn't care for my assigned seat, officer. I am here as a concerned citizen, not as a defendant." He stopped himself there as the policeman eased the door shut behind him. The small room grew smaller still and Preston felt his heart speed up.

Leaning across the table, the big man offered his hand. "I'm Nick Catesby," he opened. "Thanks so much for coming in, Mister Howard. I understand you have some information regarding our missing child."

Preston allowed his hand to be seized and released, then answered, "*Professor* Howard, officer. I am still a PhD in English Literature, though I've retired."

The younger man's face suddenly lost its animation, and Preston could see now that he was a mature man in his early forties, and a very tired man at that. He indicated for Preston to sit down and did so himself without waiting.

"Now," Nick resumed, as if Preston had said nothing, "we're kind of pressed for time here. What can you tell me?"

Preston sat a little straighter in his chair. He could see that the chief had little faith he was bringing anything worthwhile to his table. "I can assure you, officer, that my time is valuable, as well. Even so, I've taken it upon myself to attend to my civic duty and report my findings to you... should you be interested, of course." He sat back, folding his thin arms across his narrow chest.

Nick roused himself, a look of pain briefly creasing his brow. Attempting a weak smile, he said, "Of course we're interested, Professor. Please go on."

Preston grinned back, pleased with his small victory. "I may have seen the abductor of this little girl that's gone missing—

Megan Guthrie, I think the paper said. He was a boy—very odd looking, clearly indicative of the shallow gene pool we have around here."

"You saw this… boy… actually abduct Megan?" Catesby leaned forward on his elbows. "How exactly did he do that?"

Preston faltered, "Well, I didn't exactly *see* the actual act… just the prelude."

"The prelude…?" Catesby repeated.

"I'm not sure why I missed that part… I got groggy for some reason, and closed my eyes for a few moments."

"Had you been drinking?"

"That was *not* the reason—something came over me—low blood sugar probably. Do you want the facts, or not, officer?" Preston asked with a raised patrician brow and as much bravado as he could muster.

Catesby appeared to think this over; then said, "Go on then, tell me about this boy. *Where* exactly did you see him?"

Preston caught himself wringing his hands; then yanked them apart. "In the schoolyard, of course," he answered.

"When was this?" Catesby asked.

"Night before last," Preston answered.

"How old do you think this boy was?"

"Oh, I don't know… I'm bad with kids' ages… never paid them much attention, you know—thirteen… fourteen, maybe?" The chief seemed to be weighing something in his mind.

"His name?" he continued.

Preston looked up alarmed. "I don't know his *name,* for god's sake. I christened him Gabriel for lack of one. He's just some little retarded boy… didn't I tell you that already?" He couldn't actually remember if he had or hadn't.

"You *named* him?"

Exasperated, and feeling increasingly uncomfortable, Preston shot back, "It was a literary allusion that just sprang to mind; not a crime the last time I looked!"

"What was he wearing?"

Preston tried hard to recall. "A green tee shirt, I believe, none-too-clean. A pair of filthy black jeans… they were both too small for him by half."

His face thoughtful, Catesby sat in silence for several long moments; then asked quietly, "Did you ever know a kid named Seth Busby, Professor? Seven years ago, *he* was last seen wearing a green tee shirt and black jeans."

Preston's mouth opened; then closed once more.

"The night Megan went missing was the anniversary of his disappearance," Nick continued.

"I can see that you are trying to make some kind of connection," Preston managed. "But I failed to follow your logic… if there is any."

"You just described the clothes Seth Busby was wearing when he was last seen, and you've already told me that you were in the school yard the evening Megan vanished."

"Yes, but I also said that there was a…"

"… A boy," Catesby cut him off. "A boy only *you* have seen… a boy that you've named Gabriel for some reason that's not really clear to me. That's a fairly unusual set of circumstances, don't you think, Professor?"

Again Preston's mouth opened, then closed, but no sound came out.

❧

"I did it," Becky Mossberg stated emphatically, having spotted Nick before Fanny did, "but I'm not gonna give up any details without being roughed up a little." She turned to face her desk mate. "Look who's back to visit again, Fanny!"

Fanny's head snapped up from her task to find Chief Catesby looming over their shared desk. He looked uncomfortable and slightly embarrassed. He was in full uniform with navy blue trousers sporting a gold stripe down the pants legs. The shirt was a French blue that Fanny thought suited his smoky blue eyes very well. There were signs that his once-athletic build was softening with age, but he still carried himself with the careless ease of a much younger man. He appeared tired though, shadowy around the eyes, slightly pale, and in need of a razor and a hair brush; his wavy hair tossed about on his head as if by a strong wind.

Nick was taken off guard by Becky's forwardness. He was in no mood for levity, so he answered, "Actually, I was wondering if I could speak with Ms. Howard for just a moment." He turned his eyes to her.

Becky glanced at her desk mate, saying, "Of course you can! She's very helpful, isn't she? Have you already finished the '87th Precinct' series, Chief? I'm sure that Fanny here would be more than happy to direct you to some other books that you'll enjoy." Fanny flashed a warning look, but Becky happily ignored it. "Isn't that so, Fanny dear?"

Fanny was unable to lift her face to see what Chief Catesby's reaction to all this might be. "Well," she heard Catesby say, "Maybe so… the thing is I need to talk with Ms. Howard alone for a few minutes… it's not exactly library business."

Now she did look up, but only to find him studying their desktop and its scattering of papers and books, almost hiding the keyboard of her computer. A grinning papier-mâché Jack-o-lantern perched on the corner, honoring the season.

Snatching up her purse from the back of her chair, Becky exclaimed, "Police business, is it? I'll just take a trip to the little girls' room and powder my nose." She winked broadly at Fanny, then clattered down the stairs and was gone.

Silence descended in her wake, and it was only after several uncomfortable moments that Nick said, "She's got a wicked sense of humor, doesn't she?"

Risking a glance at him, Fanny smiled weakly, answering, "You should have to work with her… she never quits. I'm sorry, Chief Catesby, it's just that she wants… thinks that…" she trailed off, realizing that any attempt at explaining her friend's motives would only cause more embarrassment for them both. "You wanted to talk to me about something?"

"Yeah," Nick answered, "if you've got a few minutes. I wouldn't have come to your place of work, but I'm pressed for time. Is here okay?"

She nodded.

Looking around at the second floor reading areas to ensure that no one was within listening distance, he found only a scattering of patrons, all too far away to hear anything. Several were studying the large, uniformed officer and their librarian, but their eyes went quickly down as he swept the room with his gaze. Satisfied, he pulled Becky's chair out from behind the desk and rolled it next to Fanny's work area. Sitting down with a sigh, he glanced over his shoulder at the empty stairwell, and began.

"By the way, could you call me Nick? It always makes me feel like an old man when people I went to school with call me chief."

Fanny smiled. "But we didn't go to school together, Nick."

"Technically, that's true," he answered, "but, we *were* in the same school system at the same time. You were in the middle school when I was at Wessex High."

Fanny felt her cheeks warming, "My goodness, you certainly know the people in your township. I didn't think you knew I even existed back then."

"My little brother, Stephen, had a crush on you back when you were both in the middle-school band. You gave him one of your wallet-size class photos and it was taped to the mirror in our bedroom." Nick smiled gently in reminiscence. "It may be there still. My mom keeps that room like a shrine—nothing changes." Nick's smile grew a bit more. "You were a cute girl… I don't forget cute girls… even ones my nerdy little brother had a crush on."

"Your mom must miss him," Fanny offered. "It must have been so hard on her… so hard on you all."

Nick turned to her as if just remembering she was there. "Yeah," he said, "it was hard… who would've thought the third clarinet of the award-winning Wessex Middle School Band would join the Marines as soon as he turned eighteen—much less get killed in that dust-up in Panama?"

"I couldn't believe it either," Fanny answered. "No one could. I cried all day when I heard about it. He was very sweet."

"Yeah," Nick agreed, "he was." Shrugging, as if to shake off the memories, he turned to the subject at hand, "Fanny, I need to ask you a few questions about your dad. Would you be willing to answer them?"

Fanny sat up, her eyes widening at the mention of her father. "Has he done something, Nick? Is he in trouble?"

"I'll be truthful, I don't really know, but can you tell me if he was home with you night before last?"

"Yes," she answered, "he came home that night."

"Came home around what time?" Nick asked.

"A little after seven, I think," Fanny answered uneasily. "What is this all about?"

He answered her with another question, "Did you know that he came in to see me today?"

He could see by her expression that she did not.

"To see you?" she managed.

Nick nodded. "He said he had information regarding the missing child we've been searching for."

He watched as Fanny's face grew pale, her mind racing through the implications that could be hidden within such a statement.

Nick went on, "He said he believes that a strange boy took her."

Fanny almost sighed aloud with relief. "Well, sometimes he can get things very mixed up in his mind. He drinks like a fish, you know. Thank God, he didn't leave you with the impression that *he* was involved in Megan's disappearance. The way he wanders around here looking like a scarecrow, I worry sometime what people might think of him... that he might frighten folks. He's really harmless though, Nick..."

Nick cut her off, "Has your dad ever mentioned Seth Busby to you, Fanny?" He saw the look of confusion spread across her lean, pale face, and thought for the briefest of moments what it might be like to kiss her. "He's the boy that went missing seven years ago and was never found. Do you recall that?"

Nodding, Fanny answered, "Of course... of course I do. How could any of us forget?" She twisted her thin hands together on the desktop and Nick noticed how tight the flesh was across her knuckles, how hollowed her cheeks. "But, no, Nick, I don't think Dad has ever spoken of the Busby boy at all. The sad thing is he was probably drunk through the whole event. He's pretty much the center of his own little universe."

"Fanny," he said softly, "I'm sure that it means nothing at all... that I'm just overly sensitive on the subject of the Busby case, but your dad told me that he met this boy in the schoolyard... just around dusk." He stopped to let the words sink in.

Fanny stared at him uncomprehendingly. "I don't understand..."

"He described the boy as wearing the same clothes as Seth did the day he went missing." He watched as her face grew whiter still as the implications of what he was saying took root. "The night Megan Guthrie went missing was also the anniversary of Seth Busby's disappearance."

She stared at him for several long moments and he wondered if she might faint. Then she seemed to recover herself with a sudden intake of breath, a look of determination, of certainty, coming into her eyes, color flooding into her pale cheeks. "No," she began, sitting up straighter, "he's not like *that,* Nick. He's not a very pleasant person, not a very likable man, and I think that that's the way he wants it really. But, no, he has no interest in children. As I told you before, *Chief,* he takes little or no interest in *anyone,* or anything, other than the bottle.

"I don't have an explanation for this 'boy' he supposedly met in the schoolyard, but I can tell you this, if it is true and not a hallucination, then it was just as he said it was and nothing more."

She took a breath and Nick found himself sitting up straight in his chair like a school boy receiving a lecture on classroom behavior. Holding her head high on her long, slender neck, Fanny swung her gaze across her small dominion. Her visage drove the few interested patrons that had eased out of the stacks to take cover within them once more. That same gaze returned now to Nick, softening only a little. "He would never touch a child. He would have no interest in them. He's not made that way. I don't think he's interested in anything other than his own company, and whiskey."

Nick regarded her for several moments, sorry for what he had had to ask, and equally sorry at the result he had earned insofar as Fanny went. He had not been sure until that moment that what he felt about her was anything but loneliness seeking company. Now, to his regret, he knew better. Still, he was a policeman, first and foremost, and questions had to be asked, every possible line of inquiry pursued when it came to children gone missing.

"I'm sorry," he began. "I've upset you, I can see that. But his showing up at my office with this story, I had to follow it up. If it makes you feel any better, the identikit drawing based on his description looked nothing like Seth. In fact… it looked more like a nightmare than a boy—that may be the drink, of course.

"But I can't rule him out as a suspect at this point, Fanny, and at the very least he may be an important witness. Like you said, he wanders around out there at all hours and he may have seen something. He may even know something he doesn't understand the significance of. I'll have to hold him, Fanny. Do you understand?"

"No, Chief," she stated firmly once more, her eyes locked on his, "you're not to send him over to that jail—he's too fragile, and being who he is, he wouldn't last long in that environment; especially if the other prisoners think he's done something to a child; you know that. You let him come home—I'll see to it he's made available for you; that he doesn't leave town." She faced him squarely across her desk, her face set like flint.

"I shouldn't, Fanny, I really shouldn't... though there may be some truth to what you say." Nick couldn't believe what he was about to do, "But if you vouch for him, I guess I'll take a chance." Then added quickly, "But I'll have to question him again, Fanny, and soon."

The starch seemed to go out of her with Nick's answer and looking down at her tightly clutched hands, replied, "Yes, of course. Thank you, Chief."

"Good," he said, rising. "Well, I've certainly taken up enough of your time. I hope I haven't gotten you into trouble with your boss. Would you like for me to stop off and say something to her on my way out?"

"No," Fanny answered too loudly. Then more softly, "Thank you, no."

Nick caught the glint of tears in her eyes, and before he could stop himself he reached out and placed a hand on her arm. Fanny went stock still and it was several moments before Nick remembered himself, taking his hand away and murmuring, "Well, then, I'll..." he couldn't think of what he'd been about to say. "I'll be going," he announced, turning for the stairwell.

He brushed past Becky returning from her first floor exile. "I had hopes I was going to be interrupting something," she exclaimed, but when she crossed the landing to her desk it was to find Fanny quietly weeping.

క్ర

When Fanny arrived home that evening it was to a dark house. She could see even as she hurried up the short walkway to their peeling, white, 1930s bungalow that her father was out. On those rare occasions when Preston would decide to remain sober for more than a few hours, the reading lamp in the sunroom would be illuminated as he pored over some oft-read classic.

Sometimes, he might remain sober for two days or more, and it was easy to pretend during such essentially tranquil periods that he was just an aging, retired father, no different than anyone else's dad—smarter, maybe, certainly better educated than most. But he would never allow this cozy illusion to last, and tonight, she thought, he was at it and gone once more.

Discovering that he had left the front door unlocked, she threw it open, tossing her ring of unnecessary keys onto the side table. Out of the darkness of the hallway came the light skitter of claws, her cat hurrying as eagerly as any dog to greet her. From a frantic streak of black and white fur, and desperate yellow eyes, Loki resolved himself into the very picture of feline domesticity and welcome, rubbing his soft flanks against his mistress's bare legs while purring loudly at the pleasure of her company.

"Where's Preston?" Fanny asked, as she knelt, stroking his small, delicate skull until he began to nip impatiently at her fingertips. Standing again, she announced, "You're no different from all the other males I've known… all lovey-dovey when you want something."

She marched toward the kitchen, trying not to trip on the hungry cat as he wove his way between her feet, breaking off every few seconds to make a mad dash ahead, as if to show her the way. His purring had been replaced by the mewling of a spoilt child.

Switching on the light that hung over the table, she threw open a cabinet to retrieve a can of Loki's food. This had the effect of turning his complaints into the cries of the damned. Dumping the food into his dish, she was rewarded with instant silence as he began to eat. Wearily, she removed her jacket and took it back down the hall to a closet by the entrance.

As a matter of rote, she pulled down an old beaded change bag she had hidden under some gloves and hats on the top shelf. She routinely changed the locations within the house where she might hide money, as their secrecy never eluded her father for very long. Stretching open the mouth of the little bag, she began to count the small roll of bills it contained, finding that it had only taken her father two weeks to discover the new location. He had removed a single twenty dollar bill from within the roll of tens, twenties, and fives that had previously accounted for seventy dollars mad money. She found herself grateful for his frugality—he knew better than to kill the golden goose, she reckoned.

She had so hoped her father might be at home, and that she could gently question him about his visit with the police, his inexplicable interest in a missing child. Switching on the front porch light, she tried not to think any more about the implications of Chief Catesby's interview with her (and that's what it really was, she told herself—a police interview), she headed back toward the kitchen to open a can of soup for her own supper.

She did not see the great, glittering eyes that watched her movements from the other side of the opaque window; the goblinesque head tilting to capture the lilt of her voice, her few spoken words.

CHAPTER FOUR

Preston felt extremely fortunate to have been allowed to leave the clutches of the police, and stopped for a moment to take a long draw from his bottle. Deeply regretting having offered them any assistance, he had wandered the town looking for the boy he had dubbed Gabriel, but to no avail. Now he found himself back where his nightmare had begun.

The schoolyard and its playground were deserted, the parents of Wessex Township having taken alarm and keeping their young ones close to the nest. There would be no children playing beneath the emerging stars for a long time to come, Preston thought.

On the other side of the fence, the swings hung still in the cooling air, while the jungle gym made for an odd geometry whose purpose appeared inexplicable without children. Crickets sawed away in the quiet of the dusk, their hopeful chirping made lonely within the overarching silence. In the near distance, the windows of ranch-style homes glowed warmly as night dropped gauze-like over the deliberately emptied landscape.

From far away, Preston heard the sound of a door being slammed, followed by the laughter of a child or woman, he couldn't distinguish which, floating across the empty schoolyard like the tinkling of chimes. Turning his collar up, he took another pull on his brandy, made suddenly lonely and uneasy by the vacant tableau.

Turning right onto Ocean Street, he made his way west toward the rail-road tracks. There, he clambered over the low berm that formed the end of the street, skidding down the other side on the loose dirt and gravel. Almost losing his balance, he managed to stay on his feet, and keep a grip on the bottle all at once. He stopped to compose himself and have yet another swig of liquor.

Newly fortified against the clinging night chill he began plodding in the direction he had chosen. Though they had been out of use for many years now, he preferred to stay off the tracks themselves due to the ease of walking the well-worn paths on either side of them. These had been made by countless quads and dirt bikes used by the local kids to travel from town to various abandoned gravel and sand mining pits. These sites, all remotely located throughout the county, had provided generations of teenagers trysting and drinking spots.

That these lonely places had also been the scenes of assaults, rapes, and even the rare murder, only served to add to their cachet and provide fodder for local myth and lore.

For Preston, the tracks also provided a surreptitious shortcut leading through the heart of town. It skirted the edge of the old Baptist Cemetery, whose original stone markers dated back to 1767, and took him within a block of his home. He felt his bed calling.

Immediately ahead of Preston lay a small switching yard grown over with wheat grass. This waved like faded yellow seaweed in the dusk. Two silver passenger cars overlooked the main track like forgotten, discarded toys and had done so for many years, resting amongst the weeds awaiting an engine that would never again return.

In the near darkness they appeared without blemish, but Preston knew that by the light of day their silvered corrugated hides were festooned with spray-painted obscenities. Their windows were blackened by fires set by tramps to keep warm, as well as those resulting from vandals setting alight the cracked, cushioned seats. Within, he heard the almost delicate sound of glass being broken and made to hurry by—he had met enough of his fellow travelers over the years to be leery of night-time encounters.

Though most of the hoboes and vagabonds that stumbled unknowingly down the dead tracks into Wessex Township were harmless, there were those that were keenly predatory. These were men that would never again be a part of any society; men so isolated and depraved that there was nothing they would not do, or stoop to, in order to continue their lifelong binges. Unlike the happy tramps that would sometimes accost Preston as a brother, offering to share their cheap wine, the others shambled along like starving beasts, their eyes bright red with rage and thirst.

More than once, Preston had had to surrender one of his pints to escape the company of such men (It was apparently unthinkable to such creatures, that he might have *two* pints hidden on him). Shuddering at the memory, he promptly stumbled over something that lay unseen in his path.

Falling headlong into the dirt and crushed gravel, he threw out his hands to break his fall, flinging the near empty pint bottle into the weeds. His hands skidded out before him, the palms being painfully grated through the small, sharp stones and other debris. He grunted aloud as his chest impacted with the uneven earth and he came to rest. From somewhere to his left, and somewhat above him, he heard a quiet chuckle followed by a whisper.

Kicking away what he thought to be a bicycle that had tangled his feet; he scrambled up; reflexively clutching the remaining pint that rested in his inner coat pocket to ensure it was still intact. The familiar tactile outline gave him reassurance and he shuffled hurriedly away without looking back.

"You broke my bike, you old bastard," the chuckling voice informed him, the humor gone from it now. Preston slowed, knowing that he had no hope of outrunning the speaker. As if reading his thoughts, the voice continued, "You'd better not try to run away." Preston halted altogether. He turned to face his accuser, dread creeping along his spine like a caterpillar. The new moon had only just risen and now the clearing and its train cars, glistening with early dew, lay revealed in the pale white glow.

Connor Lacey leaned within the doorway of the closest car, his arms folded across his broad chest, his face a disapproving mask in the ghastly radiance, his eyes burnt holes. He was tall for a fourteen-year-old, athletically built, his blond curls giving him the appearance of a Roman bust, both beautiful and cruel. He was immensely popular at school, though mostly feared outside of it due to a casual recklessness that sometimes took a sinister, and even vicious, turn.

His creature, as Preston liked to term him, waited restlessly at his feet, a wiry boy of about the same age, but noticeably less physically developed than Connor. He wore spiky black hair and, even in the moonlight, the spots on his narrow crooked face appeared as purplish eruptions. Glaring at Preston as if he had hated him his whole short life, he flung a shiny piece of metal at the old man, catching him on the ankle with it. Preston yelped like a dog, bending down to grasp his injury as the boys laughed softly together.

"You know that had to hurt," Jared Case remarked good-naturedly to his friend. Preston moaned, his hand coming away with something moist and sticky on it. In the moonlight his blood appeared black.

Raising himself painfully to his full height, Preston managed to say, "I know who you two are." He hated himself for the quaver in his voice, the trembling of his legs. "Don't think for a moment I don't. Last time, I didn't say anything to the police. I let bygones be bygones. I'd hoped you'd learn your lessons without having to do time." He was referring to an incident some months before when the two of them had beaten him nearly unconscious in the deserted 4-H grounds, robbing him of his money and whiskey. They had gotten *both* his bottles.

"I'd hate to do it," he continued weakly, feeling cold and afraid, "but naturally I have to think of the community, too. We can't have this kind of hooliganism in Wessex you know… it's just not right." As these words died on his lips, silence reigned.

Both boys watched him, their expressions unreadable. They reminded him of dogs on point, immobile yet vibrating with menace.

Connor broke the spell, dropping down to stand next to his smaller friend. Placing a hand on Jared's sharp shoulder, he said equally enough to Preston, "I'll kill you if you if do that… try it and see." It was as if he was assuring Preston of the reliable delivery of his morning paper. Preston took a small step back. "I'm also going to cave your fucking skull in if you run from us, old man," he added flatly. Reaching down, he selected a good-sized chunk of broken concrete, weighing it in his hand.

Preston halted and stilled himself. He could hear his own ragged breathing; feel the warm trickle of blood down his ankle. "What…" he began hoarsely, "what can I do?" He hated himself for pleading.

"You can start by sucking my giant cock," Jared snorted.

"He's not getting that nasty-ass mouth of his anywhere near my Johnson," Connor stated plainly. "No," he instructed Preston, "you can hand over those bottles to begin with."

Preston winced in spite of himself. He had only the one left, he thought, and he'd be damned if he'd…

The larger boy interrupted his thoughts. "You'll also have to pay Jared for his bike… that's an expensive piece of equipment you broke."

Even in the weak light that seeped through the trees, Preston could see that the bike was undamaged. "I think its fine; I don't believe I actually broke anything," a note of complaint entered his voice. "Besides, I don't have any money left."

He couldn't understand why he was lying, as he knew it would do him no good. He wished now with all his heart that he had listened to Fanny the first time he had survived these boys, and had told the police about them. But he had been humiliated and terrified by the experience and had just wanted to put it behind him.

Preston had also feared the trouble that might have followed… the things that the boys had promised to say about him if he "ratted" to the police—the things that they had been willing to allege. He understood how easy it was to become the target, the pariah. And didn't Chief Catesby remind him of it once again just this morning?

The empty beer bottle was no more than a blur of motion before it struck Preston in his narrow chest. He cried out, sitting down as hard as if he had been shoved by a giant. Grasping his bruised breastbone, he heard himself sob aloud with the pain and humiliation of his predicament.

Preston heard Jared boast, "Dead on center of mass. If that'd have been a bullet he'd be a dead man. Game over."

As the moon cleared the tops of the trees that lined the tracks, Preston watched in dread the boys detaching themselves from the shadow of the train cars, beginning their self-assured approach. He saw, too, in a haze of misery, that Connor still retained the chunk of concrete, so it must have been Jared that had thrown the bottle. Connor hoisted his burden to shoulder level as he came, appearing to weigh and consider its potential crushing power.

Preston didn't know why, but he understood that something had changed in just the last few seconds. Perhaps it had been his threat to go to the police, or perhaps this was simply the moment that had to happen for these particular boys—if not now, then later, and if not to him, then to someone else, but he was sure now that Connor was going to kill him.

He struggled to rise, gasping for the breath that had been driven from his lungs. Shooting his arm out, palm forward, as if to ward off his attackers, he wheezed, "I have whiskey!"

Preston fumbled to retrieve the bottle even as he tried to gain his shaky legs. "Unopened," he cried, producing the bottle with a flourish. Preston felt ridiculously happy that Jared's bottle had not broken his own, a sickly smile spreading across his face.

"That's good," Connor observed in his agreeable monotone. "I wouldn't want my lips on anything yours have been on." His elongated shadow fell across Preston while he was still twelve feet distant. The shadow of his smaller partner danced at his side like a black goblin.

"These old bums like to suck each other," Jared opined. "They'll rape little girls, too, because they can't get any from a grown woman. What did you do with that little Guthrie girl anyway, sicko?" He stopped and turned to Connor. "Wouldn't it be cool if we found her body? This old bastard probably did it, you know. He's always creepin' around everywhere. What'a ya say we bash his fingers on the rail with your rock, one at a time? I bet he'll tell us then what he did with her."

Connor halted as well, appearing to give his little friend's suggestion serious consideration, then shook his head decisively.

"No," he declared evenly, "I think I want to kill him now, but I like the idea about the rail. We could do the same thing with his skull."

Preston heard all of this in a kind of waking horror. They were speaking of him as if were not actually present, as if he were already dead. Staggering to his feet at last, Preston felt a warm trickle of urine run down his leg. The boys turned back to him. They seemed affronted that he had the temerity to rise.

Connor resumed his advance as Jared appeared to search the ground at his feet. "I'll need something to…"

Something that glowed whitely in the moonlight sprang from the undergrowth and onto Jared's bent back. As Preston observed this, too amazed to speak, Jared staggered forward with the unexpected weight of his sudden burden, brushing past his companion who had witnessed nothing of what had occurred behind him.

Stopping, Conner looked after Jared, who appeared to have thrown himself into the jimson weed and thorn apple that grew in rank profusion beside the tracks. A strong musk scent descended upon the scene. The following silence was both puzzling and terrifying.

"Jay…?" Connor began hesitantly, taking a few tentative steps in the direction of the other boy's disappearance. He gave Preston a warning glance, saying, "Don't even think about it," and then said again, "Jay… you asshole, what the fuck are you doin' in there?"

The only answer was a steady, stealthy rustling of the rank plants, as if something squirmed within. Taking several more steps towards the sound, he stopped again, leaning forward in order to see. The old man began to back quietly away.

Preston heard Connor speaking again, a note of incredulity in his voice now, "Hey…" he began, "what are you doin'… Jared?" Then, "Who the fuck are you, asshole?" In spite of the fear that Preston could now hear in his voice, Connor nonetheless raised the concrete chunk in one hand while reaching into the weeds with the other. "Git off him," he commanded, seizing something and giving it a hard tug.

Preston recognized the streaked pale face, the tangled hair, and the glittering great eyes of Gabriel rising from the undergrowth. The head turned owl-like to regard its captor, the chin glistening dark and moist. Preston thought of how his own blood had looked on his fingertips just moments before. The larger boy hoisted the concrete up and began its descending arc.

Before Preston could break himself away from this mesmerizing tableau, he saw Gabriel's long arm streak forth like a serpent, seizing Connor's throat, snapping his head back with the force of it. The larger boy appeared to toss the concrete bludgeon away, so feeble was his response to Gabriel's attack.

Rising up, from what Preston could only surmise was the body of Jared Case, Gabriel drew Connor to him in his languid, unhurried manner. The bigger boy's face grew dark with engorged blood, as Gabriel's hand encircled his neck with its talon-like fingers. The vomitus scent of his musk blossomed like a freshly opened grave.

Using his last shred of will-power, Preston wrenched himself from the scene, turning and stumbling away, scattering stones before him in a clatter, terrified that he too might find the feral child suddenly riding his back like an incubus. Risking a backwards glance, he saw Gabriel's head snap round at the sound of his flight, his attention as focused as any predator. Then, having gauged the activity as unthreatening, he turned back to his newest captive.

In that same moment, Preston also saw the silhouette of Jared Case sit up from the weeds, even as Gabriel squatted on his legs while drawing Connor closer. Without bothering to turn, Gabriel's other arm snapped out and pressed the smaller of his victims back into the earth. Before Preston could tear his eyes away, he saw the child's frog-like mouth drop open into an impossible gape, much like a snake unhinging its jaw in order to swallow a prey of much greater size. With a cry, Preston fled the tracks and into the woods, his only thoughts of life and escape.

Stumbling on, his arms raised protectively in front of him, Preston pushed through low-hanging branches. Even above his own ragged breathing the crashing of his footsteps through the dry litter of the forest floor sounded loud, but he didn't dare look back to see if he was being followed. His only thought was to put distance between him and what was happening back there at the railroad tracks.

A long way off a thin cry rose into the velvety night sky, and this, more than anything he had so far seen, gave him the strength to go on. In that terrible, brief wail he recognized his own terror of mortality, and ran on, heedless of direction or destination, concerned only with escape and survival.

Breaking out onto a deserted two-lane blacktop, head swiveling from right to left, Preston looked for some clue as to which direction he should choose. To his left, at the end of a long corridor of trees, there appeared to be a greater lightening, as if it might open out into a neighborhood, a place where there might be people and shelter. While in the other direction the darkness appeared unbroken, mute and threatening. In the gloom beneath the great hickories that sheltered the street from moonlight, he thought he detected a movement, a shadow a lighter shade from its brothers. He turned to his left, staggering on.

His heavy breathing and pounding heart prevented him from hearing the surf, so he stumbled on past the stop sign at the end of the street. When he saw the oily black expanse of the Delaware Bay heaving beneath the newly revealed moon, he stopped, sinking to his knees. It was high tide, and the narrow strip of remaining beach afforded him no further room for maneuver. His only choice was to turn back, retracing his footsteps up the long darkened street, and this he could not do. Even if his fear of encountering Gabriel could be mastered, he simply lacked the strength.

The shacks and cottages that dotted the shoreline were dark and boarded-up, their owners having returned to their homes in Pennsylvania and North Jersey several weeks before. No one walked the lonely beach beneath the now-bright glow of the moon. The only sign of human life lay far out to sea, where distant lights winked like stars from the bows and sterns of fishing boats and commercial trawlers. With a groan, Preston sank down onto the grainy damp sand and lay there panting like an old dog.

Then, also in the manner of a dog, he rose to his hands and knees and began pulling himself toward a fallen tree that had washed up on shore many years—perhaps hundreds of years—before. It lay gray and smooth as a giant's femur bone, and he sought its meager shelter where it rested beneath the windows of a faded yellow house. With a sigh, Preston laid his long frame beneath its huge trunk, supported as it was by several stumpy appendages that must have once been great limbs, and then closed his eyes, falling promptly to sleep.

CHAPTER FIVE

It was the smell that caused his eyes to fly open, and he knew without seeing him that Gabriel was nearby. Preston had no idea how long he had slept, but he could see that the moon had climbed to its zenith in the cold twinkling sky. The shadow he lay in beneath the petrified tree was as inky black as a deep hole in the earth. Trying not to betray his presence by breathing too loudly, he noticed to his alarm the night had grown crisp and chilly, revealing his breath in tiny, silvered puffs. A movement to his right caught his eye and he cautiously swiveled his head to try and take in its cause.

Squatting on top of a downward twist of the huge, felled trunk, Gabriel studied something he clasped in one of his long, furred hands. He was no longer wearing the ill-fitting clothes Preston had last seen him in but wore jeans only a little too short for him now, a jersey marred only by some dark stains at the collar. This last hung on him scarecrow-like. Preston felt his bowels twisting as he recognized Jared's trousers; Connor's shirt.

The boy turned his head to peer down at Preston in his disturbing owl-like manner, something dark and sticky-looking on his chin. With a gasp, Preston edged his way further beneath the great trunk. As if making an offering to the old man, or possibly an enticement to come out from his useless burrow, Gabriel held out the object he had been so solemnly regarding. The moonlight made it glow whitely, revealing the fissures, the empty, forward-looking sockets, the few remaining teeth still affixed to the upper jaw. The lower jaw was entirely missing.

"Jesus Christ," Preston whispered.

Gabriel's chuckling had the liquid sibilance of a brook running over smooth stones. He thrust the skull closer to Preston in his hidey-hole, saying, "It's not *you;* not human."

At these words, Preston saw it at once—the skull was too low and narrow to have been human, the teeth too long. Smiling now, revealing his own long teeth, Gabriel pointed out to the dark water, the receding tide. He made an undulating gesture with his hand and arm, the rubbery effect made all the more uncanny by the eerie setting. Preston stared uncomprehendingly until the boy barked twice in sharp succession, making him jump.

Preston gaped, before recognizing the obvious. "A seal," he cried in relief, "it's a seal, isn't it?"

Gabriel nodded happily at having been understood, bringing the bleached remains within inches of Preston's face. Raising his hands, the old man said, "I thought it was one of the…" he stopped himself, "… how nice that you have a seal skull… good for you."

Gabriel withdrew the offering, still smiling. After a moment, his mouth fell partially open and he began the gentle panting Preston had noted before, but his eyes remained fixed on him.

Preston squirmed, struggling to sit upright and remove his remaining pint from his jacket. He had to slide out somewhat from the cover of the beached tree to accomplish this and he, in his turn, kept his eyes on the boy. Even so, he felt Gabriel's behavior was not as threatening as he had at first feared. The strange boy appeared relaxed, content to sit at his perch watching Preston. Like an animal, his repose was alert, but seemingly untroubled.

"You won't hurt me," Preston said as he uncapped his whiskey. "You're a good boy, I think. I know you don't want to hurt anyone." Connor's anguished wail was still in his ears.

This last made Gabriel smile once more, the crowded mouth ghastly in the moonlight. Preston recoiled.

Still the boy did nothing, and after several more moments Preston dared to continue, "Thank you for helping me back there, Gabriel." He had said the name aloud without thinking. Surely the boy had one of his own, Preston thought. But before he could ask, the boy repeated it.

"Gabriel," he said, turning to stare out across the empty bay.

Preston followed his gaze to see that even the boats had vanished from the horizon as the night had deepened, and now the wind from the east danced across the black waters, throwing up small whitecaps beneath the distant stars. The world might have been empty of people but for the two of them, he thought. Yet, as he took his first long and welcome pull from the bottle, he wondered if, indeed, there were two "people" sharing the beach at that moment. In a sudden burst of bravado and camaraderie fueled by his near escape and the brandy, he thrust the uncapped bottle beneath the boy's nose saying, "Care for a shot?"

Gabriel's head reared back, the eyes opening wide, the nostrils distending with an animal-like snort. Preston felt his hand seized in a grip so stern and merciless that he thought it would surely crush the bottle within as well as the brittle bones beneath. He let out a small, stifled cry, even as he was released to fall back against the smooth log. Gabriel's smile had entirely vanished, and the seal skull now lay in the sand at Preston's feet, forgotten as a child's discarded toy.

"I'm sorry," Preston pleaded, anxious to restore their relationship and ensure his own safety. "That was foolish of me… you're… you're too young for alcohol. You were completely right, absolutely correct. I don't know what I was thinking. Sometimes I drink too much myself, you see, and do foolish things. This was certainly one of them. Let's not give it another thought, okay?" Gabriel turned his face seaward once more, as if having lost interest in the entire matter.

Preston watched him for several moments longer, then feeling the crisis had passed, thought to satisfy his curiosity about the boy. In any event, he didn't feel comfortable enough to try leaving his company just yet. "So, the question having arisen naturally enough… just how old *are* you…" Preston asked, "… fourteen, or so?"

Dropping silently onto the sand, Gabriel stretched his arms wide and yawned, his great maw turned to the heavens. When he had finished, he shuddered his entire length then set himself down, making use of the skull as a stool for his narrow rump. Gripping his bony knees, his filthy talon-like nails showing a full half-inch beyond his fingertips, he sat facing Preston. The freshening breeze spared Preston his puzzling odor that could at one moment be repugnant and in the next strangely beguiling and lulling.

"I have many more years than you, Preston," Gabriel answered clearly enough, in spite of the lisp inflicted by his crowded teeth, "Many more I am certain." Then he added more cryptically, lifting a corroded-looking claw to point at Preston's thin chest, "You will die soon, I think. You always die soon."

Preston sat up straighter at this chilling response, forcing himself to smile, and said, "I was never good at guessing ages."

He swiftly changed subjects, "By the way, I can't keep calling you Gabriel, you know, I'm sure that you have your own name. Would you mind sharing it with me... now that we're good friends?"

"Gabriel *is* my name." The boy smiled back at him, adding, "I have never had another, and it pleases me."

Preston considered this response as equally unlikely as the previous. Taking a good long swallow of liquor to steady himself, and lubricate his thinking, he asked, "What do your mother and father call you then? What name did they give you?"

Gabriel appeared to consider this for a moment, his shaggy head tilting to one side as if he were listening to something beyond Preston's hearing. "She had not learned any speech that I recall, and so, did not name me," he answered.

"What about your father then?" Preston persisted.

Gabriel shook his head, saying, "No, there was none but her."

"There's a lot of single parent families these days... more common than not." Preston murmured. He hoped he didn't sound too condescending, but doubted the boy was intelligent enough to grasp it if he did. "What does your poor mother do for a living? Does she work in the area here?"

Gabriel appeared to weigh Preston's question, rolling it around heavily in his mind. "Do?" he repeated, then after a pause said, "She fed me her own blood... before I was able to hunt for myself she would allow me to sup at her throat. There were not so many of you here then," he clarified, "and she might be gone for several nights before she could return. She would hide me away and I would await her. She had no speech," he repeated. "There were few to speak with."

Preston stared silently at the boy, unable to account for his astounding, nonsensical, eloquence. He's as mad as he is simple, he thought, even as events of earlier that evening returned in a new, even more sinister light. "Where is she now, Gabriel… your mother? Does she know that you are out so late at night?"

"She departed many, many sleeps ago," he answered, "and never came to me again. But it was no matter, Preston, as I had learned to hunt small things by then and could fend for myself. After each sleep, I found that I had grown a little and was stronger. There were also more of you around each time I awakened. This made things easier for me… for a while, at least." He regarded Preston with an unreadable expression and the older man grew uneasy once more.

Even so, his curiosity had been piqued by the bits and pieces of the boy's strange ramblings. "That's very tough circumstances to be in … to be left behind by your mother. When was this exactly? You said something about several 'sleeps' ago… How long are your sleeps?" Gabriel continued to watch Preston as if he expected something more from the older man. "Days… weeks…?" Preston offered.

"I sleep when I am no longer hungry… I arise when I am. My days are not your days, Preston… my years are not your years."

Preston shook his head in bewilderment when suddenly it struck him that Gabriel had been using his name. "How did you know that I am called Preston, son?" he asked. He was certain he had not spoken it in the boy's presence during their earlier encounter.

Gabriel smiled once more, his dragonfly-green eyes glittering. "I listen at windows," he giggled like a naughty child, covering his huge toothsome grin with a blood-specked hand.

Preston was brought up short by this latest revelation. The thought of the feral boy creeping around his home in the darkness, peering in windows, listening in on conversations was unsettling. He had seen with his own eyes what Gabriel was capable of, and his thoughts went to Fanny.

Something flew low and unseen over their heads, its passage a mere whisper of wind through feathers. Preston shuddered and asked, "Why don't we have a fire, Gabriel? Would you like that? It's a bit chilly out here tonight."

"Fires are nice," the boy agreed, but Preston detected an unmistakable discomfort cross his features, his great eyes growing wary once more.

Rising a little unsteadily, Preston began to cast about for driftwood. When he turned back to see if Gabriel intended to offer any help, the boy was gone. Preston turned this way and that but could see nothing that might be Gabriel. In the silvery light of the now-descending moon, the beach sand glowed whitely, revealing nothing. In the opposite direction the yellow marsh grasses swayed with the gentle on-shore breeze, the landscape empty but for the presence of a few black and twisted trees struggling at the dune line.

The boy moves like a shadow, Preston thought, gathering an armful of dried wood from the high tide line, and glancing over his shoulder from time to time. The thought of trying to leave did not tempt him, as he recalled the long, dark distances he would have to traverse. Knowing where the boy was proved far more comforting than not knowing.

When he had gathered enough for a small fire, he scooped out a shallow bowl in the sand, filling it with wind-dried twigs. Afterwards, he stacked the wood together above this nest of tinder and put a kitchen match to it—dozens of nights of "roughing it" had taught him the lessons that every hobo had to learn. Within a few moments, the tinder flared and the breeze fanned it into a blaze that caught quickly. Soon he was warming his hands at a crackling fire.

Satisfied, Preston retrieved his bottle from inside his coat, uncapped it, and brought it to his chapped lips. As the amber warmth tumbled down his throat, he realized with a start that

Gabriel had returned and was perched once more on the beached tree. He gasped and choked, while managing to say, "My God, boy, make some noise when you're around, will you?"

Smiling down at him, Gabriel answered, "That would not be wise, Preston. I like to come and go as I please." Preston noted with disgust that the blood on Gabriel's chin appeared refreshed, moist and glistening.

Preston considered this and said nothing, sitting himself carefully down next to the fire's cheerful blaze, the bucolic scene marred by the presence of the skull. Even so, he had grown more confident in his odd relationship with the strange boy and could not contain his curiosity. "Have you cut yourself?" he asked, pointing at his own chin.

Raising one of his own freakish digits, Gabriel dabbed at the blood on his chin. He regarded the result for a moment before flicking out a long and facile tongue to taste it, his cat-like eyes glazing with pleasure. Preston could not turn away from the boy's obvious and disturbing enjoyment, watching in horrid fascination as Gabriel's serpent tongue cleansed his chin of gore.

"No," Gabriel answered at last, "I have not hurt myself, Preston, but I was not yet finished with my feeding when you ran away. You are my good friend now, and I didn't want you to be hurt in your haste so I followed. I went back to secure my prey."

Preston blinked. "Your prey," he repeated. "Have you harmed those boys, Gabriel… you know what I mean… killed them?" He felt a twinge of guilt when he found himself half-hoping that he had.

"That would be a waste of blood to kill them, Preston. It does not keep in the dead," he replied with his little half-smile. "I wished to be sure they were too weak to escape before my return—they are young, and we have many nights yet to play together."

The older man stared at the younger in both confusion and horror. "I don't understand you, boy," he began, "I want to, but

I don't. Perhaps, now that we are friends, I could ask you some questions, and you could answer them for me... as best you can, of course, then maybe I could get a clearer picture of ... what... that is, who... you are, exactly. That would make us even better friends, wouldn't it?" he finished with a smile.

"Would it?" Gabriel smiled back, adding, "If it will please you, Preston, I shall."

In spite of his newly revealed aptitude for speech, Preston noted that the boy still appeared to speak as if English might be a second language, haltingly, rummaging through his mind to make the correct selections. Even more puzzling was the archaic pattern of his English usage. Preston found it reminiscent of early American literature, colonial, perhaps, certainly no later than Hawthorne.

Who would have taught him to speak in such a manner? He wondered. What's more, who *could*?

Preston leaned forward in anticipation, collecting his thoughts. "That's very kind of you, Gabriel, very kind. You are a good boy, I think." Clapping his hands softly together, he began by reviewing what he already knew, or at least had been told. "So, you have no name, and don't remember your age. Is that right?"

The boy disagreed. "Gabriel is my name."

Preston waved him off. "No," he corrected him, "that's the name *I* gave you. I am referring to your own... your *real* names—first and last. You don't know either of these?"

Gabriel turned his face away from Preston and whispered stubbornly, "Gabriel."

Preston chose to ignore the boy's petulance and continued, "Yes, all right then, we'll leave that for now, but what about this mother of yours? What was she called? *She* must have had a name."

Gabriel shook his head once, dislodging several dried leaves from the tangle of his hair. "She was called nothing. We had no speech then. I told you that there was no one to speak with… or very few in any case."

"Your mother never spoke to you at all?" Preston asked. "Was she a mute, then?"

Gabriel shrugged his indifference. "What would we have spoken of?" he asked in his turn.

"About a name for her child, maybe," Preston barked. Glancing up at the boy, a little fearful of the tone he had used, he saw that Gabriel remained placid and unmoved. Preston rubbed his hands together to make a new start.

"Now then," he resumed. "Now then… how about these others you mention… these neighbors of yours? Wasn't it necessary to speak with them?" A sudden thought flashed into his mind, an inspiration. "Your neighbors weren't Amish were they… or something like that?" Linguistics was not his specialty but maybe that would explain the boy's unusual speech.

Dashing his hopes, Gabriel answered, "I don't know Amish. Are they the dark-skinned ones who daubed themselves with clay and soil when they searched for me? Are those Amish?"

Preston stared open-mouthed for several long moments, gathering his wits about him. "Daubed themselves?" he asked at last. "Searched for you? What are you talking about?"

Standing suddenly on his log, the boy feigned the unmistakable drawing of an invisible bow, the release of a phantom arrow. Even through the wind, Preston heard his whistled mimicry of an arrow slicing through the air. Gabriel looked down at Preston to see if his pantomime had been effective, then raising his nightmarish arms to the inky heavens, he howled, "Hoo, hoo… hoo, hoo!"

Preston fell back in surprise and shock—the boy made a terrifying picture as he clawed at the heavens and hooted like some great owl.

"I was smaller, then," Gabriel crowed, "and very swift, and they could not pierce me! I made their children my prizes!" The flickering light of the fire painted the boy in shifting shades and colors.

"Gabriel," Preston whispered, "that would make you several hundred years old, you know, to have had… encounters, shall we call it, with the Lenape. They left this area in the 1700s."

The boy nodded in agreement, but as to what part of his statement Preston couldn't guess. Gabriel continued, "Once, when I awoke, the painted ones were gone and they never returned. But…" he glanced slyly at the older man, pointing a long, filthy finger at him, "there were many more of you by then.

"At first, I fed well, as you did not know me, but in time I was seen. Then things grew difficult and I had to be very careful. I listened at windows to learn of your habits and tongue, and this proved useful—wearing garments and saying words helped the children to come to me." Gabriel looked into Preston's face. "In the days that I kept them, we would converse and I would learn more."

Preston thought of the little girl gone missing and the two boys he had left behind on the tracks, and a fine sweat began to form on his brow in spite of the breeze. "You don't really hurt them, then?" he asked. "You don't… kill them, do you?"

"Oh yes," Gabriel assured him. "In time they must die as they no longer have blood enough to live… by then they have gone stupid," he added, "and no longer care."

The calm cruelty of the boy's words struck Preston's heart as cold as anything he had so far witnessed or heard. He returned to his questioning, repulsed and intrigued, fearful of what he might learn, yet unable to turn away. "Why do you keep them, Gabriel? Is it for company, are you lonely?"

Gabriel reached deep into his borrowed trousers, scratching earnestly at his genitals and staring up at the sliver of moon sailing through the sky. After satisfying his itch, he answered, "Their blood goes bad too quickly when they're killed outright. They have other uses as well."

"Such as," Preston ventured.

"Their speech, as I said, but also for…" Preston noted the hesitation; the slyness that crept into the boy's smeared face, "…decoys." He finished this statement with a coy glance at Preston from the corner of his slanted eyes.

"Decoys," Preston repeated, "what do you mean? I don't follow."

The boy was silent for several long moments, as if considering the wisdom of continuing. "When I am hunted, Preston, it is useful to give the hunters a quarry. Many sleeps ago, after the painted people left, I saw that the new ones hunted me where they buried their dead. I didn't know why, until a child wandered away from me when I had gone a-hunting myself—she had been stronger than I thought—so when I returned and found she had taken herself away, I went in search of her.

"As I neared your village, I beheld the burial place was lit by men carrying torches and crying out to one another. They had found my girl wandering amongst the stones that mark your deaths, and they were sore afraid. I watched them from the trees and saw her stumble and moan at their coming."

Preston could easily picture the scene, as he had no doubt that Gabriel was referring to the Baptist Cemetery, no more than two miles distant, containing the crypts and burial places of Wessex County's first settlers.

"She fell and lay prostrate, and after a while they drew close to her and spoke in whispers that I could barely hear. These men said that it must have been she that had lured their other children away, that she was unclean and undead. One man did not like this, but the others pushed him aside. They listened carefully for her heartbeat, but could not detect it. Then she spoke some words, but they made no sense, and this affrighted them even more. They did not know that when the blood is drained away the children become insensible and I could smell their fear.

"I was impatient for them to go away so that I could fetch her back before she died, but they did not leave, only went some little distance away from her, where they conversed amongst themselves. After a while, one man separated himself from the others, while several more led the other, the unhappy man, away. Then, before I could think of how to get my prize back, this man pierced her heart with his knife. When she screamed, he leapt up and ran some several feet away before stopping once more with the others. They had all become as white as my prey.

"I thought then of how I wished to drink from this man since he had robbed me of my food. But I dared not approach as there were so many, and none were pups. Then the man with the dagger knelt down and sliced the throat of the girl through and through until her head fell away. They all marveled at how little blood she contained and spoke aloud of this as the cause of her hunger for their children. This last made me know them even better, so now I knew how to trick them and lead them away from my trail." Gabriel glanced once more at Preston to see if he understood, then said again, "Decoys."

"You mean to say that you would leave your victims to be murdered by their own friends, their own families?" Preston asked.

Gabriel watched the dying flames with interest. "Not all of them, Preston," he answered, "only those necessary to throw off my pursuers. The others I finished myself as I am needful... but in these times, I am seldom sought for amongst the stones. I have *other* ways now to confound my hunters."

"So they don't become like you, Gabriel... they don't be-come... *vampires*?" Preston watched for the boy's reaction to the word.

Gabriel stared blankly at him for a moment, then said, "No, they do not become like me, Preston. They become dead."

"My God," Preston heard himself saying, "The hurt and misery you must have caused."

Gabriel replied with animation, "I, too, was sore hurt once—my very heart shot out." He lifted the ill-fitting shirt to reveal his narrow waist and the great rib cage that swelled above it, and placed one of his fingertips into a thumb-sized depression. "See here, Preston, what was done to me. This hunter knew to aim before me so that I would spring into the path of his ball. He had stalked me for an entire season and learned my habits. I did fear him so."

Preston stared hard at the puckered, faded scar that surrounded the tiny crater and thought of a musket ball's spherical shape and density. He had seen dozens displayed at the county museum. "It's right over your heart," he murmured, "how could you have…?"

Answering his unfinished question with a smile, Gabriel said, "I have two, Preston, one in either breast. I have seen the innards of both man and beast and know myself to be alone in this. The hunter, though he had studied me well, did not know this.

"It hurt me sore, Preston, but I drank all that man's blood for his troubles, and then I went to my sleep early that season. When I awoke, I was once more whole and strong."

Preston turned up the bottle with shaking hands, draining it. The shock of the events of the evening, combined with the effect of the two bottles of brandy, made his head swirl and he tossed the empty onto the sand. He could see the night tide was drawing away from the beach revealing a series of sandbars, like arising islands, as the swift current ran south into the Atlantic Ocean.

"It can't be," Preston whispered, "it just can't." Turning once more to the boy, his curiosity near even with his loathing and fear, he asked, "How can I believe without proof? You must show me that you are not… one of us, Gabriel."

The boy hesitated, but just a moment, before sliding down from his perch to present himself to Preston. He smiled his panting half-smile, and Preston, assailed by his rancid breath, forced himself to approach.

Cautiously, in much the same manner as he might have neared a suspect dog, he reached out, gently taking Gabriel's hands in his own. The tops, besides their extraordinary length and claw-like nails, were narrow and thickly corded with tendons, the numerous hairs long and coarse. They resembled the feet in almost all respects, but for the facility of their digits. When he turned them palm up, he found that the pads of Gabriel's fingertips were dark and cracked, without line or whorl— he possessed no fingerprints.

Still holding onto Gabriel's hands, Preston glanced up into the boy's mesmerizing eyes to find the child leaning close in to him, the fearful tongue lolling from his mouth, the nostrils distended and questing. Startled, Preston drew back, releasing the hands and gasping, "You won't harm me... you said you wouldn't."

Gabriel regarded the old man for several moments, then, as Preston watched, the broad face grew more relaxed and the panting quieted. Gabriel answered, "So I did, Preston... but it is wise to remind me." The smile returned.

"It's true, then, isn't it?" he asked aloud, though he required no answer. "You *are*... something... apart from us." The enormity of his discovery (because he did consider Gabriel *his* discovery) suddenly overwhelmed Preston and he staggered back against the log, nearly stepping into the dying embers of the fire. "But..." he began, as a sudden thought occurred to him, "how... how do you feed, Gabriel? I see a lot of teeth, mind you," he giggled drunkenly, "but no *fangs*! How do you explain that, my boy? With those ragged choppers of yours you'd chew their heads off, wouldn't you?"

Sitting down hard on the sand, he laughed aloud as the last of the alcohol he had consumed that day released itself into his bloodstream. He had been drunk often enough to know that he had, at last, reached the end of his endurance for another day.

Gabriel squatted before the older man, shadows twining themselves across his face from the last of the fire, and opened his great mouth, the jaw impossibly unhinging itself to achieve a nightmarish gape. As Preston watched, stupefied, the tongue emerged like a thick, raw serpent, lifting itself to gently touch the tip of Gabriel's nose. Then he saw the two viper-like teeth that lay buried within the flesh of the underside of the tongue. Like twin hypodermic needles they lay sheathed within the muscle and were retracted once more as he watched. Gabriel had answered his question.

Groaning in terror at what he had witnessed, Preston began edging crab-like away from the boy to the useless shelter of the beached tree. He pointed desperately at an edge of red that lay to the east of them, just visible on the low horizon. "The sun is coming up, boy! You'd better go now don't you think? Hurry now or it will burn you up!"

Gabriel stood, looking to the rose-colored tinting of the eastern sky and chuckled, saying, "I don't like the sun, Preston, it makes my eyes tender, my skin raw, but it will not kill me. Still, it is time for me to go," he agreed. "It is not good for me to be seen in the daylight."

Relieved, yet still reeling with fear and shock, Preston managed to ask, "Where do you go to, Gabriel? Do you rest in a grave?"

The boy, or creature, as Preston now understood him to be, appeared to grow pensive, answering, "I would not like that, I think, Preston. How would I breathe? Once, many sleeps ago, I dwelt in a house with wings. I liked it there. The sound of the wings was nice, but then it fell into the creek bed one night and I sought other shelter."

"Wings," Preston repeated, "I don't understand." But the boy had already begun striding toward the line of maritime forest that lay nearby. "Where can I find you, then?" Preston called after him.

Stopping, Gabriel turned and waggled a long finger at the old man. "That would be telling," he said. "I'll find you when I have need of you."

"Need of me… need of me for what?" Preston shouted back, but Gabriel was already bounding swiftly through the dune grasses, only to vanish within the stunted trees of the twisted, windswept woods.

CHAPTER SIX

Father Gregory Savartha watched Preston stumbling hurriedly down the street in his direction. It was warm in the early morning sunshine and he was content to wait a few moments before entering Wessex Coffee. He hoped to engineer a meeting.

The little priest knew the other man only as the "Professor," a title which Father Gregory respected greatly, especially as he understood it to be for advanced degrees in English literature. He was a great admirer of Dickens and Harding, Greene and Austen.

Though English was not his native tongue, he had made a thorough study of it during his seminary years in India. These lessons had not been wasted and he had discovered a world of literature of which he had become very fond. Less happily, his command of the spoken tongue had not kept apace.

"Ah, Professor," he called out cheerfully to Preston as the older man shuffled past him without as much as a glance. "It is a beautiful day today, I find! Will you not halt with me for some moments?"

Preston half-turned to take in the plump little man who had accosted him, and saw Father Gregory in his black suit and Roman collar beaming at him, his small hand gripping the door handle to the coffee shop. "Please, come join me for a coffee," he clarified, while making a sweeping gesture with his free hand. "Please do."

Stopping altogether now, Preston regarded the foreign priest sourly. He had noticed the dark little man listening intently to his diatribes in the library from time to time, but they had never spoken. He also realized that he was very hungry, and his head was beginning to pound from an incipient hangover. He had only slept for a few hours on the damp beach before the cold had awakened him, sending him scurrying for home. Nightmarish visions of Gabriel and their night by the sea dogged his steps, pursuing him like a bad conscience. But the thought of a cup of hot coffee and something to eat, added to the fact that his pockets were empty, decided him. Even so, he felt compelled to add conditions to his attendance.

"I have no respect for your office, little man, and will not tolerate a recruitment speech," Preston warned, his tongue clacking dryly. "You have already inducted my only daughter into your cultish practices, so consider that I have already 'given.'"

Father Gregory's smile grew brighter yet as he realized that he had received some form of acceptance. "Splendid," he crowed. "It is all settled then, shall we say?" He held the door as his imperious guest strode past him into the shop, and followed happily.

Several patrons turned to witness their entrance, and Father Gregory noted a distinct line of worry crease the owner's forehead at the sight of Preston. He took the older man's threadbare sleeve possessively and led him to a table that was being hastily abandoned. Father Gregory thought he recognized one of the librarians from across the street as she scurried past them. "Good morning," he called after her in puzzlement.

As they settled themselves, a young couple at a table facing the priest suddenly decided to leave as well. It was then that Father Gregory noted the sour fishy smell that emanated from his contentious guest's clothes and skin, as well as a slightly musky, more mysterious odor. Whispering too loudly to the girl with him, the young man said "Oh my God," wrinkling his nose at the same time to make his point. The owner, a crumpled looking man standing behind a glass counter, shook his head in either resignation or disgust.

Within moments the small, warm establishment was largely empty. "I am Father Gregory Savartha," the priest introduced himself.

Preston turned in his seat, as if nothing had been said, to glare at the proprietor. "Service," he shouted, turning back to his befuddled host. "A café au lait for me, thank you, and since you're offering, a bran muffin, toasted and buttered."

As the owner was already standing over them, it was not necessary for Father Gregory to repeat it, so he simply nodded apologetically to the man, adding, "My usual, Mister Charles, if I may please."

Charles, having come within the bloom of Preston's less-than-hygienic person, backed quickly away while jotting something onto his order pad. "It'll be right out to you," he promised.

Having had a few moments to digest Preston's earlier words, Father Gregory alighted upon their meaning. "Your daughter is one of our parishioners? What is her name, may I ask?"

"Fanny," Preston answered, glancing impatiently over his shoulder.

"Ah," the little priest cried, "yes, I know her… she is a very charming young woman… very devout! Fanny Howard! You must be very proud of her."

Preston turned back to his host and snapped, "Of course I am, and I also forgive her for her ridiculous lapse of reason as regards the Roman Church."

"I see… yes, it is good to be tolerant of one's children." Giggling, Father Gregory added, "Of course, I would have no way of really knowing, would I?" He smiled broadly across the table at Preston.

"No," Preston answered as their orders arrived, "you wouldn't." Charlie managed to spill some of Preston's coffee in his haste, but was already returning to the safety of the kitchen before Preston could chastise him. In any event, Preston found he was famished and began devouring his muffin.

Father Gregory joined him by eating his pastry with equal relish. After several mouthfuls, he mumbled while patting his round stomach, "I really should not be eating such things. I am growing fat here."

Preston did not think his remorse convincing and stared through the sheen of warm moisture that coated the plate glass window of the store front. Outside, vehicles and people were hurrying this way and that in what passed for a rush hour in Wessex Township. How mundane and ordinary their lives were, Preston mused, as the bloodstained image of Gabriel, crouching on the moonlit shore of the Delaware Bay, flickered through his mind like a primal memory. Father Gregory's words only belatedly entered into his consciousness.

"… And now, so the paper says, two more children have not returned to their homes. It is all most troubling, wouldn't you agree?"

Preston turned his attention back to the priest. "What children?" he asked after a pause.

"Two boys this time, it seems," Father Gregory replied. "Not as young as the little girl however, and the police say they are very perplexed at these goings-on."

"Two boys," Preston repeated, "How old?"

"They were both fourteen years of age," Father Gregory answered. "It seems they have run away before," he added disapprovingly, "and have caused their parents and the police great worry. Perhaps that will be the case this time as well. The police state most empathically that they are searching diligently for all three and rule nothing out. The police are behaving most commendably in this matter, I believe."

Preston snorted his amusement, "They have no idea what they are looking for."

Father Gregory studied his guest for several moments as he sipped at his heavily sugared coffee. "I see," he said, "You have a theory, Professor?"

"A theory," Preston countered, "hardly. I know…" he began; then stopped. He raised one of his patrician brows at Father Gregory and recited, "There are more things in heaven and earth, Horatio, than are dreamt of in your philosophy."

Father Gregory nearly sprang from his chair with excitement. "That is Shakespeare," he cried, "The Tragedy of Hamlet, if I am not mistaken—a most unfortunate young man!"

"Very good, Father," Preston smiled at the priest's enthusiasm… if only he had had students like this strange little man, he thought.

Father Gregory regained his composure. "But, why have you said this to me, Professor Howard? What is the meaning here?"

"You, of all people, should know," Preston replied. "Your almighty church has built its golden edifice upon the unknown… nay, the unknowable—angels and demons, saints and miracles! Why should anything on this earth be a surprise to you? What of Cain's descendants… *his* inheritors? Now there's a thought for you!" He slapped the tabletop with a force that rattled their cups, and the owner shot him a warning glance.

The cleric raised a hand, saying, "You have perplexed me greatly, Professor, I must confess."

"For God's sake, call me Preston," the older man snapped. "I only have the morons call me Professor these days—for that matter, it was mostly morons that called me Professor when I actually taught." He barked a laugh.

Father Gregory smiled, once more genuinely pleased to have been granted the privilege of Preston's Christian name. "That is most welcome," he said. "You honor me greatly… Preston." He gulped down the last of his coffee, replacing the cup in its saucer.

"My English is not as good as it might be," he began quietly, "and so I often struggle with the inner meanings of things that are said." He glanced up at Preston from beneath his white eyebrows, the blackness of his skin made all the darker by the color of what remained of his hair. "Perhaps, then, it is the case now that I have misunderstood once more, but, and here please correct me if I am mistaken, you seem to indicate some secret knowledge as regards the missing children." He studied Preston with a mild expression.

Preston looked down into the dregs of his own cup, caught off guard. He thought of the creature he had christened "Gabriel" realizing that it was with a terrible sense of pride… even ownership, that he did so. Was there any other man in the world that knew what he did at this moment, possessed such "secret knowledge," as the priest put it?

Glancing up, he said, "You have a better grasp of the language than you let on." He ran a paper napkin across his chapped lips, pushing away from the table. "This is a mystery for the mind, Gregory," Preston murmured, as the cleric smiled warmly at the use of his name, "and, therefore, foreign to you theologians, accustomed as you are to practicing mumbo-jumbo."

He shook his large shaggy head, reminding Father Gregory of a lion with a worrisome, but delicious bone. "Sometimes, there are those moments when the right man is at the right place—serendipity we call it. When such a moment occurs… well, a man would be a fool to desist, to let go of his discovery before the time is right, before its true meaning has been plumbed." Rising to his feet, he towered over the much smaller and seated man. "So, let's just leave it at that for now, shall we?"

Father Gregory was not to be put off. "Perhaps," he ventured, "such a man might wish to share his secret knowledge with others in order to alleviate their sufferings. Surely, it would be wise, and most kind, to do so, if indeed he has such knowledge."

Preston looked down the length of his long nose at the curate. "*If*," he repeated. "I assure you that *if* doesn't enter into it, little man. Please do not trouble yourself further, but leave it up to those with the intellectual capabilities and secular education to do so—to put it bluntly, *Father*, this is not a matter for churchmen."

He turned to walk away, but the priest reached over the small table, snagging the greasy sleeve of his jacket, stopping him. "I have offended you, my new friend, and I had no wish to do so. But, I must say this plainly to you, Preston… if you have knowledge of these missing children, you must speak. This is not just for their sake alone, but for your own. Do not allow pride to rob you of your humanity—God would not wish such a thing."

Snatching his arm free, Preston glared down at the priest, then answered, his voice seething with emotion, "If there were a God, then there would *be* no missing children, Priest, surely that much is obvious! God has no power here," he swept a long arm across the room, indicating the whole world. "It's all left to nature in the end, don't you see—nature is both god and devil!"

Charlie came out from behind the counter, removing his apron and looking hard at the older man. But, before he could reach him, Preston stalked out the door and into the crisp beauty of the autumn morning, his leonine head held high.

"No offense, Father," Charlie said, "but I'd really appreciate it if you didn't bring that wino in here anymore." He swept up the money the little cleric placed on the tabletop and began to clear away the cups and dishes.

"He is in a very excitable state," Father Gregory replied while watching the older man's long-legged progress down Mercantile Street. "Perhaps it is I who has upset him."

"Don't trouble yourself about *that* guy," Charlie reassured him. "Everybody knows he's got a couple screws loose... and that's when he's *not* drinking... which is never," he concluded.

Father Gregory rose to his full five foot, four inch height, saying, "Thank you, Mister Charles. The coffee was excellent, as usual." As he reached the door, he thought to add, "Oh yes, and the bear claw... this was most enjoyable. By the by, do you have a dietary version of this pastry?"

Charlie grinned at the priest and answered, "Sorry, Father, I only serve the kind that makes you fat."

Father Gregory patted his stomach for the second time that morning, and in unconscious imitation of a famous literary bear, responded, "Oh dear... dear me."

Walking the two blocks to the rectory, his thoughts were on Preston and his mysterious words, and no matter which way he turned the professor's allusions around in his mind, he was unable to come to any true understanding. He was troubled now and didn't know what he should do about it, so fetching his Rosary beads from his pocket as he strolled beneath the saffron colored leaves of the elms, he began to pray.

&

The hushed murmur grew in intensity as Chief Catesby descended the stairwell, resolving itself into individual voices as he entered the first floor of the police department. From behind every door of the long hallway there arose the hiss and squeal of suppressed anger, the barely contained fear of men under pressure.

Every available office had been pressed into use as interview rooms to accommodate the number of registered sex offenders, tipsters, and other "persons of interest," who had been rounded up and brought in. Many of the voices were complaining loudly at having been included in the roster at all, despite their previous histories—these last had the most to lose, either in terms of their carefully constructed reputations or the conditions set down in their paroles—any offense, pertinent or not to the current investigation, might send them back to prison.

Nick continued down the hallway with its grimy linoleum and scuffed green walls. At shoulder-level, someone, probably his secretary he surmised, had strung a banner of black and orange cardboard cut-outs, depicting gleeful witches astride broomsticks and idiotically grinning jack o' lanterns. The tape securing it to the cinderblock wall had already begun to give way and it drooped in sad neglect. Nick halted before the last door he came to. It was closed and he listened. Inside he could just make out a subdued conversation, but not individual words.

The door held a plaque that read simply, "Interview Room." Nick had instructed that the particular individual within be given pride of place and not be wedged into one of the administrative offices that had been pressed into service. He had also specifically requested that his friend, Jack Kimbo, sit in on the interview.

When he opened the door Jack looked back over his shoulder at him, his normally expressive face blank, and Nick understood instantly that no progress had been made. The subject of Jack's frustration sat opposite, facing the door, his fear and stubbornness revealed in equal parts by the quivering of his hands, the set line of his mouth.

From down the hall someone shouted angrily, "Sit down," and something clattered onto the floor… a door slammed. The little man's eyes widened at the commotion, then sought his own shoes. Nick eased the door shut with a click.

"Do you mind?" he asked. "It's awfully noisy around here today."

The shaking of the other man's head was barely perceptible. Nick saw that his fingers were tightly knit together.

"Good… all right then," he murmured, glancing over at Jack. "I'm Nick Catesby, Mister Albright, I'm the Chief here." The other man's eyes flickered up briefly to take him in before returning to his hands, his shoes. "I just wanted to thank you for coming in today to help us with this matter. It's a very important matter, I think you'll agree."

Mister Albright nodded.

Nick studied him a moment before proceeding. He saw a man of roughly his own age, not much more than five foot seven, maybe a hundred seventy pounds, with thinning dark hair that Nick was fairly certain had been dyed. Combined with his ashen complexion this gave him the look of a corpse prepared for a viewing. He was nervous to the point of hysteria. Nick had seen this same look dozens of times in his career, many of them in this very room. In his estimation, this was a man who had something to hide—something important. His fleshy face twitched at the corners of his pursed mouth.

"May I call you Bob, Mister Albright?" he asked, sliding into the chair opposite.

"I don't really understand why you wanted me here," the man answered, his voice a whisper. "I came in like I was asked to, but as I've told your…" he stabbed a finger at Jack, "…your… your man, here, I really don't know anything about all this… about what's been going on… what's been happening." He waved a hand helplessly at the small room. "My wife will begin to worry if I'm not home soon," he promised.

"Would you like to call her and tell her you'll be a little late?" Nick asked. He slid the desktop phone in his direction. The little man stared at it, but made no move.

"Didn't you tell your wife that you were coming here?" Jack asked. "I sure would've... I'd have damn sure told my wife." He leaned back crossing his arms.

"I didn't think I'd be very long," Albright said after a while, then, "I didn't want her to worry."

Nick now reversed the direction of the phone and returned it to his side of the table. After a moment, he opened a drawer and placed the phone inside and slid it firmly shut. He looked at Albright for a moment as the smaller man began to fidget.

"Worry," Nick repeated at last. "Megan's parents could probably tell us something about 'worry.'" Albright's head popped up at this, then ducked down once more. "Bob, why don't you tell me and Agent Kimbo what you were doing in the parking lot at the elementary school the night she went missing?"

"She..." Albright whispered hoarsely.

"Yeah, *she*, Bob," Nick snapped back. "You know who we're talking about, don't you?" Albright remained silent. "Megan, Bob... we're talking about Megan Guthrie here. Would you mind saying her name aloud for me, Bob?"

"Now that's a simple enough request," Jack added, smiling.

The room went silent as they waited. At long last, Albright murmured, "Megan."

"Good," Jack said, reaching over to pat the other man's shoulder. Albright flinched as if he had been struck. "You're doing real good, Bob."

"Now that we have that out of the way," Nick resumed, "maybe you'll tell us what you were doing there that night."

Albright's feverish looking eyes flicked from one to the other of his interrogators. "Who says I *was* there?" he asked in a small voice, with just a hint of petulance.

"Your car was there, Bob," Nick replied. "A neighbor saw it and wrote down the license plate number. He said that he's seen the car there before... usually after dark. He got suspicious and wrote it down—he has a perfect view of the school grounds from where he lives. After Megan went missing, he thought to report it. Why would he lie to us, Bob? Why would he have made it up?"

"I don't know," Albright whispered. "I... I just..."

Jack cut him off, "Someone else use your car, Bob? If you loaned it to someone, we could just have a chat with that person and that would explain everything, since your car *was* there... there's no real question of that, is there Bob?" Albright seemed to be considering something, his rubbery features squirming.

"It wasn't reported stolen, I checked out that angle before we even asked you in here," Nick picked up the questioning again. "So what were you doing there... you don't have a kid in that school, do you, Bob?" Nick already knew the answer to this as well.

"No," Albright moaned, "I don't. I just have the one boy, and he's in high school. He doesn't have to know about this... does he?"

Jack shrugged elaborately at his question, as if the issue was in doubt, something out of his control, perhaps.

"Know about what, exactly?" Nick countered. "Maybe if we knew why you were there, we could help you, if you would just explain it to us."

Both policemen watched as their primary suspect writhed and twisted in the molded plastic seat. His hands flew to his face several times as if to knead and mold his features and were returned to his lap with obvious effort. Nick noted his chewed, unclean nails, even as he witnessed his struggle. He *was* a small man; it suddenly occurred to him—could this be the "boy" Preston saw in the dusky light?

Nick was almost afraid to move, to say another word, for fear of breaking the tension that was clearly driving Albright to the brink of confession. He could hardly believe that it was going to be this easy, feeling the sweat break out beneath his armpits. What was the agonized little man going to say... what did he have to tell them? Could it really end up being this simple?

When Albright did speak again, it was with surprising vehemence. "I want you to let me go... right now," he squeaked. "You haven't even offered me a lawyer, and I know that you have to!" He stared wild-eyed from man to man, coming to his feet for the first time, his legs shaking, his voice a vibrato. "I'm not even under arrest—I came in because you asked me... because I'm a good citizen!"

"Relax, Mister Albright," Nick stood also.

"What are you so worked up about, anyway?" Jack asked, crossing his legs and leaning back in his chair. "We were just talking, weren't we... just having a conversation?"

"Conversation, my ass," Albright's voice rose to a falsetto of outrage and fear. "You two are trying to frame me for this... this..." he appeared unable to finish.

"For what...?" Nick asked. "Just what, exactly, do you think we're trying to frame you with?"

The little man fumbled with the zipper on his jacket, unable to get it started. "I'm leaving," he began to cry, "I'm walking right through this door, and no one," he glared defiantly at his captors, "no one is going to stop me! I'm going home to my wife," he wept.

Nick stepped aside, throwing open the door. "All we needed was an explanation of why you were there, Mister Albright," he said, his voice seething with anger. He watched in disgust as the weeping man swept by, stumbling for the exit and wiping the snot from his nose with his jacket sleeve. "We'll be in touch... *soon*," he promised. "We're not done here."

Joining him at the door, the FBI agent said with genuine regret, "He was *right* there, Nick; I mean *right* there—then something happened. I don't know what though, because I have never seen a guiltier, conscience-ridden sonofabitch than that one! Five more minutes, that's all it would have taken… five more minutes," he sighed.

Nick took in the tired, pouchy face of his friend, then said, "Jack, I've got to get back to the search party, but see if the prosecutor will okay a search warrant for that bastard's house and car, then get it to a judge. We've a least got enough for that much—he was there when it happened and has offered no reasonable explanation as to why. I think we've got enough.

"Tell the judge we'll be looking for anything that could have been used to abduct and secure a little girl… you know the profile, the type of things he would have needed… duct tape, gloves, children's toys, cut lengths of rope, that sort of thing."

Nodding, Jack grinned and said, "I was hoping you'd say that."

☙

Nick staggered into his office long after dark. Not bothering to turn on the overheads, he collapsed wearily into his desk chair. Through his office window he witnessed the moon as it rose over the steep pitch of library building, three stories high, bathing the slate roof and its peeling, wooden cupola in a roseate glow. The moon's yellowish, pock-marked surface appeared stained with blood, like the yolk of a fertile egg.

The tall windows of the building opposite bled light onto the shrubs that crouched round it, shaking and swaying in a wind that had arisen off the sea with the fall of night. On the great portico, standing beneath a giant lantern gently swaying on its suspending chains, a lone man smoked a cigarette.

Behind the windows, figures passed from time to time, clutching books, magazines, or DVDs, and Nick yearned to cross the street and join them, to immerse himself in quiet normalcy. He wondered, too, if Fanny Howard might also be within those walls, and the thought of her made him feel a small spark of gladness. Leaning back into the leather of his chair, Nick ran a hand through his hair, closing his eyes.

Darkness had once more halted the search for Megan—a search that had expanded with the disappearance of the two boys, but appearing no more likely to achieve success. His officers and volunteers were exhausted and their ranks thinning. Dogs, helicopters, boats, infrared scopes, trained and experienced trackers… nothing, and no one, had managed to find a single clue as to the children's whereabouts or fate. The mood of his searchers had become morose, and more than once Nick had heard mention of Seth Busby.

Across the street a burst of laughter drew his eyes once more to the library, and he noted that the smoker was gone now as a group of adolescent boys and girls burst forth from the building. They sprinted across the street and out of Nick's sight just as his cell phone began to ring.

It was Jack Kimbo. Flipping it open, he said, "Tell me something good, Jack."

There was too long of a pause before the agent answered, and Nick felt his heart dropping in his chest. "I wish I could, Nick, but I'd have to be one hell of a liar to pull that off." Nick remained silent… waiting.

Jack continued, "While we were executing the search warrant, Albright killed himself… went out to the garage after we cleared it and hung himself from a rafter with an extension cord. It was the damnedest thing, his feet were actually touching the ground when his son found him, and so the best we can figure is that after securing the cord, he just leaned forward until he passed out from lack of oxygen, then let his own body weight do the rest. The M.E.'s out here with him now."

Nick couldn't speak for several moments as the image of the frightened little man from that morning filled his mind's eye. At last he said, "No one was watching, Jack? How'd that happen?"

"We were short-handed with all the search teams out, and just trying to do a thorough job of it—he waited until we were busy, distracted, then walked out. It was only the work of a few minutes. I'm sorry, Nick."

"And the search itself," Nick asked, desperate for something salvageable, something useful.

He heard his friend sigh before answering, "No joy in that direction either, I'm afraid. It's not good news. We found what was making him so antsy during the interview, but it's not what we'd thought... what we'd hoped for in this case."

"What was it?" Nick persisted, already dreading the answer.

"Photos, magazines... all gay porn stuff... most of it hidden in the garage where he hung himself. I guess his wife and kid didn't have a clue. The worst part was that he had included some amateur action in his collection that featured him and different 'companions'. I'm guessing that one of these met him after dark in the school parking lot and drove him to a motel on the night in question. That's why his car was there, I'm thinking.

"We found nothing to do with kids, though... he wasn't bent that way, I guess. Can you believe it... this day and age... a guy goes and offs himself over something like this... where's the sense in it? Nice fuckin' surprise for the family, huh?"

"What a nightmare!" Nick answered, as the senseless tragedy of it rolled across him like a black wave. "Poor son..." he breathed, "... poor wife. Give me a few minutes and I'll be out there."

"Don't," Jack said with force. "Everything's about wrapped up out here and as soon as they finish bagging him up we're outa here, too. I've already got some family members and their minister coming this way anyhow—they... the wife and son, don't want to see any more cops tonight, Nick, not even the chief. Besides, you'd do yourself and everyone else a lot more good by going home and getting some sleep for a change. You're worn out, Buster, and need some shut-eye. This is a federal agent telling you this, so you know it's gotta be true… just do it and I'll see you tomorrow." He disconnected.

Nick closed the phone and brought his hands to his face, the action reminding him of Albright earlier that day. Bringing them away once more, he stared into the opened palms as if something might be divined there, some explanation for all that had happened over the past several days. Then, placing his head down on the desk, he closed his eyes.

❧

Nick started awake at the sound of Weller's voice, momentarily confused as to his whereabouts and the time of day.

"Sorry to wake you," his second-in-command continued, though he didn't sound it. "I guess your boy has already filled you in on the fuck-up out at the Albright search?"

"My boy…?" Nick managed to ask in his turn, his mouth dry and cottony. He struggled to sit up in his chair and recover his senses, a spark of anger at Shad's tone fueling him. "If you mean Special Agent Kimbo, then yeah, I've been briefed." He glanced at his watch, noting that he had been asleep half an hour. "I guess I dozed off waiting to get the word from you." He saw Weller stiffen.

"I wanted to tell you in person," Weller returned, "considering the nature of the news and all."

Rubbing his creased, stubbled face with both hands, Nick struggled to his feet. He understood why Weller wanted to tell him in person—he liked nothing better than to be the bearer of bad news—especially when it was to the man who had, in his mind, stolen his promotion from him.

"Well, I'm sorry you made the trip for nothing, Shad, but I think I'll head on home now—I've got to think of what to say to the press tomorrow."

"Yeah," the other man agreed, "that won't be easy…" He let the statement hang there unfinished for a moment, then added, "The Atlantic Courier and the Wessex Scribe have both been on the horn today asking questions… I put them off and told them you'd be in touch soon."

Nick stopped with one arm in the sleeve of his jacket. "Today?" he asked. "You mean before Albright killed himself?" Weller nodded and Nick thought he could detect the beginnings of a smile even in the semi-darkness of his office. "What kind of questions, Captain?"

Hesitating for just the briefest of moments, Weller said, "About suspects, Chief, about who we've been interviewing, that sort of thing… who we had let go."

"They know we're not going to be giving out the names of people we're interviewing. They know better than that, Shad. Hell, we don't even have someone that could be genuinely classified as a suspect now that Albright's eliminated."

His captain guffawed at Nick's wording, saying, "Yeah, he's *eliminated* all right!"

"You know what I meant," Nick shot back, suddenly and genuinely sick of Weller's long, lined face, his small, cunning eyes. Thrusting his other arm through the sleeve of his jacket, he strode past his second-in-command. "Close the door behind you when you leave," he spat over his shoulder.

"They want to talk about Preston Howard, Chief… I thought you might want to know that, at least."

Shad's words brought Nick to a halt. He turned slowly and asked, "And how did they come to know that we had talked with him, Captain?"

"I wouldn't know, Chief… but people are talking out there." He pointed vaguely at the window and the street beyond. "People are a little perplexed, I can tell you."

"People," Nick repeated, studying Weller's shadowed face. "And what are the *people* saying, Shad?"

Weller found Nick's eyes with his own now. "They're saying that you had the right man in the beginning, Chief, that Preston Howard is that man. *They*," he added his own emphasis, "are saying you dropped the ball and that it has probably cost the lives of two more kids." Nick felt himself flinch, but Weller continued, "*They* think that you let your relationship with Howard's daughter influence your decision in releasing him." He allowed himself the beginnings of a smirk. "What… did you think you were flying under the radar with Fanny Howard, Chief? Everybody talks in this town, you know… even librarians."

Nick could feel the blood drain away from his face and felt his legs go rubbery for a moment. Shad Weller's hatred for him had never been more naked nor his malicious handiwork more obvious. But what was even worse was that every venomous thing he had said contained an element of truth—was something that Nick himself had had doubts about.

"And you, Shad," Nick managed after a moment. "What about you? What do you say?"

Weller hardly hesitated, "Since you're asking, chief—I couldn't agree more."

The two men stared at each other for several long moments before Nick asked quietly, "Do you honestly think that old man could've handled Connor Lacey and Jared Case, Shad? If I believed that, he'd be in custody right now—I'm not clearing him by any means, but I'm keeping an open mind, something you might give a try." Then continued, "If I ever find you giving out unauthorized information to the press, Captain Weller, I'm gonna bring you up on charges and bust you down to sergeant. If I had the time, which I don't, because I'm actually trying to find out what's happened to these children, I would pursue the matter right now."

Pausing to casually zip up his jacket, he added, "But don't push your luck, Shadrick, or I may find the time in spite of it all." Nick stepped out into the hallway, jamming his shaking hands into his jacket pockets, and striding for the stairwell exit without a backward glance.

❧

Nick was passing the parking lot for the library when he heard someone calling his name, "Yoo hoo, Chief Catesby, yoo hoo!"

Turning in the direction of the voice, he found Becky Mossberg standing at the open door of her car. Another figure stood in the shadows on the passenger side.

"Yoo hoo," she repeated as he approached. Smiling widely she said, "Oh how lucky that you were passing by! I was just telling Fanny here," she swept an arm in the direction of the other person, "that I couldn't possibly give her a ride home tonight, as I'm already late for my stylist," she patted her blown, yellow hair, "and she's a little nervous about walking, you know, with all that's been going on.

"So when I saw you there, all by your lonesome, I thought, who better than the Chief of Police to get her home safely... hmmm?" She continued to smile brightly even as she slid into her seat and started the engine, backed out of her spot, and sped off, leaving Fanny standing in the now-empty lot.

Nick read the embarrassment and discomfort in her frozen posture. She clutched a book to her breast like a shy schoolgirl and, in spite of himself, he felt all his irritation drain away—after such a day, he thought he had never been so glad to see someone.

"She's relentless, isn't she?" he ventured.

Fanny wore a long belted sweater that reached to her thighs and her chestnut hair was swept back into her usual ponytail, and when she stepped into the yellow glow of the streetlamp, he thought that she was breathtakingly beautiful.

"She is the most awful friend anyone could ever have," Fanny answered. "I can get myself home just fine, Nick… honestly."

Nick waited until she had taken the few steps to reach him then turned with her in the direction of her street. They walked together in silence for a while before Nick spoke again. "I guess I'm not as subtle as I'd like to think, Fanny, and Becky's just calling me on it. She must think I'm pretty ridiculous, really… and I probably am."

Fanny glanced up at him, her dark eyes throwing off glints of light from a nearby lamp. "You're not ridiculous at all, Nick," she reassured him, "it's me."

Smiling, Nick shook his head. "I owe you an explanation at the very least—you must know by now that the reason I've been coming to the library is because of you."

Fanny remained silent and Nick studied her long, slender neck. "When you're the police chief of a small town there's very little that goes on in your life that isn't known… and what isn't, is made up out of whole cloth to fill the gaps."

He saw the faintest of smiles cross Fanny's lips at this, only to vanish once more. "What happened to your marriage?" she asked. "You don't have to tell me, but I would like to know… I can see that the hurt is still fresh. It might help us, you know."

Nick nodded and they walked on in silence for a while. Then he heard himself saying, "Donna couldn't have children. It wouldn't have mattered to me if it hadn't mattered so much to her. We'd been married five years before we finally had the tests done to see what the problem was—she was devastated when the doctor explained the results."

Turning right at the next corner, they found themselves walking beneath the low hanging branches of the ancient elms, oaks, and maples that lined the sidewalks. The houses on either side of them were mostly two-storied Victorians whose tall windows glowed warmly. Some sported jack o' lanterns on their porches, their expressions flickering in and out of darkness.

"When I tried to talk with her about possibly adopting children," Nick went on, "she would just cry and cry. I never knew that anyone could cry as much as she did. So, after a while, I stopped bringing it up—we stopped talking about it altogether. It seemed like things were going along okay after that, and for about two years I thought we were going to pull ourselves through it. Then, one day, she came home from work and accused me of having an affair.

"After that, she would sometimes stay out all night, or even for days at a time. I never asked who she was with; though I often knew—that's one of the awful things about being a cop… you hear things you wish you hadn't. I understood what she was doing, and even why. In a way, I think I felt I somehow deserved it because I could never think of how to take her pain away—to fill that awful emptiness she felt inside her."

A gentle breeze brought the aroma of burning wood, even as it stirred the dried leaves at their feet.

"I wasn't cheating. I never cheated on Donna, ever." Nick stopped and stared down at his feet for a moment before looking up once more. "I'm not asking anything of you, Fanny, though I do have feelings for you. I think about you all the time. The only picture I have of happiness anymore is you." He couldn't think of anything else to add.

Fanny took his hand into her own, then leaned down and kissed the back of his hand. The simple gesture took his breath away.

"You don't need to ask anything of me, Nick—I've already decided to offer you what I have… such as it is," Fanny said quietly. She studied his face for several moments, before continuing "Neither of us are kids anymore, are we? We've both been banged up a little bit—you by things going bad with your wife, and some tough breaks at work; me by circumstances that have always seemed just beyond my ability to control—my father, mainly." She smiled a little at this last and they resumed their stroll hand in hand now.

"I'm not without some experience, Nick, but I won't be treated like a mistress, you understand that, don't you?"

Nick nodded. He was surprised to discover a side of Fanny he had not seen before. "I just want to spend time with you, Fan."

Her laughter contained a nervous trill. "And I with you, but I suspect that you are going to try my faith at some point, Nick… at least, I hope so."

Now it was his turn to laugh, and he answered, "Yes, I suspect I will."

She came to a stop, and a little belatedly, Nick realized that they had reached the end of their journey—they stood outside the bungalow Fanny shared with her father. She shrugged. "I would invite you in, Nick, but I can see by the lights that dad is at home tonight. I guess I should be glad, but I'm not so much."

"It's all right," he assured her. "I've got a lot of thinking to do tonight, and maybe, if I'm lucky, I'll catch a few winks as well. I doubt that I could do that if I stayed with you." He leaned down and kissed her.

After several moments, Fanny disentangled herself, stepping back. "I'm going in now," she whispered, pointing at her home.

Nick nodded. "Okay… right. I've got to be going, too." He studied Fanny's face, taking it in; then added, "So, I'll see you tomorrow."

"Tomorrow then," Fanny answered, hurrying for the door.

Nick turned in time to see Preston pass a window, the shaggy, imperious head reminding him of Weller's words earlier that evening—he *was* involved with the daughter of a possible suspect. But he couldn't begin to think of setting Fanny aside now. If it had been possible before, it wasn't now.

⁊

Fanny found her father in the sunroom, absorbed in a book that lay open on his lap, seemingly unaware of Fanny's presence as she swept up the desperate Loki. The cat's mewling meant that her father had not bothered to feed him.

Turning to leave the room, Fanny was surprised when he called after her, "Fanny, come here, I need your attention for a few moments."

Puzzled at both the request and the tone, she turned back to her father. His lean face appeared uncharacteristically flushed, his dark eyes blazing. Leaning forward, he pointed to a chair opposite his own. "Put down that silly cat and join me."

Fanny glanced down at her burden and found Loki regarding her father with open disdain, his golden eyes haughty with his current favored status. "I'll just hold on to him for now, Pop," she answered, "he's starving. Its way past his dinner time, you know."

"Oh, damn that beast," Preston spat; then exclaimed, "Do what you will then, but do sit down!"

"Let me remind you," Fanny replied evenly, "that you'd be in jail right now if not for me. I suggest you adopt a more civil tone, mister, and I mean right now!"

Glancing up at her through his spiky brows, Preston nodded meekly; then added, "I'm a little excited, Fanny... I'm... I'm sorry."

Fanny sat, settling the large feline in her lap while stroking his sleek skull. "What is it, Pop? Is everything okay?" She had not seen her father so enthused in a very long while and the sudden change was unsettling.

He thrust the large book he was holding out at her in apparent answer, snapping it shut—she thought she recognized a history of the original families of Wessex County. Loki flinched in Fanny's lap and eyed Preston darkly. "I've met someone," he announced.

Fanny stared for a moment. "What do you mean, Pop... a woman—you've met a lady friend?" She couldn't begin to imagine the kind of woman her father might meet in his ceaseless wanderings.

"A woman?" he replied, "Hell no! God save me from women. He's a boy!"

"A boy?" she repeated, a small shrill alarm sounding in her head. Her hand ceased its stroking and Loki squirmed in her lap at the sudden withdrawal of affection. "What boy?" she managed at last.

"Didn't I tell you about him just the other day? The child I met on the school grounds—Gabriel!"

The pieces began to tumble together in her head—this was the boy he had gone to the police about, the boy that had made Nick suspicious that her father knew something about the missing little girl, and maybe even had something to do with Seth Busby's disappearance seven years before.

Fanny had thought he had been suffering from a hallucination, or at best, that he had been seriously confused over some innocent encounter with some neighborhood child. Now here he was speaking about him again.

"Why are you talking with a boy?" she managed at last. "Who is he?"

Leaning forward in his eagerness, Preston fired back, "*What* is he, Fanny? That's the real question—*what?*" His eyes shone with a feverish quality. "I call him Gabriel for the lack of anything more suitable, though he could be called Cain or Grendel. Hell, for that matter," he barked, "he could be Mrs. Leeds's thirteenth child!"

Fanny felt herself shrink back into her chair. Loki had sprung to his feet at Preston's sharp laughter and was now regarding the man warily from her lap. "I don't understand what you mean, Dad," she said. "Who is Mrs. Leeds?"

Preston assumed his lecture voice, "The legend goes that she lived in poverty in the Pine Barrens during the colonial era, and that when she learned she was pregnant with her thirteenth child, cursed him, saying she hoped the devil would take him. When the child was born it was a monster. The story claims the creature escaped into the woods where it has dwelt ever since, preying on the unwary traveler—maybe this is how the early settlers explained Gabriel, how they tried to understand him."

Leaning toward his daughter, he clarified, "The Jersey Devil, Fanny—they name local football teams after him, you know."

"Pop," she began; truly afraid now of what she might be about to hear, "you're scaring me. Are you saying that you've met the Jersey Devil and that he's a little boy?" The fact that Preston appeared and smelled sober frightened her all the more.

"Whatever he is, Fanny, he's certainly no boy. I'm not even sure he's really human! As to what he is *exactly*, I have to figure out. That's where you come in… I need your help. You have access to the archives at the library and I think that somewhere in those old histories and local legends we'll find the footprints of Gabriel's passage."

"But, Pop," Fanny whispered; "why would this… this boy… Gabriel, be mentioned in the county archives? How could he be? Some of those records are over three hundred years old."

Preston rose from his chair in his excitement, causing Loki to flee at last for the quiet and comfort of the kitchen. "It's fantastic, Fanny, I admit that, almost inconceivable really, but nonetheless, he's out there." He pointed at the darkened panes of glass that formed three sides of the room. Fanny saw only her own white, stricken face peering back. "And he's been out there for hundreds of years… I know, daughter, because I've met him… and spoken with him—by god, Fanny, he's even allowed me to examine him!"

Fanny felt as if she, too, might be going mad, and tears began to leak from the corners of her eyes. "Dad, what do you mean, 'examine'? You mustn't touch other people's children you know... they wouldn't understand. You haven't actually done that have you?—what with all that's been going on around here?"

"I haven't touched anyone's *child*!" Preston shouted. "What have I been telling you all along—he's not human to begin with! He just looks that way so that he can get close to us, I think.

"You're just like that fascist, Catesby! You think I've had something to do with these children going missing and I haven't, but I do know what *has* happened to them which is far more than I can say for that ass of a policeman!"

Fanny winced at the mention of Nick and found that she was shaking. "What do you mean, Pop... who... *who* has been taking the children?"

Preston regarded his daughter for a long moment before answering, "It's Gabriel, of course. What's more, I think he's been at it for hundreds of years. It's what he does, Fanny, most probably what his kind has been doing since the dawn of man, or before—they hunt us—they drink our blood, and when they're done, they sleep, for years at a time, I think. Gabriel may be the last of his line... certainly, by his own account there are no others like him left here."

Then, sitting once more, and as Fanny listened in stunned silence, he recounted his evening with Gabriel on the beach.

When he was done he rose and took Fanny's hands into his own. "I know you don't believe me, girl. How could you? But if you think anything of your old man at all, you'll help me research this thing, help me to find the clues that show Gabriel has been among us here for a very long time, and help to illuminate what he is. At worse, you'll prove me wrong, even though I know that's not possible because, sooner or later, I'll convince him to show himself—I'll introduce him to the world. It will be a remarkable meeting!"

"What about those missing children, Pop? Where are they? Do you know?"

Preston flinched and looked down, his seamed face paling. "The children..." he repeated, "... the children... yes... oh God, I'd almost forgotten them." Raising his eyes again to Fanny's, he said, "I believe they are still alive... according to what he told me they should be. All the more reason we have to learn more about this creature, Fanny. The more I know about him the greater chance I have of getting them back. I think he trusts me, Fanny... maybe there's a way I can save them."

Fanny nodded, unable to stanch the tears that continued to flow down her pale cheeks. At least in this manner, she thought desperately, she could keep her father close, and perhaps, come to understand his role, if any, in the disappearance of Megan Guthrie, Jared Case, and Connor Lacey.

CHAPTER SEVEN

Holding aloft his right hand, Father Gregory intoned, "Bow your heads to receive God's blessing." He observed his small flock to rise and obey, the crowns of their mostly grey heads exposed in their humbled postures.

"Bless us, o' Lord, with Thy gracious bounty," he continued, "and open our hearts that we may be recipients of Your Grace. Teach us to be thankful for the abundance of Your blessings and for the Gift that raised the world from darkness, Your Son, and our Savior, Jesus Christ. Amen—In the Name of the Father, the Son, and the Holy Spirit." He sketched the Sign of the Cross in the air and concluded the Mass with, "The Mass is ended. Go in peace to love and serve the Lord and one another."

The small gathering that regularly attended weekday services responded by raising their heads once more, crossing themselves, and murmuring, "Thanks be to God." Turning to the altar, he bowed to the sanctuary that held the Host, then proceeded down the aisle to the entry where he would greet each of his parishioners as they exited.

It being a weekday, Father Gregory had no altar servers or choir, so he proceeded in what he hoped was a stately silence to the entrance lobby. He was fully conscious that he did not cut the same imposing figure as Monsignor Mulcahy, as his small, plump body in its billowing vestments was no match for the ancient Irish giant that was Our Lady of the Visitation's senior, and ailing, pastor. Nonetheless, assuming an expression of gravitas that he thought might somewhat outweigh his physical disadvantages, he managed not to smile until reaching the lobby. Once there, however, he relaxed and looked forward to having a few words and handshakes with the doggedly devout that had welcomed him so warmly to the United States.

Human contact and interaction almost always made him happy. He was grateful to have been blessed with an incurable cheerfulness, even though he was aware that some mistook this blessing for silliness.

Freed now by his passage, the worshippers each genuflected in their turn, following their little priest to the entrance. Father Gregory enjoyed the image of their approach, bathed as it was in the dappled colors of the stained glass windows. The morning sun painted his fellow Christians in blues, reds, greens, and golds taken from the Garden of Gethsemane, the Annunciation, and the wedding feast at Cana. Behind them all, a bloodied Christ watched their exit from His cross, flanked by Mary, his Virgin Mother, and Joseph, her earthly husband.

Most stopped long enough to take his hand, wishing him a good day, even as he returned their wishes and engaged in brief murmured conversations—he had only been visiting pastor for two years but knew almost all but the very shyest by name.

Father Gregory had not known what to expect when his application to Rome had finally resulted in this assignment, but had applied out of financial want for his own parish in Mumbai. The money he was to be paid to minister to the Americans so far outweighed the pittance he received in India that, eventually, it would allow him to build a school there, perhaps even a clinic. The commitment had been daunting, requiring as it did five years at Our Lady of the Visitation Parish.

What he had not expected was the warmth with which he had been embraced by his American wards. They were not as television had prepared him for: there had been no fistfights or shootings, and he had yet to encounter a cowboy or gangster that he recognized as such.

He stood framed in the large arched doorway watching his parishioners find their separate ways to their cars when he first noticed that something might be wrong. Several had discovered colored pieces of paper beneath their windshield wipers and were removing them with varying degrees of annoyance. The less observant drove off with the gaily colored papers fluttering in the relative wind of their departures.

He turned to go inside when something told him that things were not as they seemed—that all was not well. With one hand on the door handle he was stopped by the image of the antiquarian Mrs. Spenser blanching a shade whiter than was normal, even for her. The paper she clutched in her wizened fingers trembled with shock and with a small cry she flung it away like an unclean thing.

From the opposite side of the parking lot came a choked curse, "Sonofabitch!" Father Gregory turned in time to see Larry Seldon, normally the most restrained of gentlemen, wadding his flyer up with a shocking ferocity. Noticing that Father Gregory was watching him, he stuffed the offending paper into a jacket pocket and climbed into his car with a strained expression. Similar pantomimes were occurring at cars across the length and breadth of the lot. Father Gregory stood rooted in bewilderment as an unaccountable sense of dread crept over his heart like a cloud across the sun.

When the last of them had fled to work or home, Father Gregory shook himself into belated action, hurrying down the steps. The flyer he picked up was a garish shade of pink. Turning it over he was greeted by a crude rendering of a man in a priest's cassock looming over what must have been meant to be an altar. The artist's meager skill had failed him at this task, and rather than an altar and its hangings, he had only managed to draft what looked like a kitchen table with a ragged cloth thrown over it.

But the artist's skill was hardly the issue with his creation as he had certainly accomplished his goal to shock and outrage. The malicious depiction of the towering priest was unquestionably intended to be Monsignor Mulcahy, with his mass of curly hair and thick brows, though the mouth was full of filed and sharpened cannibal teeth. Blood ran down his chin in dark rivulets and his eyes were crazed with primal lust. Yet even this was not what lay at the core of its creator's travesty—that was cradled in the prelate's giant blood-stained hands—a child ripped from sternum to pelvic cradle, its organs spilling out from its sprung rib cage—this was what the false priest feasted upon, a black Eucharist of murder.

Father Gregory just stopped himself from flinging the filthy paper away, but instead carefully folded it up and tucked it away beneath his vestment. Turning once more to his beloved church, he walked slowly across the empty asphalt, stopping only to retrieve those flyers that had been tossed down by his parishioners in their outrage. Trudging up the few steps to the massive oak doors of Our Lady's, he found that for the first time since coming to America he felt truly afraid, and sick at heart at the thought of having to share this pornography with his desperately ill superior.

☙

Becky raised a finely plucked eyebrow at her desk mate and asked, "He walked you to your door… that's it?"

Fanny nodded while pretending to read through a catalogue she had received touting the latest technology in converting microfiche to PDF. The translation of the library's ancient archives of film to electronic format was long overdue and a project Mrs. Cohansey had asked her to research. "Yes," she murmured without taking her eyes from the page. She felt Becky's skeptical gaze but resisted the impulse to look at her.

After a long pause Becky resumed, "So… you two shook hands and went your merry ways then?"

Fanny put the catalogue in her lap and glanced across at the mostly empty tables in the research reading area. No one was watching them, no one could overhear them. She felt her face grow hot nonetheless, but said nothing, just gave a curt nod of her head while pretending to return to her article with renewed absorption.

"You are such a little liar," Becky announced loudly. "Look at you—you're blushing! Oh my god! How old are you two anyway? You sound like a couple of school kids! Did he carry your books for you?"

Fanny turned to her with widened eyes. "Hush! You want everybody in the library to hear?"

Becky was not in the least dissuaded. "I bet he planted a good one on you, didn't he? He looks like a good kisser. Believe me, I've had a little experience and I can spot a good one a mile off." She leaned into Fanny, lowering her voice only a little. "Then what?—did you give him a tour of your home… or *anywhere else*?"

Fanny stood up, the catalogue sliding down her skirt to the floor. "I'm going to take my lunch break now if it's all the same to you," she stated. "I have a little research to do upstairs." Turning for the elevator to the restricted third floor, she walked away from Becky's provocative laughter.

Her work mate called after her in a stage whisper, "We don't currently carry the kind of research material you and your policeman need, honey, but I will be happy to provide the material Warren and I use."

Fanny poked the illuminated up arrow and the door slid instantly open. "I'm never sharing anything with you ever again," she promised Becky.

"Sweetheart," Becky returned with a broad smile, "when you two finally get down to business, you won't have to. It'll be written all over your sweet face."

The door slid shut with a hiss and Fanny felt the slightest of jolts as the car began to rise to the top floor of the building. When it opened once more, she stepped out into a silence even more rarified than that of the public floors.

Fanny was glad that Becky had been distracted by her lusty curiosity and had not inquired as to the object of her current research. She would not have known how to explain it. All night she had tossed and turned in her bed, alternately replaying the moment of Nick's hungry kiss and her own willing surrender with that of her father's strange story, his vehement demand that she assist him in proving the existence of the feral boy. Now, here she was, exhausted with worry for the one even as her heart sang with the touch of the other.

It was an absurd task, she knew, but Fanny felt as if there were no alternative. Clearly, her father believed what he was telling her, but Fanny feared that he might have been speaking in some Freudian code of guilt, or complicity, that masked a darker, if more mundane, truth.

Yet her mind recoiled from this thought. No one knew the faults of Preston Howard—and there were many—better than she. His arrogance and insufferable conceit, his alcoholic gluttony, and his preening hunger for adulation, were all things she had witnessed and endured.

But, she reminded herself, he had never been violent—even at the very worst of times between her mother and he, Preston had never laid a hand on his wife or child. And as to some sick obsession with children, Fanny knew both from her own experience growing up, as well as having lived with the man as an adult, that Preston virtually ignored their existence. He had never shown the slightest interest in children, his own or any others. Yet, his talk had deeply frightened her and she didn't know what else to do but follow through on his bizarre request. Perhaps the research might shed some light on his thinking, and its deeper meaning, than was now apparent—he was her only family, after all, and she had to try.

Fanny walked across the slightly sagging floor to a research station. All morning she had pondered how she should proceed, finally arriving at what seemed a clear direction—she would research the newspapers for reports of missing, and murdered, children as far back as the library's resources allowed. In keeping with the relative antiquity of the county's history, at least by American standards, she knew that the local, and very parochial, newspapers had served the people of Wessex County for nearly three hundred years. It would be time-consuming, but she was determined to mine what information those that had been photographed onto microfiche might contain.

Fanny began with the Seth Busby case, as he was the only other child she knew of to have gone missing in recent times. The microfiche revealed a grainy photo of a child not more than seven, obviously a school portrait. Smiling at the camera in the artificial manner common to such sittings, he nonetheless managed to convey a beguiling humor, a certain engaging mischievous quality.

He was not a handsome boy, but healthy-looking even in the black and white of the reproduction, with full cheeks, and eyes that appeared clear and gleaming with intelligence. Fanny thought he could have used a haircut to manage his thick shock of light-colored hair. She knew, of course, from the police posters that he had been blonde-headed and had a small scar over his right eye from a fall into a rose bush as a toddler. The scar was hidden in the photograph by his long bangs.

There was nothing in the article that she did not already know and nothing in the past seven years had occurred to add to it. Seth's life had simply stopped mid-page, as if the author of it had risen from his desk and never returned. Fanny thought of Seth's mother still waiting after all these years, and how she would still be waiting for another seven, or perhaps until the end of her own time if she must—her story, too, suspended.

Sighing, Fanny flicked off the projector, swiveling round to the desktop computer. She clicked onto Wessex County Library Resources and chose Microfiche from the menu. This presented her with a table of contents for all those files and she clicked on "newspapers" and another array was displayed. Typing in the word "murder," she hit enter, and was rewarded with hundreds of selections from the papers that covered the tri-county area. She typed in "Wessex County," hitting enter once more. The selection became instantly more manageable.

Having lived in Wessex County her entire life, Fanny knew that murders here were extremely rare, averaging less than one a year. And with a population that had only recently exceeded one hundred thousand, every murder, or disappearance, was something to be remarked on and remembered. There was no such thing as casual violence in Wessex County; only the barrier islands with their sudden and large influx of visitors during the summer season offered anything like that, and then only briefly.

Fanny began making notes of the stories that she would subsequently, and laboriously, locate on the microfiche. When she had completed this task, she intended to do the same under the heading of "disappearances." Glancing once around the empty aisles of the large room, she lowered her face to her work, the buzz of fluorescents and the soft cooing of pigeons on the windowsills providing her only accompaniment.

❧

Commandeering an entire table to himself in the reference wing, Preston spread all of the books he had collected across its surface. Though the table was certainly large enough for four, no one contended with Preston for space. Hovering over his finds, he picked up one, then another, to examine its contents.

After several of these forays, his face grew suddenly still, and he began flipping pages rapidly, reading and absorbing the material as if in a race. The book he had seized upon was a locally published history of Wessex County that had been written in the 1970s. It claimed to have been drawn from sources, both written and oral, that went back to the early 1800s. Preston noted that the cheap paper of the pages was already yellowing and disintegrating near the binding, its stiff cover sporting a broken corner like a useless wing, the book's title almost completely worn from the spine. Its title page revealed that it was the third of only one hundred published, and was dedicated, in a careful longhand, to the patrons of this same library in which Preston now read the work.

His large, dark eyes raced from page to page searching for any clue that might have been left by Gabriel's long passage through history—an unsolved murder, tales of missing children, anything that might lend credence to what he knew, logically, could not be, yet was convinced existed.

Having almost reached the end of the book, Preston came across an account that made him stop. He began to read more carefully. It was a chapter dealing with the earliest of the European settlers.

The passage recounted an interview by a Methodist pastor and self-styled anthropologist with a "colored" man who had gone by the name "Lappawinsoe." This fellow, it seemed, had been a farmer with a small holding in Wessex Township in 1824 and claimed to be a descendent of a great Lenape chief of the same name.

Even with so lofty a claim, the settlers of that period, having had little or no contact with the aborigines that had formerly hunted and fished the area, called him Winsloe, an obvious corruption of the name he had offered. They believed him to be of Negro stock. According to the Reverend, Winsloe was generally thought to be a man of dependable work habits and was often sought out for his skill at carving decoys for marsh hunting, as well as his uncanny and useful ability at locating lost objects.

It was also generally known, it seems, that Mister Winsloe did not have a head for strong drink but was happy to receive payment for his services in the same. He apparently lived alone without benefit of family, though it was rumored that a wife, whom no one could recall with any accuracy, had deserted him many years before during one of his tumultuous binges.

It was Winsloe's claim to Indian heritage, however, that had brought the good reverend to the door of his cabin, as he had taken it upon himself to document the story of what might be the last of Wessex County's red men. Winsloe, in support of his claim, had assured his learned visitor in no uncertain terms that he was indeed a descendent of a people now scattered as far west as the Susquehanna Valley, and even to the White River in Ohio.

The author of the current history, Preston read, noted that a Chief Lappawinsoe had, indeed, lived and ruled a band of Lenape, but that he had died in 1755, throwing Winsloe's lineage into doubt. Were Winsloe a son of the great chief, he would have had to have been at least sixty-nine years old at the time of the interview, though probably older—a great, and improbable, age for those years.

Preston read on nonetheless.

Winsloe explained to the pastor that he had been raised to the north of Wessex County on the Brotherton reservation, until his people had decided to join with some Mahicans near Oneida Lake in New York. His mother had been ill at this time and he was loath to leave her alone, so he had remained behind until her death a few years later. By this time he had lost touch with the other members of his tribe in faraway New York and the reservation lands had been sold from beneath him by the New Jersey Legislature. For his part he received twenty dollars with which he bought a parcel of land in Wessex County upon which to farm. He removed himself there, though with great trepidation that was only overcome by the cheap price of the land.

At this point in the narrative, the preacher expressed disappointment that Winsloe was not, indeed, a native to the county but a relatively recent migrant. He then pursued a line of questioning regarding Winsloe's initial reluctance to relocate to a region that others (European settlers, to be exact) had found so wholesome and bountiful.

According to the curate, Winsloe grew restive and assured him that he was Christian and would not proceed without the reverend's acknowledgement of this fact. Puzzled by this strange request, he reluctantly gave his assurance that he understood the Lenape to be a fellow Christian, though he had never seen him attend services at his own small church on Blue Creek Road.

Satisfied that he would not be viewed as a heathen, Mister Winsloe was at last persuaded to continue. Firstly, he had corrected his interrogator, the Lenape—more often referred to as the Delawares by the Whites—had never maintained permanent settlements in southern New Jersey in general, and Wessex County in particular. In fact, he assured the minister, had it not been for the abundance of shellfish available on the barrier islands, as well as the great numbers of shad and sturgeon to be caught in the Delaware Bay, they would have avoided the peninsula altogether. It was these food sources, in their dried and salted forms, that supplied much of the peoples' protein through the cold, lean months of winter and were, therefore, indispensable despite the great risk in the taking of them in this haunted region.

The reverend gentleman, his curiosity aroused, insisted on knowing the meaning of Winsloe's words, and of hearing the tribal lore that had been their inspiration. Then, after another protracted, and tiresome, declaration of his Christian status, followed by the minister's equally tiresome assurances, Winsloe delivered himself of his knowledge.

Leaning forward from his perch on a small wooden barrel on his front porch (having given the preacher his only chair) he offered an explanation for the absence of permanent settlement in these parts by his near-forgotten brethren. "It was on account of the snow boy," he had emphatically stated.

"Snow boy," the curious man of the cloth had repeated. "Is this some demon that your people once worshipped in these parts?"

Winsloe had shaken his head at this. "He is a spirit that is to be placated, not worshipped. Yet, in these parts, he would not be still, but was always restless and would not leave the children alone.

"In good times," he went on to explain, "and in the good places, the snow boy would provide the fresh snow for us to track the beasts of the forests, so that we might make our kills and feed our people, but here, he would not act as our brother, but tracked us instead, as if we, too, were beasts of the forest.

"My ancestors offered the sacrifice of our first fruits—the first buck slain in the season—but this would not satisfy him, as he disdained meat, and recognized no taboos. In the grey hours of dusk and in the blackness of night he would hunt out our little ones and remove them from their mothers' care. Once gone, they were never found alive afterwards, though on those few occasions when their bodies were recovered, they appeared unharmed but for the draining of their life's blood—empty as the husks of the corn dolls they clutched."

Preston sat back in his hard chair, letting out a long breath—here he was, he thought, I have found his tracks, I am not mad after all—he does exist. He had to restrain himself from holding the book aloft and crying out in excitement, "I know this creature… he is my discovery and I have named him Gabriel!" It occurred to him that Christopher Columbus might have had similar feelings upon first sighting the Bahamas and knowing, at last, that he and his crew were not about to sail over the edge of the world.

He returned to the book and read on.

The preacher persisted in his questioning, "So, this demon drove your people away from this area, you say?"

Winsloe nodded his head vigorously in agreement, but then explained, "We tried to make war on him, Reverend, but he would not be found in his resting place, and heard the arrow before it was released from the bow. He came and went like a breeze that turns leaves but does not rustle them, and struck like a serpent at the heels of my people—they never knew when or where the danger might lay.

"Sometimes he might be glimpsed at the crossings of a deer trail or warrior path, still and white as a column of snow, appearing no older than his victims, perhaps seven years of age, waiting for some young boy hunting squirrels, or girl-child out looking for roots or nuts for her granny's cook pot. Once he drew close they could not escape him, but simply awaited his touch. This was attested to by frantic parents who had come upon these scenes and called out to their young of the danger. Their cries were unheeded... no one knows why this was so, but it was believed the snow boy practiced great magic on his victims—casting a scent that rendered them senseless.

"In the first days of this, in the time of my great-grandfather, the snow boy might be accompanied by a woman as white as he, who would remain behind him and many paces away, hiding and watching from the underbrush. But in my father's time she was seen no more.

"After many years of this, so my father said, our medicine men conferred with one another, and with every band that hunted south of the Raritan, and declared that this was 'Blood Ground' to be left for the evil spirit that ruled here. They ordered the tribe to stay north or west of this area, as we were never a numerous people and could not spare our children. So the people did so and were happy to leave and never return."

"But you did," the minister seized upon this fact, "so you must not have believed in this pagan nonsense?"

The old man chose not to answer directly, but replied with careful deliberation, "When I decided to come here, my people had long left me behind and I did not know how to find them again, and as the land was cheap and I had no place to stand upon because the government had sold it out from beneath my feet, I came here."

According to the preacher's narrative, here the elder had stopped and glanced from the corner of his eye to see his reaction, then seeing none added mildly, "I had no children and was no longer one myself. Besides, by that time white devils were everywhere."

The shocked preacher, feeling by this statement that he had been "tried on" to use his own words, had excused himself of

Winsloe's hospitality, but recorded his tale for posterity none-theless in the hopes that it had contained some nugget of actual Indian lore.

The writer of the history that Preston held in his hands added that more modern anthropological research had indeed proven the Lenape belief in the "Snow Boy" spirit was an ancient practice. But, he added wryly, the adaptation of the legend, as told by Winsloe, might also be seen in the context of a Native American parable of the violent encroachment of European culture into the Lenape homeland. He strongly suspected that Winsloe's tale had been concocted for the benefit of a nosy clergyman, and perhaps better illustrated White/Indian relations of that era rather than shedding any new light on Lenape spiritual practices.

Preston shut the book and clutched it to his chest, smiling. "Idiot," he said aloud.

The head librarian, Mrs. Cohansey, who was making a point of passing by in order to keep an eye on her most troublesome patron, threw him a murderous look, but continued on. She carried a few books in her arms and began slamming them loudly into their places on the shelves.

Preston glared after her, but was not annoyed. He was too enthralled with his discovery, this evidence that, in his opinion, supported what he already knew… that *only* he knew. As the librarian moved deeper into the stacks, he fished a pint of bourbon from his jacket pocket, cast a quick glance around, uncapped it, and took a deep victorious swallow. The glorious burn of it rode silkily down his throat and, like a magic vapor, rose from his warming innards to his brain.

Hearing the clacking footsteps of Cohansey returning he hastily returned the bottle to his pocket. She eyed him as she passed, but Preston let it go, fearful she would smell the liquor on his breath and have him removed from the building. He could not afford to anger her today, he reminded himself—not when he was so hot on Gabriel's trail. He kept his eyes downcast as she returned to the stairs, descending to the first floor.

Preston re-read the old Indian's words, *perhaps seven years of age*, he had said, while the events he had related were at least three hundred years before. Now Gabriel appeared not much more than thirteen or fourteen, Preston mused. Somehow, he ages much more slowly than we do, his thoughts continued, the years passing like days for him as he matures as slowly, as imperceptibly, as an ancient oak.

He remembered Gabriel's evening with him on the beach, his talk of "sleeps," of "painted people." He's like Rip Van Winkle, Preston realized, sleeping for—how long?—years?—a generation?—then rising again to find a new world, even a new people awaiting him. Gabriel not only heals and grows during these hibernations, Preston surmised, but his existence in the memory of man dies away as well—he and his acts fade to nothingness so that he is both new and unexpected when he rises once more. What a marvelous facility, he thought.

Is Gabriel a member of a species grown incredibly adaptive and successful, he wondered, or the last in an ancient chain of creatures that has somehow survived against all odds? It occurred to him that either answer would be as remarkable as the other.

The only other reference he came upon that appeared to shed any light on the creature was a thin, flimsy book of local legends. There, sandwiched in between the usual stories of the "Jersey Devil," and tales of hidden pirate treasure buried along the coast, he found a brief mention of a "Phantom Child" haunting the Great Pine Barrens. Appearing as far south as the salt marshes of Wessex County, but no further north than the Raritan, bounded on the west by the Delaware Bay and River, the child was a very local, if roaming, ghost. The recounting of the legend lay the brief tale out in the simple, unembellished manner of the pamphleteer.

The child, so the legend went, had roamed this vast region since some of the earliest White settlements. Its restless travels raised questions amongst those same people as to whether he had been the victim of savage red men, or perhaps murdered by his own parents. In any event, he was a phantom to be greatly feared, as he craved the company of his own peers—when he was known to be in the area, it was a near certainty that a child would soon vanish. He was, as one purportedly authentic colonial witness attested, a ghostly child seen only "twixt dusk and dawning."

Preston slipped the slim volume into the jacket pocket that did not contain his liquor, hiding the larger history beneath his shirt. Confident that he would not be searched, he felt justified in his theft by his scholarship and cause. He marched out of the reference section anxious to meet with his daughter and compare notes. Arching an imperious eyebrow when passing Mrs. Cohansey's desk, he said loudly, "An occasional dusting of the stacks wouldn't hurt," before sailing out the door to the street beyond.

ℰℒ

Pleading a sudden case of nausea, Fanny left work early. It was just past five in the afternoon, but the sun had already vanished behind lowering clouds, shrouding the landscape in a fine grey mist. Fanny felt herself hurrying against the coming darkness, spooked as she was by her father's strange story of a feral boy, the missing children, and now by the scarlet threads she had found woven into the tapestry of Wessex Township's history.

After her afternoon's research, the small town she had always found so staid and dependable threatened to drift apart like a mirage. Even without the unifying theme provided by her father's bizarre story of an ageless, predatory child, the history of the region, when viewed through his prism, was dark and unsettling.

With the darkness and its sheen of moisture, the lawns and porches of the homes around her grew unfamiliar: the harmless ghosts suspended from the trees of front yards, the carved faces of the pumpkins that watched her progress, alien symbols—indecipherable warnings posted along her path. The clapboards of her cottage glowed whitely near the opposite corner ahead, and Fanny hurried to reach her door before the last of the feeble light was drawn down and true night began.

From the corner of her eye she noticed a movement between the houses. Without stopping, she turned her head in time to see a boy, dressed as a scarecrow it seemed, trotting through the backyards of the homes, matching her pace. Before she could completely take him in he disappeared behind the next house she would have to pass. Without thinking or questioning her own actions, she crossed the empty street between the parked cars and to the opposite sidewalk.

Clutching her cloth book bag to her breasts, she chanced another look as she overtook the driveway of the house the boy had gone behind. With a start, she found him waiting at the top of the drive. No one appeared home as there was no car parked there, no lights within.

The boy regarded her in silence and stillness. It was too dark now to see his expression and Fanny had no wish to—her sunroom glowed like a beacon just two houses away. But, before she could tear her eyes away from the apparition, the boy raised a hand, whether in greeting or farewell she was past considering. She broke into a run.

Within moments she was throwing open the front door. Clattering into the foyer, she was greeted by her father from the back of the house, "Fanny, you're home at last! Come in here and see what I've found."

Closing and locking the door behind her, Fanny dropped her bag and gulped down air. Loki sped toward her down the hallway, then slowed and eyed her warily from a distance. After a few moments, Fanny chanced a peek from behind the narrow curtained windows that framed the doorway.

The boy, whoever he was, had vanished, swallowed up by the wet night, but she could not forget the image of his raised hand, the astonishingly long fingers.

❧

Her father took no heed of Fanny's blanched complexion or the slight tremor in her hands as she joined him in the kitchen. Like a proud storekeeper with his wares, he stood over the books he had stolen. They were laid open on the kitchen table to the passages he wished her to read.

Filling the kettle, Fanny set it on a burner; then crossed to her father giving him a small kiss on his grizzled cheek. She smelled alcohol, but his words had sounded clear enough. He wasn't drunk yet. "Hi Pops," she murmured. Unloading her own findings from her book bag, she set them on the table without comment.

"You're home early," he commented. Then, before she could explain how upsetting her day had become and, more importantly, tell him about the boy who had followed her home, he continued, "All the better! I've located some substantiating documents that I think shed some light on this phenomenon of Gabriel. I'm sure you'll agree once you've had a chance to review them." He shoved the books across the table in her direction.

"Oh Dad," she began when she saw that not only had he taken them without permission, but had marked certain passages with yellow highlighter as well.

"No one will miss them," he muttered.

Fanny bit her tongue and sighed, turning back to the stove-top and the now whistling kettle. The kitchen felt warm and comforting, and her recent fears faded somewhat. "I could have checked those out for you, Pop," she admonished Preston, while brewing her tea. "You didn't have to steal them... honestly, sometimes ..." She left the thought unfinished, adding some milk and joining him at the table.

As soon as she sat she noticed that the windows that looked out into their small backyard were black mirrors now. She thought of how she and her father must look to someone standing outside in the darkness, framed as they were in the golden glow of the room. Rising suddenly, she pulled the yellow curtains together to shut out the darkness and all that it might contain—the image of the boy hovering like an indecipherable warning in her mind's eye—the long, attenuated fingers like claws raised in a black benediction, an ominous farewell.

"What's wrong with you?" Preston asked, studying her face. Then, pointing to her papers, remarked eagerly, "I've been waiting all afternoon for you to get home. What have you got for me?"

Regaining her composure, Fanny sat once more, spreading out the photocopied pages of her own research. Then, after taking a sip of tea, began to tell him of her findings:

"There was a series of missing children cases in Wessex County in the 1930s, during the Great Depression which were blamed on tramps passing through the area. And until the disappearance of Seth Busby, those kidnappings, or murders, or whatever they were, were considered isolated events—except that while everything appeared quiet here, there were children vanishing in ones, twos, and sometimes threes, all across the southern part of the state. They were all separated by years, even decades, and so there was never any reason to connect them, and I'm not sure there's a reason now... I hope there isn't," she added quietly.

Raising his face to his daughter once more, Preston listened to the summation of what she had discovered in the library's archives. Loki, having followed his mistress into the kitchen, now regarded her owlishly from a perch atop a counter. Forbidden from kitchen surfaces, he instinctively recognized when the normal laws of the household were in temporary suspension. Refraining from purring lest he break the spell, he watched in contented silence with his large, golden eyes.

"In the next county north there was another series in the 1850s that made the papers of the times and achieved a great deal of notoriety. These disappearances were thought to be the work of Black slaves escaping from the South via the Underground Railroad. Apparently a rumor was started that a settlement of these refugees had brought the practice of Voodoo with them and were kidnapping and sacrificing White children to their African gods. Lynchings were only just prevented by the intervention of federal troops, though they were not able to stop the looting and burning of a number of homes belonging to the escapees. No evidence was ever discovered to support the allegations and the crimes remain unsolved to this day."

Fanny paused to catch her breath and allow her father to read the supporting documents. Preston snorted in derision several times as he perused the material, and she heard him murmur, "Idiots," from time to time.

Taking a long sip of her cooling tea, she selected a copy of an article printed at the time of the events concerning the "Runaway Colony." Fanny slid it across the tabletop to Preston.

"I probably shouldn't show you this," she said. "What you've told me about Gabriel can't be true, Dad. You must know this… I know it, but…" her fingers remained on the article. "I can't explain all this either, but it can't mean what you think it means. It's just not possible. So when you read this remember what you've always told me, 'Be skeptical.'"

Preston snorted more loudly, "This from a Catholic, by god! If that's not irony I don't know what is!" Snatching the paper from beneath her fingertips, he brought it up to his face.

It was written apparently by the same reporter who had covered the disappearances attributed to the so-called Voodoo cult, and had been crafted in the free-wheeling, highly-opinionated prose of the 1800s. Preston understood within a very few sentences that the reporter was performing an investigative follow-up on the tragic events he had reported upon earlier.

"Dear readers," he began, "as regards the woeful acts that have befallen our small communities of late in this dreadful and, as of yet, inexplicable loss of our children, it has behooved me to investigate yet further than our constabulary seem capable of accomplishing. Firstly, I must report that we, the people, have acted inexcusably in the matter of the Negro colony that has of late been established on the banks of the Wendigo River. Whereas, the Good Book exhorts that all men are our brothers and that it is our duty to aid the poor and downtrodden, we have not just failed to do so in their case, but rather have acted the role of Herod or Pilate, torching their meager shacks and foodstuffs, beating and whipping men, women, and children, and driving off their livestock. The people involved in this outrage were just prevented from heinous and indiscriminant murder! Is this how we fulfill our roles as Christians? These poor folks were better off under the lash of their hated slave masters than while in our barbarous care! Yet more damning, not a scintilla of evidence was found against them! They did not possess our missing children nor were any human remains discovered, even after their homes had been knocked down and razed, and their gardens dug up and despoiled! The only symbol of religious practice that could be found was not of the black arts of Africa, but a small chapel with the cross of Christ Jesus hung above its simple altar!"

Preston glanced up at Fanny. "I hope there's more to this than a sermon?"

She nodded and he returned to his reading.

"Perhaps it is they, the former slaves that came to us for succor and comfort, that should instruct us in the proper practice of Christianity! Dear reader, these dreadful events of late have succeeded in exposing our greatest weaknesses and heathen superstitions. As an example, I was approached of late by several of our eldest citizens with an explanation as to the mystery of our missing children that I would not dare repeat but as an illustration of the godless thinking that we must avoid in these dark times.

"It would seem, according to these ancient wags whom shall remain nameless to protect their reputations, and perhaps to prevent their being locked away in a closet as feeble-minded or mad, that at the turn of the last century our community was beset by identical crimes to those we find ourselves victim of today. They assure me, dear reader, that the perpetrator had been both identified and dealt with and was nothing less than a child that dwelt in their own midst!"

Fanny saw her father flinch and sit up and knew what passage he had come to.

"A young girl, in fact, whom the public had thought to be a victim, yet was seen wandering the cemetery at night by a most reliable witness—God save us from such witnesses! It would appear that we have recently relied on just such witnesses, have we not? But this is not the end of the horror, but only the beginning, for this same poor, and quite probably deranged child, was purportedly found reposing in one of the mausoleums with the blood of her victims upon her lips. Dear reader, according to these unseemingly gleeful informants of mine, the child was promptly decapitated without benefit of trial or even of the most rudimentary trappings of justice. Can you imagine the horror of her dear parents upon learning of the dreadful news? Is this what we are coming to now? If so, let us draw back from the precipice before it is too late!

"Perhaps it satisfies our astute constabulary to settle for vampires or practitioners of voodoo as their elusive villains, but a more enlightened people will insist that facts, not fancy, rule the investigations of our hapless constables into such dire matters. Shall we blame our Jersey Devil, as well? After all, Mrs. Leeds' thirteenth child is also missing and remains at large! Certainly his great wings would be an asset in eluding our slow-plodding lawmen, though Lord knows, he would hardly have need of them!"

The opinion piece masquerading as investigative journalism sputtered to a halt with this last exhortation and Preston set it down once more. Fanny saw that he had paled and his eyes were unfocused.

"Dad," she began.

"He told me about this," Preston whispered. "He thought it was a clever trick leaving one of his victims in the cemetery to take the blame for him."

Fanny reached across the table, grasping his arm. "Pop, it can't be. It just can't." The image of the boy clad as a scarecrow flitted across her memory, his face the blank undulating grey of a filthy pond, and she shuddered.

Shoving the two books at his daughter, Preston said, "It was him, I swear, Fanny," he pecked at the open pages with a finger "The stories are real, and so is he. As real as you and me."

Seizing his veined hand in her own, Fanny looked into her father's bloodshot eyes. "Dad," she whispered, "Are we losing our minds, you and I?" Preston made to pull free, his mouth turning down in disdain. "Because I think I may have seen him, too. I think he may have followed me home today."

Preston snatched his hand away. "Followed you? Why on earth would he follow *you*? He has no use for you—you don't even believe he exists!"

Fanny turned her face away, her eyes coming to rest on Loki at his forbidden perch, his golden eyes fixed unwaveringly upon the curtained window and the night beyond.

❧

Nick sat in silence in the small fusty room, the two priests watching for his reaction. The little one had left a message on his voice mail earlier in the day and requested he stop by the rectory. He had not given any details on the phone, but had politely insisted that his presence would be most appreciated by both he and Monsignor Mulcahy. Now, as the light rain had hastened the end of another day's fruitless search for the missing children, Nick found himself damp and deeply depressed, sitting in a worn overstuffed chair in the rectory's office.

The image he regarded without actually touching lay atop the small spindly end table at his elbow. A crucifix with its bleeding transfixed Christ looked down upon it as well from the near wall, prompting Nick to think, "The fight goes on." As he no longer regarded himself as a religious man, the thought surprised him.

"It appears that evil is very enterprising in Wessex Township," Father Gregory offered, as if reading Nick's thoughts, "but without artistic merit, I'm afraid." Smiling, he appeared to be waiting for Nick to appreciate his quip.

"It's clear enough it's meant to be me," the larger priest boomed from his wing-backed chair. He dwarfed the little Indian who sat by his side in a kitchen chair brought in upon Nick's arrival. Father Gregory looked like a plump dark child next to his superior. "He's done a good enough job for that much," the older man concluded.

Nick could hear the phlegmy rattle deep within his lungs. Though he was still a huge imposing man, it was evident that he was wasting. His once-thick neck was corded and thin, his Roman collar no longer gripping his flesh but simply providing a reference to measure his diminishment. The complexion that Nick had once thought of as comparable to rare roast beef was now the powdery white of a man who sees his own waiting grave—the thundering Irish giant was clearly dying.

"Is there any chance you two *didn't* handle this with bare hands?" Nick asked.

The two priests glanced guiltily at one another before Father Gregory answered, "I should have known better, Chief Catesby. It was very stupid of me, of course... unforgivable." He began to wring the offending hands in distress.

Pointing one of his large fingers at Nick, the monsignor said, "He's the bloody policeman, he should have caught the bastard while he was making free with our parking lot! If he bothered coming to Mass, maybe he would have!"

Nick had long since become immured to the monsignor's chastisements, having endured them in his younger, more impressionable years. Even so, he refrained from pointing out to his old confessor that he had fallen away from the Church long ago—sometime around the time his brother Stephen had been killed in Panama, he thought. "We'll have to get both of your prints, you know, in order to distinguish them from the possible culprit." He looked at them without expression and again both men grew silent and shame-faced.

"Whatever you say," the monsignor croaked, "you're the chief after all. We're just poor men of the cloth; even Christ Himself cooperated with his executioners."

"Meaning...?" Nick asked.

The old man shifted in his seat and Nick noticed Father Gregory glance at him before turning away to study his shoes. The sunburst clock on the wall became suddenly audible in the tiny, makeshift office. The patter of rain struck the window in a sudden gust, like a handful of pebbles.

"Well?" Nick persisted.

"It's not easy, Nick, talking frankly with a boy… a man, that is, like yourself, that I've once served communion to, taught in catechism class. You see what I mean, don't ya? You take my meaning?"

"I do not," Nick responded in the priest's own manner.

Father Gregory nodded to the Monsignor as if this was something they had discussed prior to Nick's arrival. The older man nodded in return, appearing to think for a few moments, before clapping his big hands together and saying, "Well, it would'a come out anyway, you bein' a policeman and all, so I may as well be the one to tell ya.

"It's like this, Nicky, many years ago, back when I was still a young priest and assigned to a parish way the hell over and gone in West Jersey, that certain allegations were made against me."

Feeling the room grow warmer, Nick experienced a slight dizziness that was only partly due to his not having eaten since morning. He tried to keep his expression blank.

"Ah," the old priest remarked, "I can see by your face that you've got a notion where I'm going with this. Well," he leaned back gripping his bony knees, "I can imagine what you might be feeling with what I'm about to tell ya, havin' been a boy in my own parish, but then you must also know before I've said it that the allegations were untrue." He halted to cough, fishing out a handkerchief to wipe at his mouth, then caught Nick's gaze with his own. "I've never touched a child, Nicky, never, not once. I'm just not made that way and doin' without women does not a pedophile make, no matter all the fancy theories about celibacy that they spew on the television."

Nick willed himself not to squirm in his seat.

"There was never no police involvement that I knew of, Nick. Back in those days when such things were said, ya got moved on… quietly—the last thing the diocese wanted was police involvement. That was the way it was done. I'm not sayin' it was the right way, and it wasn't the way I wanted it, of that you can be sure—you can take that to the bank!

"As I had done nothin' wrong, I wanted to have it out and be done… to save my good name! But the bishop wasn't havin' it. He sent me on my way to Wessex Township and silenced the family with money from the church coffers—a shameful business any way you look at it. But, as obedience is one of our vows, I did as I was told and came away."

He stopped to take a breath, bowing his head as if in prayer. After what seemed hours, he looked up once more, his grey wintry eyes wet with emotion. "The truth is, Nicky, I've dreaded this day all of my life, and over the past few years with all the scandal, I've feared every moment that my name, my face, would appear on the evening news programs as one of the accused, one of those damn predators. Then, just when it seemed that it might all have blown itself out at last, there's that… that thing…" he pointed at the crude ugly drawing as he groped for the words "… that abomination. When Father Gregory showed it to me, I told him what I thought it meant, and he said that I should tell you straight away. So…" he threw open his hands, "Here ya are."

Nick found it hard to meet the old man's eyes, but asked anyway, "What do you think it means, Monsignor?"

"Oh don't be thick, boy," the monsignor groaned. "What with the children disappearin' isn't it obvious? Someone knows my past and wants to frame me, and do a little more damage to the Holy Mother Church while they're about it! Can ya not see that?"

Risking a glance at Father Gregory, Nick found the little man staring at his clasped hands. "And who do you think that might be?"

The big priest threw up his arms in despair. "How the devil would I know that, Nick? Aren't you the one that does the investigatin'?" He turned to Father Gregory in exasperation. "What kind of bloody policeman have we raised in this parish?"

Nick stood abruptly as Father Gregory, smiling once more, answered, "A very good one, I suspect."

"I'll do what I can with lifting and identifying any prints on this," Nick said, as he slid the hideous drawing into the evidence bag he always carried with him, "but don't get your hopes up. I'll still need both of yours, as well, since you've seen fit to paw the evidence."

He planted himself in front of the older man, adding, "If any more of these show up, don't touch them and call the department right away. Also keep a look-out for anyone suspicious hanging around the church or the rectory. It seems as if whoever did this wants to create suspicion and distrust of you—maybe even tie you and the Church to the missing children. At the very least it smells of a hate crime, an attempt to intimidate, to smear." Nick snatched up his jacket, pulling it on.

When he reached the door, he paused and added, "In the meantime, I'd advise you to keep as quiet as you can about this, which won't be easy considering that some of your parishioners have already seen these." He shook the bag in emphasis. "In any case, don't go making any statements to the press just yet, Monsignor—maybe, if this guy thinks he hasn't gotten to you, he'll try again… and this time, as unlikely as it may seem, we'll catch him."

Monsignor Mulcahy smiled at Nick. "If it can be done, Nick, then I've no doubt that it will be you that does it."

Stepping out onto the small railed porch that led to the driveway and Mercantile Street beyond, Nick pulled the door closed behind him. Outside, the misting rain was a grey veil that twisted beneath the street lamps and he turned up his collar against the damp.

Plodding toward the street and home, a boy flashed across the end of the drive, impossibly swift it seemed to Nick in his exhaustion. No doubt, he was late for home and supper, but it worried the policeman in him that his parents should allow him out on such an evening; with all that had been happening. And it seemed especially irresponsible to have allowed him to do so without shoes on his feet.

But he was far too tired to pursue the boy and comforted himself with the thought that he was flying to a warm home. As Nick walked through the wet semi-darkness he thought of Monsignor Mulcahy and his evident and impending mortality—he had once thought of him as a titan amongst mortals—God's black clad warrior-priest, but now he found him grown old and, if not feeble, as destined for the grave as any man.

Even so, he made a mental note to add the prelate to his list of potential suspects and, though it pained him to do it, to authorize an investigation into his past. The tragedy and mystery of the missing children seeped a poison, Nick thought, which was finding its way into the bloodstream of everyone that lived in Wessex Township, tainting all that it touched—the good with the bad, the innocent with the corrupt.

Reaching his house, Nick stopped and studied its dark windows, its empty driveway. As the rain seeped through to his scalp and down his neck, he found himself picturing the abandoned, lifeless rooms within, rooms that he had occupied like a phantom for the past year—a home that had never held children. He wondered about Megan, Jared, and Connor, about what kind of night they might be having, whether they were still alive. Then suddenly it dawned on him—it was the anniversary of his divorce.

Turning away from the empty house, he began to walk again. It didn't really matter to where.

CHAPTER EIGHT

Preston stood outside his daughter's bedroom door listening. From within he could hear a faint susurration that, after several puzzled moments, he identified as Fanny's slumberous breathing. Satisfied, he tip-toed down the hallway to the mud room at the back of the cottage, avoiding the floorboards that creaked along the way.

Preparing for his nocturnal outing with coffee and brandy, he felt confident that he was sober enough, without being uncomfortably so, to achieve his mission—seeking out his elusive discovery. Since his conversations with Fanny about the children, his conscience had begun to prick and worry him. Perhaps, he thought, Gabriel could be reasoned with on this account, besides which he wanted to compare his notes of the day with him.

Removing a hooded jacket from the coat peg, he pushed his arms through the sleeves, fumbling with the zipper. Grunting and cursing he at last managed to align it and close the front, then turned for the door. Loki awaited him there, anticipating an opportunity for an unauthorized night out.

Preston regarded the little beast with disdain, while Loki attempted to charm his adversary by purring loudly, his golden eyes glowing with artificial affection for his mistress's father.

"You must be joking," Preston said aloud, shoving the cat away with a booted foot. Loki hissed at him. "Wouldn't it be nice to have an opposing digit?" he asked, turning the door handle and slipping into the misty night. Before closing the door behind him, Preston added, "Or the power of speech, for that matter? Then you could have, at least, argued your case—too bad." He drew the door closed, the large cat glaring at him through the narrowing aperture.

It was not the kind of night he would have chosen to pursue his studies, he thought, but field-work made its demands and they could not be ignored. Fanny's mention of a strange boy watching her, Preston took as a summons. Flicking the hood over his dampening pate, he strode off toward the front of the house and the street beyond. In spite of the lateness of the hour, Preston felt energized and suffused with an enthusiasm he had not experienced since his earliest days of teaching. How quickly the bloom falls from the rose, he thought ruefully, and how rare for a man to receive a second opportunity.

Drawing in a breath moist with a rain so fine as to be almost invisible, he thought of his quarry with gratitude. "Gabriel," he said aloud, as if to conjure him up from the darkness, setting forth to find a boy who had already lived for three hundred years.

Walking first to Gambol Street, he then turned north on Chapel, away from the small town center. His goal was the cemetery Gabriel had alluded to in his alternative history lesson on the night beach. He couldn't really say why, but he felt that it was as good a place as any to find the creature on such a night.

In any event, if it had indeed been Gabriel that Fanny had seen, then Preston had little doubt that he was nearby and watching—he would make himself known at the time and place of his choosing. He was, after all, an animal, and like any animal would take every precaution within his means to protect himself.

Taking a pull from the brandy bottle he had brought along he pushed on, and within minutes reached Cedar Drive. Cars went whizzing past in either direction, their passage marked by the hissing of water beneath their tires. When the road was clear, he stumbled from the curb and hurried across.

Reaching the far side, Preston stepped over the railroad tracks that paralleled Cedar, crossing to the sandy access road that formed the perimeter of Wessex Baptist Cemetery. A peeling wooden sign, only some decades old, but already looking at home in the ancient burial ground, announced that it was founded in 1769. Preston halted to catch his breath, leaning against the sign and studying the scene that lay before him.

At his end of the cemetery most of the graves were burials of the last century, each successive row growing older as one walked north or east toward Cedar Drive. The newer section lay to the west and on the opposite side of Chapel Street, populated largely with severely simple markers, but ornamented here and there with the fashionably whimsical lighthouse or engraved portrait of the deceased.

Recovered somewhat, Preston pushed off and began making his way north toward the distant wood line. He left the access road walking carefully between the drunkenly leaning stones, their inscriptions blackened by centuries of soot and rain. Stones that grew older and older as he stumbled toward the cemetery's heart. Some had sunk so far into the earth that little of them remained above ground. These appeared designed to catch at

Preston's dragging feet, causing him to stumble, almost falling onto the damp soil.

From time to time, an obelisk would appear as an exclamation in the darkness, its strange Egyptian geometry foreign and perplexing. Here and there lay enclosures encompassed in wrought-iron, the jumbled family groupings within still protected from interlopers by the rusted spear points of the fencing. Increasingly, the ground grew more treacherous, made lumpy and uneven by the roots of trees older than the oldest inhabitant of the necropolis they shaded. And it was toward the largest of these that Preston made his way.

His goal was a tremendous oak lying at the very edge of the cemetery, a tree three times the size of any other for miles around. Its great twisting limbs, largely bare, were lit from below by a street lamp planted where the perimeter curved back to the west. Viewing its strange, sky-clawing bulk, Preston shivered. He thought of its ancient network of roots stretching dozens of yards in every direction, and of the morbid nourishment fueling its titanic growth. How many coffins, he wondered, had this monster pried open like nuts to feed upon the moist kernels within?

And with that gut-churning thought, Preston no longer wanted to be in the graveyard, his desire to encounter Gabriel having grown as sour and tainted as the corpse oak. Turning, he began to hurry in the opposite direction, desperate to be away from this place. Like a man suddenly awakened to find that he is not in his own bed, his own home, Preston's only wish was to steal away unnoticed before encountering the legitimate and rightful resident.

꿍

Fanny heard the knocking as something infinitely far away and moaned that something so remote should have anything to do with her. Tugging her blanket tighter, she burrowed deeper into the softness of her own bed. She felt Loki spring to his feet with annoyance, or alarm, she couldn't tell which and didn't care. She moaned softly once more in her troubled sleep.

Suddenly, as if time had telescoped from some distant memory to the immediate present, the faint knocking became thunderous in her ears. Her eyes flew open and she found herself sitting up with her feet already seeking her slippers. Fumbling with her housecoat, the tapping resumed, and she realized that the summons had been barely audible all along, a gentle, almost tentative, rapping on the panels of her front door.

Throwing open her bedroom door Fanny hurried down the hallway with Loki skittering along at her heels. She could see at a glance that the figure partially silhouetted in the small panes of glass framing the entrance could not be her father. The man (she felt certain that it was a man) was about his height, but possessed of a thicker, more powerful-looking frame. Her heart catching in her throat, she thought she recognized Nick Catesby's outline partially captured by the nearest street lamp. The figure turned and began to move away.

"Who is it?" she called out, her voice high, the quaver it normally contained heightened by the anxiety of being awakened in the middle of the night. The figure halted, appearing to hesitate before turning back to her door.

"It's me," she heard Nick say softly through the door, "Nick."

She unlocked and partially opened it. Nick peered in at her clutching the robe to her throat, her long hair tousled with sleep, a stray tendril having become caught in the corner of her mouth. As he stared, she self-consciously tugged it free and attempted to sweep the rest out of her face with her slender hands.

"I was just out walking," he said, his face a study in embarrassment and confusion, "and I saw the light on in the back of the house—I thought you might still be up… sorry. I hope I didn't wake your dad, too."

Fanny managed to find a scrunchy in her housecoat pocket and, in one smooth motion, expertly seized her unruly mane and snapped into a pony-tail. "That's all right," she answered. She looked back over her shoulder towards her father's room, still shaking the fog of sleep from her brain. "I think he went out... I thought I heard him slip out the back around eleven." She turned to face Nick once more. "He does that, you know. Unfortunately, I can't lock him up like Loki here." The cat sat on the floor several feet behind her, his glowing eyes studying the odds of successfully escaping through the partially open door.

Fanny took note of his intentions and said, "Come in, Nick, please." She reached out to take his hand and she felt it jump at her touch. "You're cold," she observed with some concern, tugging him through the opening and into the shadowed hallway. Nick allowed himself to be pulled in as Fanny eased the door shut behind him. She flicked on a light as she led him toward the kitchen and saw that he was wet as well, his dark hair sheened with moisture, drops of it running down his neck and beneath his collar.

"Sit down," she commanded, vanishing round the corner only to return moments later with a towel. She handed it to him and watched as he began to towel-dry his hair and face. "You look tired," she murmured.

Nick smiled at her, the lines around his dark blue eyes crinkling, and nodded. "Yeah," he agreed, his voice hoarse, "I am... it's been a long day."

Looking down at him from the other side of the table, her arms folded across her chest, she asked, "Would you like to tell me about it, Nick, or would you rather just sit here for a while?"

Nick glanced around the large, warm kitchen, with its scoured butcher-block table and racks of hanging pots and pans, the flourishing plants that lined the windowsills, and thought, 'I'd rather sleep right here in this kitchen than in my own bed.'

But he answered aloud, "I'd just like to sit here with you, if that's okay. I won't stay long."

Fanny pulled a chair next to him taking one of his broad hands in her own. This time he did not flinch. "You can stay as long as you like. Dad's not likely to come back tonight… he rarely does once he's gone out. Besides, Nick, this is my house, I just let dad live here."

"Okay… good." He studied their meshed fingers with apparent sadness.

"Would you like some coffee… or tea?"

Nick shook himself. "No… no thanks, but if it's not too much trouble what'd I'd really like is a drink. Is that possible, or am I asking for the exact wrong thing in this house?"

Laughing, Fanny stood once more. "Are you kidding? I know every 'secret' hiding spot dad ever thought of… and some that he's even forgotten about—name yer poison."

Nick laughed too, saying, "Well then, make it a whiskey, Miss—a double if you please. And pour one for yourself, if you've a mind to."

Fanny let go of his hand and curtsied, "You're very kind, sir."

Returning with the promised bottle, she found Nick asleep, his head cradled on an arm thrown across the tabletop. She stood watching the rise and fall of his back and shoulders for several moments before hiding the bottle once more. When she returned, she grasped Nick's arm, gently but persistently, tugging him to his feet. He rose with a grunt to stare uncomprehendingly at her and the room around him.

"You're exhausted, Nick," she whispered, "and it's time we got off to bed."

"Couch…" he mumbled.

"Don't be ridiculous," she said, guiding him down the hallway to her bedroom. For the briefest of moments, she wondered what Becky would say to her dragging a man off to her bed by main force, and couldn't help but smile at her imagined approval.

છ

Preston aimed himself toward a street lamp, this time one that lay near the railroad tracks and the southeast corner of the cemetery. Once there, he had only to cross Cedar once more to be back in his own neighborhood, and this was something he now greatly desired.

Like a curtain the low bank of clouds suddenly parted to reveal the brilliance of the hunter's moon, throwing generations of dead and their small earthly holdings into sharp relief.

As if cued by this event, something small and white stumbled into Preston's vision. A doll, he thought with a frisson of horror, a large doll, as wobbly as a puppet on strings. It occurred to Preston that he might have gone mad, that drink had at last driven him round the bend. The creature tottered unsteadily into his path and before Preston could change his course to avoid it, it was suddenly caught up by a more familiar figure.

Sweeping the little girl up into his arms like a protective older brother, Gabriel turned to regard Preston, his large glittering eyes seeming to penetrate his motives, his now-wavering loyalty.

He said nothing, however, but gently lowered the child to sit drunkenly on the edge of a marble vault. Preston could see that her long brown hair was roped by moisture that ran down her stuporous, ashen face in rivulets. Her clothes, some sort of pink stretch pants with a matching top featuring a romping kitten, were similarly damp and stained by dirt, as well as something dark and tacky-looking. Turning away to avoid seeing what that "something else" might be, Preston had no doubt that this was the missing Megan Guthrie—the little girl from the schoolyard.

Gabriel held up a long, taloned finger and Preston stopped edging away. Again, with a studied approximation of tenderness, the boy reached down and patted the girl-child on top of her small head, whispering something that Preston could not hear.

Then, looking up once more at Preston, he smiled—a ghastly display of teeth as jumbled as the headstones that surrounded them, the tongue flickering redly within the cavernous mouth. Preston recoiled in horror. My God, he thought, my God! What have I been thinking? He *is* a monster.

Seemingly unconcerned, Gabriel loped off toward a mausoleum, disappearing into the moon-shadow it cast and leaving Preston alone with the near-bloodless Megan. He stared in silence at her for several moments before it occurred to him to simply take her hand and lead her away from the place, but fear made him hesitate and in those precious moments he observed Gabriel returning.

Still smiling, Gabriel led the two boys out into the bright moonlight and down the slight slope to where Preston and the girl waited. Preston recognized them at once.

He watched their coming as if in a dream, Gabriel leading them by their hands, something neither of them would have tolerated in normal circumstances. Gabriel the gentle shepherd, the loving caretaker of these stolen children—children that he intended to drain of every last drop of their life's blood. Preston grasped this now in a manner that was no longer intellectual, but gut-wrenchingly visceral.

Taking in the full horror of this moonlit, incongruously pastoral scene, he understood that he must stop this creature if he could. But even as he thought this, he doubted his own ability to accomplish such a thing. He had never been in a position before that challenged his actual physical courage, and now feared he had none at hand. Preston heard himself moaning in dread at the trio's approach.

Dancing ahead of Connor and Jared as they stumbled in his wake, Gabriel made a terrifying Pan for his stuporous followers. Jared's spindly legs were bare and pebbly in the freshening breeze, his jockey shorts wet and dirtied. While lurching along behind came the husk of Connor Lacey, bare-chested in the chill night air, his desiccated torso smeared with mud and old leaves. It was quite clear where Gabriel had obtained his current wardrobe.

Blue veins pulsed faintly beneath the boys' marbled skins, and like Megan they appeared barely able to stand, the whites of their eyes gone grey with dying. They all reeked of decay.

Bumping into Gabriel, who now stood in front of Preston, the boys shuffled to a halt. Again, the vampire raised a filthy forefinger, this time to his wide lips, and Preston understood that he was to remain silent.

These boys will never threaten me again, Preston thought, they will never threaten anyone. But this thought gave him no satisfaction because he understood also that none of these children could survive Gabriel's ghastly ministrations much longer. And in that moment he began to hate the creature that could visit such misery on them. In a rare burst of empathy, he even thought of their terrified, sorrowing parents, and the new agony of their existence.

Turning, Gabriel gripped the boys by their shoulders, making them sit on the muddy earth, before spinning round once more to Preston. "Sudden and loud noises afflict them with ague," he whispered, "and they are easily startled now—but soon," he promised, "they will rest more easily and not rise again."

Preston began to speak but found he couldn't, then cleared his throat and tried again, "Gabriel," he whispered hoarsely, "how did you know that I would come here? Were you watching my home?" In the presence of these dying children the thought of Gabriel lurking near his own home—and his own daughter—took on terrifying possibilities that he had not fully grasped before.

"I watch many homes," Gabriel lisped, "yours as well."

Preston mulled this over for a moment beneath the bright moonlight. "Yes, but did you wish for me to join you here? Is this why you showed yourself to my daughter… to get me out of the house?"

Gabriel squatted onto his haunches amongst the boys, a position, Preston noted, that appeared to be his normal resting posture. Looking up, he replied, "I saw you come out and followed you. When you came to this place, I thought to show you my catches—they are healthy and good, are they not?" He placed long fingers to the neck of each boy, the yellowed nails indenting their panting flesh. Each of them flinched, but made no move to escape.

Feeling a touch of nausea roil his stomach, Preston sat back onto an upright headstone, his mind racing. "Healthy? No… I wouldn't say so," he disagreed, forcing a sickly smile. "They have grown sick and weak, Gabriel. That much seems obvious."

Gabriel turned his head from one child to the next as if examining them for proof of Preston's words, a slight crease forming between his extraordinary eyes. When he was done, he turned his gaze once more to Preston. "Their hearts will stop soon," he agreed.

Leaning forward, his narrow rump still resting on the edge of the lichen-covered grave marker, Preston concurred, "Yes, yes, that's exactly right, Gabriel. But in the meantime, their hearts slow and their blood thickens, does it not?"

Gabriel appeared to give this some thought, nodding his shaggy head once in puzzled agreement.

Megan began to cough as if to make Preston's point about the state of the children's health. Gabriel's head snapped round to regard her coldly.

"See… see, my point exactly," Preston persisted. "Not that I'm an expert on these things, of course, but I suspect that as they grow weaker and weaker that their blood not only grows more torpid, but loses its original vitality and taste. Would you agree with that?" he asked. He slipped off his parka, draping it as casually as he could over Megan's damp, shivering shoulders.

Gabriel observed this last with a growing frown. At the same moment, Jared began to fidget and mumble something unintelligible. Connor lay across the cold, brilliant earth with his arms thrown back, unmoving, his breath barely visible as a faint, rising moisture on the cooling night air. Scowling openly at the children and Preston, Gabriel pronounced, "They are passing good, I like them well enough for all that." He flicked a sinewy hand at his prizes.

"Of course you do," Preston hastened to reassure him, "of course you do, and why shouldn't you?" He dared now to raise a finger himself. "But consider this, my friend—what if, rather than... than drinking from the bottom of the barrel, so to speak, you were to release these poor specimens back into the wild? After all, what's the point of carrying on to the end? There's nothing really gained, is there? It's a matter of diminishing returns, don't you see? You've kept them past their expiration date, beyond their expected shelf life—time to cut the old losses and strike out fresh, I say!"

The boy-like creature listened to Preston's speech with rapt attention, his filthy neck stretching upward as his eyes grew wider still. When he was done, Gabriel brought his awful hands to either side of his head clasping his own skull and gaping at Preston.

"Your words are like birds in a church, Preston," he answered, at last. "They flutter and fly, battering themselves on the painted windows, but find no place to rest—I must not give up these children."

Mesmerized by Gabriel's words and his terrible Bacchanalian face, Preston was unable to reply. Even in the cool night air, he could feel the sweat running down his spine.

"That's j-j-just it," he stuttered at last. "Why not?—May as well before you poison yourself!" Rising unsteadily from his perch, he took Megan by a thin arm. "This one," he bluffed; his voice shaky in spite of his best efforts, "she's outlived her usefulness—that's obvious. I'll just take her off your hands before she sickens you. You're not looking well, did you know that? I noticed it right off." He tugged Megan to her feet to sway uncertainly at his side, his jacket brushing the wet ground.

"As to those sad-looking specimens," Preston waved airily at Connor and Jared, "I may as well take them off your hands, too. What do you say?" He gave Megan a slight shove in the direction of a distant street lamp, and hearing the faint scuffle of her small shoes, turned for the boys. The corners of Gabriel's frog-like mouth turned more downward still.

Ignoring this, he leaned over the creature to seize the arms of Connor and Jared, his heart thumping and straining within his chest. "Come along, boys," he admonished them. "Stop wasting Gabriel's time and endangering his health, you've done enough harm here already." Jared began to struggle up, but Connor lay as heavy as death, his eyes fixed upon the cold, alien moon. "Up, up," Preston commanded, "time to be on our way."

Gabriel shot out an arm, pressing his long white hand into Connor's bony chest and seizing Jared by his thin wrist in the same moment. "None may leave here," he hissed at Preston, pulling the smaller boy back down beside him, wrapping an arm around his quaking shoulders. Connor moaned from the pressure of the vampire's hand upon his heart. Preston staggered back.

"It cannot be that any return home. Now, return me my blood-calf," he cried, pointing a dirty fingernail at Megan's back. The musky bloom that Preston had come to associate with the vampire rose like a miasma amongst the drunkenly titling stones. Preston felt himself growing stupid and slow.

"I'm only thinking of you," he slurred, "Haven't I made that much clear? You are poisoning yourself with these sickly brats!" From the corner of his eye he saw that Megan had somehow made it halfway to the perimeter road, his jacket trailing like a cape on her tiny frame. She appeared to be following the beacon of the distant street lamp as if on instinct.

"No, the thing to do here is to cut your losses… move on to better choices. Only the weak-minded, or lazy, keep making the same mistake when they've been told better. That's absurd on the face of it." Blathering on, he was determined to buy the little girl as much time as he could—after all, did Gabriel understand any of this to begin with?

"I'm only trying to help, to be of some service," Preston struggled against the malaise that was enveloping him. "And far be it from me to tell you your own business, but if I were to be asked…"

Springing to his feet, Gabriel swept Preston aside. The old man stumbled backwards, falling over a headstone and landing on the ground with a burst of exhaled breath. "Christ," he managed to gasp, as Gabriel rushed past him like a wind. He struggled to sit up and catch his breath once more.

From his low vantage, he could see that the creature was already upon the little girl. Though she was now but yards from the sporadic traffic of Cedar Drive, Gabriel overtook her, scooping her small, weakened frame into his nightmarish arms.

Turning to the near insensate boys, he croaked, "Get up and run… do you hear me? Connor… Jared, get up and run—he can't possibly manage all of us at once! Go!" Neither boy stirred, while already the creature was rushing back with his prize, bounding across tombstones and vaults like an elk.

"Run," he pleaded once more, as Gabriel bore down upon them, but still the boys sprawled amongst the markers, insensible to the impending danger.

Crawling to some old fencing that surrounded one of the family plots, Preston strove to pull himself up, straining to find his feet as the poison of Gabriel's presence dissipated. The upright he clung to separated itself from the rest with a tired groan and a scattering of rust, flinging Preston onto the muddy earth once more.

As Gabriel closed the final yards to their location, Preston discovered that he held a short rusted spear in his grasp. "Run... please," he managed one last time, but the ancient predator was upon them.

Tossing Megan to the ground with a sickening thud, Gabriel stood looming over Preston. "They will speak of me should they live," he declared, his breathing easy in spite of his exertions, "and this they must not do."

Even as the old man heard these measured words, he thrust upwards with the corroded paling. It was a poor position in which to gain the leverage he needed to kill the thing, but he knew that this might be his only chance. The point, with its heart-shaped flanges, flew towards the creature's breast as Preston cried, "Die, Goddamn you!"

Raking a furrow across the vampire's ribcage, the crude tip brought a dark stain to the filthy shirt that clothed him. But Gabriel was quicker yet, twisting away from the point like a serpent while seizing Preston's thin wrist and squeezing until the sound of grinding bone could be heard. Preston screamed like an animal as the impromptu spear went flying from his fingers.

Retrieving the makeshift weapon with his free hand, Gabriel raised it on high, his wide jaw unhinging as if to swallow the moon. In spite of his excruciating pain, Preston understood that he had arrived at the end of his life, and gritted his teeth in anticipation. Yet Gabriel hesitated, the lower jaw reconnecting with a nauseating snap of cartilage.

With a shrug, he tossed the iron spike into the tall yellow grasses, saying, "Soon enough you will take responsibility for these children, Preston Howard. Meanwhile, say nothing of my prizes to those that hunt me—these children belong to me now. Betray me, old man, and your own child shall surely die."

The languor that he had experienced earlier returned and Preston felt himself swooning into unconsciousness. He saw the glowing white moon sailing above him in the starry sky, a dark cloud reaching out to shroud it like a tattered funeral pall. Then, in the fast fading light, Gabriel's broad pale face appeared inches from his own, his breath reeking, and Preston felt something warm dripping onto his shirt front. The scent of blood filled his nostrils.

"I will require another before I sleep again," Gabriel said quietly, his eyes never leaving Preston's own, "and when that time is nigh, I will come to you. Until then, remember your own daughter… as I certainly shall."

Then the darkness that lapped at the edges of Preston's consciousness rushed over him, sinking him into the crushing black depths of a subterranean sea.

CHAPTER NINE

Awakening to sunlight filtering through the yellow curtains, Nick watched Fanny's bedroom glow into coherence. Lying in the warm bed, he wished he could be suspended in time, encapsulated in this moment that divided rest and pleasure, stress and responsibility. Fanny's smooth backside was fitted against his hip, the naked flesh of her shoulders and long neck exposed by the ardor of their earlier exertions. Remembering his confused earlier waking in the small hours of the morning, he smiled.

He had found Fanny studying his face from the pillow next to his, her eyes warm and dark in the faint light. How natural it had seemed to find her there at that moment, he thought. He had reached out for her and she had responded without reservation, and now he couldn't recall having opened his eyes more happily on a new day in a very long time.

Not wishing to disturb Fanny, or hasten the end of this interlude, he lay his head back down as softly as he could. But a gentle shifting beneath the covers told him he had failed in one thing already. Turning to see, he found Fanny regarding him with eyes narrowed in concern, her emotions flickering in rapid succession across her pale face. Nick knew, without a word, that she was wondering if she had done the right thing. It was clear she did not give herself lightly.

Smiling warmly, Nick touched her cheek, and she took his hand within her own, pressing it against the softness of her flesh. "Good morning," he said.

Fanny smiled back. "Good morning."

"Do I know you?" he asked pleasantly, still smiling. "Have we met?"

Fanny's eyes widened.

"I will say that you look familiar," he continued, stroking his chin in thought. "Ever been arrested?"

She punched his bicep… hard.

"Hey," Nick cried out, "that really hurt! There are laws against assaulting police officers, you know."

The trill of her laughter flew like a bird around the early morning room. "I don't see a badge," she countered, arching an eyebrow at his nakedness.

"No, no badge…" he agreed, lifting the covers and peeking beneath them, raising an eyebrow in return. "But I do have a nightstick, madam… and I'm not afraid to use it."

Fanny snatched up a pillow and reared back.

Nick sat up and threw his arms out. "Wait, wait! It's coming back to me now… I'm beginning to remember." He looked hard at her pouting face. "Let me see now… *Franny* is it? Did I get that right?"

She flung the pillow at him. "I'm gonna kill you," she promised, laughing once more, the upper half of her body springing free of the entangling blankets. Nick saw in the soft glow of the rising sun what he had only glimpsed in the earlier shadows of the night. She was beautiful—slender and fragile, with near pen-dulous breasts, her hair a wild tangle, her face alight with passion and happiness.

He caught up the next pillow before she could hurl it, pull-ing her to him—on this morning he was not tired.

☙

When Nick awoke for the third time, it was to the ring tones of his own cell phone. Carefully pulling himself free of the tangle of Fanny's long legs and arms, he felt for the trousers that he last remembered being on the bedroom floor. After several attempts he finally snagged them, searching the pockets for the persistent summons. Locating it at last, he glanced at the still-sleeping Fanny, before whispering, "Chief Catesby, may I help you?" Fanny stirred.

"Chief?" the voice on the end inquired. "Is that you?—I can barely hear you."

Nick recognized the rasp of Captain Weller on the other end. "Yeah, Shad, it's me," he answered, raising his voice a little.

"Are you coming in today?"

"Yeah, I'm coming in… what… what time is it anyway?" Nick looked around the room for a clock.

"It's nearly eleven," his second-in-command chuckled. "You tie one on last night or something?"

Nick got the impression that Weller was speaking for the benefit of others in the room with him. "No," he snapped, "I did not tie one on… or something. What's this about… is there a problem, Captain?" He had overslept terribly. He should have been out with the search parties hours ago. Thank God he had Jack Kimbo heading up that effort—he would take care of things until he could arrive.

"Depends on how you look at it," Weller replied. "We've got that old drunk down here—the 'professor.' One of the patrols picked him up about dawn this morning—he was passed out in the Baptist cemetery. He's a real piece of work, that one."

Stiffening at the news, Nick glanced at Fanny. Her eyes were open now and she was watching his face. He smiled easily at her, stroking the curve of her hip beneath the blankets. She mouthed the word, "Problem?"

Nick shrugged, shaking his head. "That's not all that unusual, Shad. What's so special about this time?"

"That would be the blood, Chief. He was found with blood on the front of his shirt and we can't find a scratch on him. We thought that was a bit suspicious." A long pause built up between the men.

Nick knew he was being played, but had to ask, "What else, Shad? I get the feeling there's something more to this… want to fill me in?"

"Yeah," Weller agreed, "there is something else. About thirty yards from the old man we found his parka. He identified it without batting an eye. He also demanded the brandy bottle we found in the pocket be returned to him forthwith… that was the word he used… forthwith." Nick heard Weller's sour chuckle in his ear.

"You mind wrapping this up, Shad?"

"Oh sure, Chief, yeah… there was a shoe underneath the jacket… it was a little girl's pink sneaker with kittens on it. I thought it might be important so I called you."

Nick thought he heard suppressed laughter in the background. The sneaker sounded identical to the one Megan Guthrie had been wearing at the time of her disappearance. "Who's there with you, Shad?"

There was a too long pause, "Nobody, Chief… why?"

"No reason," Nick lied right back, sliding out of the warm bed and snatching up his pants on his way to the bathroom.

Once inside he shut the door with his shoulder and said, "Except for this one, Shad—all the info you just told is strictly confidential to this investigation and I hope for your sake that you're keeping it that way."

"Are you threatening me, Chief?"

"No, Captain. I'm reminding you. Now, has Howard been questioned yet?"

"No, we were waiting to hear from you."

"How about the shoe," Nick asked, struggling into his underwear and trousers, "has that been shown to Megan's parents yet?"

"No, it hasn't."

"Dogs…?"

"They were brought to the scene and did what they've done every time… they tracked from the scent item a short distance before starting to tremble and whine and walk in circles—they were useless. Fuckin' Sheriff's Canine Unit ought to all be fired, if you asked me."

"Has the blood on his shirt been collected for evidence?"

"Yep, that's been done… anything else… Chief?"

"Nope," Nick answered in the same laconic tone. "I'll be there shortly, just keep everything as is until I do."

Returning the phone to his pocket, he felt his heart pounding at the first real break in the case. In the same moment, he thought of where he was and who he had spent the night with and felt the excitement changing to dread. He splashed some cold water on his face, toweled off, and turned to the door, his mind racing. When he threw it open, Fanny sat up in alarm. She read his expression instantly.

"Was that about dad? Is he down at the station?"

Nick nodded, crossing to her and taking her hands. He hated himself for what he was about to do, but he had three missing children, possibly and quite probably murdered. "Do you believe in your dad's innocence, Fanny? Do you truly feel that he's had nothing to do with what's happened to these children?"

"Of course I do, Nick," Fanny answered pulling her hands free of his. "I've already told you this, you know I do!"

Looking directly into her eyes, Nick asked, "Then let me search his room, Fanny. You have the legal authority as the owner of this house to give me permission. If you believe as you say you do, and really want to help him, then you'll give me that permission."

"Is that what this was all about Nick?" Fanny's gaze took in the wrecked bed. "Is that why you're here?"

He seized her hands firmly in his once more and wouldn't let go, "No it isn't... I think you really know that, Fanny. But they've found your dad with blood on his shirt and a little girl's sneaker... possibly Megan Guthrie's. Do you understand? This isn't about us at all—it's about those kids."

Fanny looked back at Nick, her struggles dying away. She thought of Preston's stories of Gabriel, his wild boy of the woods, and of her own research that appeared to bolster his crazy beliefs. She thought of the boy dressed like a scarecrow standing in the misting rain, his terrifying hand raised in mute greeting, his skin glowing as whitely as a slug's. She thought of those children gone missing, both now and in the past, then she said quietly, "You have my permission, Nick, but I know you won't find anything. He's not like that. I know he's not a good man... my God, I've known that my whole life... but he's not like *that*.

"I'm not sure what the truth is, Nick, but maybe dad's stumbled onto something out there... but I know he didn't harm those children... I know that much."

Pulling her housecoat around her, she stood up. "Come on, I'll show you." Taking Nick's hand in her own, she led him down the hall to her father's room.

❧

Sliding his shoeless feet off the narrow metal bunk, Preston placed them gingerly onto the grey cement floor, pushing himself upright. The cold seeped immediately through his worn socks and he flexed his toes to circulate the blood in his feet. His head felt as if it might burst with the steady unrelenting throb of his hangover, and his stomach was percolating with gastric acids.

Staring at the toilet bolted into the corner of his tiny cell, its steel surface spattered with the squalid effluvia of earlier occupants, he prayed that he would not have to embrace this awful receptacle. Above this woeful throne, the unblinking lens of a camera observed his movements from within a plastic globe. The globe was speckled with tiny balls of moistened toilet paper. Preston glared up at it for several moments with a defiant expression he did not feel.

Shivering now, he clasped his torso with his thin arms and began to rock himself. It was only then that he noticed he was in his undershirt, and that his shirt and parka had been taken along with his shoes and belt.

"Bastards," he murmured, his chapped lips adhering to one another. "Could I, at least, have some water?" he challenged the cloudy globe.

"I know you people can hear me," he said a little more loudly, causing the throbbing in his head to worsen. "Bastards," he repeated more softly now.

As if only waiting for this simple request, he heard the metal door to the cell block clang open. Startled, he wondered if they heard what he said. He set his expression and hoped that it did not reveal his alarm.

He heard a quick confident tread, and then a young uniformed officer arrived at his cell door. They looked at one another through the bars.

"Well," Preston managed, "am I being released? On what charges are you holding me, I would like to know, and where are my clothes?—I demand them back this instant."

Smiling, the younger man began unlocking the cell door, replying as he did, "No sir, to your first question. As to the second and third, I'll let the chief explain about all that." He held out a hand, but Preston shrugged it off. "Will you come with me, Professor Howard?"

The officer's respectful address caught Preston off guard as he struggled to his feet. "Do I know you?" Preston asked. The officer was tall and slender, with sandy colored hair worn just long enough to comb, his eyes a washed-out blue. Preston thought he was pleasant looking enough without being in the least remarkable.

"I doubt that you'd remember me," the officer replied, leading Preston into the corridor and out into the hallway, "but many years ago I was in one of your English Lit classes. I didn't do very well, but I did manage to pass... just barely—you gave me a 'D'."

"Did I?" Preston replied, while holding up his pants with one hand. "Well, no doubt you deserved it... I was probably being too kind at that."

"Probably," the policeman agreed, chuckling.

"And you ended up here," Preston observed, as if this was the inevitable outcome of stunted academic prowess.

"I did," he agreed, "... as did you." He grinned at Preston without the least malice, ushering him into the same cramped room he had been interviewed in just days before. He pointed to a chair, but as the other was occupied by the chief himself, it was an unnecessary courtesy. "Anything, Chief?" he asked as he was backing out the door.

Nick held up a hand. "Why don't you sit in on this, Beckam?"

The younger officer, smiling once more, replied, "Sure, Chief, I'd like to. Thanks." He wedged himself back into the tight room, easing the door closed behind him.

Preston took the proffered chair in the suddenly crowded room, eyeing the cardboard cups of coffee that sat before the chief of police.

"Would you care for one?" Nick asked, "How about you, Beck?"

Beckam leaned into his corner, shaking his head. "No thanks, Chief. I'm a green tea man myself."

"Are you now?" Nick slid a cup over to Preston. "It's still hot. I thought you might need it after some time in that cell—it gets cold back there."

Flipping the top off, Preston attempted to raise the steaming cup to his lips, but his hands were shaking so much that he set it back down. After a few moments, he brought his mouth down to the cup and slurped as quietly as he could. He would not look up to see if he was being watched, but flushed with embarrassment even so.

"Cream… sugar?" Nick asked.

Raising his face from the comforting steam, Preston simply shook his head. Already the caffeine was entering his system, rejuvenating his brain cells. "Would it be possible for me to have some aspirin?"

"We're not allowed to give…" Nick hesitated over his choice of words, "… those in custody any medication unless it has been prescribed by a doctor."

Preston's mouth turned down in disapproval. "I see, interrogation tactics at their finest—no shoes, no shirt, no food, no aspirin, no sleep—old school deprivation."

Nick refused to rise to the bait. "Professor, I'm going to be taping this interview." Flicking a switch on the wall behind him, a red light glowed into life on the camera perched above his shoulder. "For the record," he began without further preamble, "I am Chief Nick Catesby. Officer Timothy Beckam and I are interviewing Professor Preston Howard in reference to the disappearances of Megan Guthrie, Jared Case, and Connor Lacey, all of Wessex Township."

Preston felt a jolt go through his body at the mention of the children and the memory of the previous evening came rushing back to him with nightmarish urgency. The thought of the limp, dying children turned his bowels to water even as the vampire's words came back to him with sinister force, "Betray me, old man, and your own child shall surely die."

"Please read along with me, Professor, as I read your Miranda Warning aloud for the record." Chief Catesby's words interrupted Preston's reverie and looking down he found a printed card in his hand informing him of his rights. He listened in a kind of dull wonder to Nick's droning recitation, even as he began to understand at last why Gabriel had chosen him—people no longer believed in the walking dead of vampire lore, but they did very much believe in the pedophiliac monsters that stole and murdered their children. They saw proof of their depredations in the news every day—they would believe it was Preston... easily.

When Nick was done, he asked, "If you've understood these rights and wish to answer my questions without benefit of a lawyer being present, please say so for the recording and sign the card in your hand." He shoved a pen in Preston's direction.

"I haven't done anything wrong..."

"Then you should have no problem answering my questions," Nick replied.

"Only you wouldn't believe my answers—I tried to tell you about the boy in the woods... Gabriel. You didn't listen. Now it's too late... I can't help you. I have to think of my own daughter now."

"What are you talking about, Professor Howard? What has she got to do with any of this?"

"I should be released… I should be with her. You have no evidence against me. You couldn't, and I want my clothes back now."

"That's not possible." Nick did not attempt to soften the blow, "Your shirt appeared to have a quantity of blood on it, and your parka was found with a child's shoe. These items are going to be examined by the state lab, Preston, as soon as we can get them there." He nodded at Officer Beckam, "When we are done here, this officer is going to drive them up there as fast as he can. I've asked them to prioritize this case and they've agreed."

Preston remembered the warm liquid spilling onto his chest as he was losing consciousness in the cemetery, Gabriel's inhuman eyes boring into his own. "I will require another before I sleep again, and when that time is nigh, I will come to you. *Until then, remember your own daughter… as I certainly shall.*"

He had never felt so trapped and useless. Even if he was free to tell Catesby about Gabriel, he would never believe it. Without actually seeing him, who could? Remembering the fragile, drained children in the graveyard he lowered his head into his shaking hands and began to weep.

"What's wrong," Nick asked none too gently. "Why are you crying?"

Without raising his face, Preston answered, "Because I am such a fool… I have always been a fool."

The camera continued recording.

❧

As Nick was passing dispatch, Diana caught his eye and beckoned him with a crooked finger. "Chief," she whispered as he stuck his head in the doorway, "there's a Ms. Howard here to see you. I told her you were tied up in an interview, but she said she'd just wait. I told her I didn't know how long you'd be…"

"All right," Nick cut her off, "it's all right, D. I'll just walk her in." He could see Fanny through the smoked glass behind which the dispatchers monitored the lobby. She was slumped in one of the molded plastic chairs and looked frail in the unhealthy fluorescent glow. Noticing that she was clutching a brown paper sack from which clothing protruded, he guessed that these were for her father.

He threw open the door and she turned at the sound. "I hope you haven't been waiting long?" he asked in a more formal tone than he felt. He could feel Diana's eager eyes on him and his female visitor.

"No," Fanny replied with a weak smile, "not very long." She rose to her feet and appeared to totter. Nick took a step toward her. "I've brought some clothes for dad, Nick. I thought he might need them."

Casting a nervous glance at the smoked glass, Nick couldn't make out the dispatcher's expression. He had no doubt, though, that she would have keyed on the casual use of his name and he could already imagine the gossip that would shortly spread through the department. In for a penny, he thought... "Fanny, why don't you come up to my office? I'll have an officer take his clothes back to him while we talk. Beckam's picking him up some lunch now. You can talk to him afterwards." He reached across and took the sack from her, grasping her arm all in the same moment. "Come on through," he murmured as they were buzzed in by the ever-avid Diana.

He hurried her along the corridor, only stopping to drop off the sack with Diana, instructing her to have an officer deliver it to Preston. Diana assured him that she would, then asked archly if he would like one of his "urgent" phone calls from dispatch in fifteen minutes or so—these were prearranged calls that Nick often employed to extricate himself from the perennial complainers and crashing bores.

"That won't be necessary," he assured her.

"I see," she replied.

"I doubt it," he said over his shoulder, catching just the ghost of a smile on her lips. He returned to Fanny waiting in the hall.

Once they were safely behind the closed door of his office he kissed her gently. Fanny pulled away, saying, "Not here, Nick. I feel so frightened for dad. I know this is your world, but try and understand this is all very new to me, and I'm so worried about what might happen."

"Of course," he said. "I'm sorry, it's just that I…" he let his words trail off. What was the point? His feelings were not what were important to Fanny at this moment and he understood that. Ushering her into a comfortable chair, he sat across from her holding her hands in his own. "You want to know about your dad?"

Fanny nodded, her eyes dark, trembling pools.

Nick took a deep breath and said, "The interview didn't exonerate him, Fanny. I wish I could say that it did.

"He chose not to cooperate… he mentioned that boy in the woods again and then wouldn't speak any more. The first time he told me about him I thought he might be talking about Seth Busby—the truth is, I thought he might have been involved in that boy's disappearance and that this was his crazy way of telling me that. The clothes he described him as wearing were the same as Seth was last seen in. Now, he's been found with what appears to be Megan Guthrie's sneaker."

Fanny's head snapped up.

Nick continued, wanting to get it over with, "After her mother identifies it, the shoe will be sent, along with the bloody shirt your dad was found in, to the state lab for DNA screening."

"Oh my god… !" she whispered.

After the search of Preston's room had revealed nothing incriminating, he knew Fanny's hopes had been raised… now this.

"I'm sorry, Fanny." Squeezing her hand, Nick asked, "He seemed worried about you... do you know what that's about? Is there anything you can tell me about all this?"

Fanny nodded, avoiding Nick's eyes. "Just a few days ago, he came to me with this story of his encounter with this... boy... this creature, he calls Gabriel. He was so excited. I haven't seen dad like this since... well, it's been a very long time. At first, I thought he might be having delirium tremens or possibly some kind of nervous breakdown, but he sounded so coherent when he spoke about these encounters... he had so many details."

"You didn't believe him...?" Nick asked.

"No, not at first, I didn't." Fanny looked down at their intertwined fingers in embarrassment. "But then, he asked me to do some research for him on earlier cases of missing children... historical cases. It seemed so important to him that I did."

Nick was intrigued in spite of himself, "And...?"

Fanny glanced up at him before continuing, "So much of what he was saying was supported by historical accounts, archived stories that went back hundreds of years. I know it seems incredible... and it can't possibly be true, I know that, but Nick there *have* been children going missing in South Jersey since colonial times, and possibly before, and there are mentions of a boy sometimes seen in the vicinity of these disappearances." Taking a breath, she filled him in on the legend of the "snow boy," and the tales of the phantom child of the Pine Barrens.

When she was done, she added, "I know that it's impossible that these cases and this 'boy' could be connected and real, yet... how would dad have gotten onto this? He hasn't had the slightest interest in anything beyond English literature and the bottle in decades, he hardly even notices that other people exist, and that goes double for children."

Nick stood, releasing Fanny's hands and walking to the windows that faced the library where he watched her ascend the steps each day that he could. "I've got to admit it makes a pretty good story." He turned back to face her.

"The problem is… it's just that… a story. Even if I were to believe something so incredible, how would I go about proving it? The sad fact of the matter is that when all's said and done, everything your dad has told you could just as easily be attributed to a guilty conscience… an alcohol-addled mind." He looked down at his shoes. "I can't let him go, Fanny, I'm sorry. Because in the end he's all I've got that makes any sense."

Head bowed, Fanny spoke after a long silence, "Nick, I think I may have seen this boy, too… this Gabriel… following me last night. It was as if he wanted me to know that he was there… watching. He didn't look right, somehow… I… I can't explain exactly."

A memory flickered briefly through Nick's mind… a barefoot boy in the mist. Shrugging it off, he said, "Fanny, it was just a coincidence… some neighborhood boy trying to scare you— it had to be. It is almost Halloween, you know. He probably thought it was funny."

There was a knock on his office door.

Opening it, he found Weller. Shad peered beyond Nick to his visitor who remained in her chair, her face averted from scrutiny.

With a lazy insouciance, he returned his gaze to his superior. "Got a minute?" he asked.

"A minute," Nick replied, stepping out into the hallway and pulling the door closed behind him. "Shoot."

"You were breaking the news to her?" Weller asked with a small grin.

"What news?" Nick asked.

"… about her old man—that you're charging him with the murder of those kids."

Shaking his head, Nick said, "No, Shad, I'm not. Firstly, I'm gonna wait for the lab results. Secondly, we don't know for a fact the kids are dead."

"I understand," he replied equably enough, "you want to break it to her gently, she being your... well, *friend* and all. It must be tough on you," he concluded with a glance at the closed door.

"Actually, what's tough on me right now, Shad, is trying to keep up with where you're going with all this." Turning his back on his second-in-command, he gripped the door handle. Weller's voice froze him.

"You mean to tell me that you're going to let him go?" The venom of his tone electrified the air in the narrow hallway.

Nick spun around, firing back, "I didn't say that, Shad. I intend to hang on to Professor Howard while we continue our investigation and await the lab results... I'd also like another stab at an interview with him. At the very least, he may be a valuable witness, if he's not our kidnapper."

"Witness," Weller hissed. Nick saw the vein in his temple pulsing, his droopy eyes grow dark with suffused blood. "You're droppin' the ball here, Chief, and I'm just tryin' to save your ass. It's all over the department about your visits to the library— about you bangin' the pretty librarian." He nodded at Nick's office, shaking his head as if in bewilderment. "You must think we're idiots over here, Nick. I suspect most of the town is—or will be—talkin' about it, and soon."

Slapping Nick on the shoulder, he managed a sickly smile. "Hell, there's no one here that blames you of course, after all you've been through. No man should have to put up with a wife that humps every guy that looks her way... hell, she even gave me a shot at it!" He patted Nick's shoulder gently now.

"But don't let that blind you here, Boss. Don't drop the ball on this like you did in the Busby case. Hell, Nick, if you don't want to screw things up with the sexy librarian in there, just give the nod and *I'll* charge the sonofabitch! That'll get you off the hook and you can blame me."

Nick didn't know where to begin. He actually felt dizzy with all of Weller's words, innuendos, and revelations, but even as he reeled under the verbal assault, a white-hot flame shot upward into his consciousness, burning away the poisonous fog that threatened to engulf his thinking and paralyze him. In a single motion he seized Weller's wrist and swept it off his shoulder.

"Don't ever touch me again, you back-stabbing bastard, or I'll stuff that hand so far up your ass that it'll tickle your tonsils. Are we clear on that much, at least?"

Weller recoiled like a struck dog, snarling, "You don't know when someone's trying to do you a favor."

"Favor," Nick laughed. "You call screwing my wife a favor… spreading rumors about me, a favor? Well thanks a lot pal, but I can do without any more of your favors.

"As to *this* case, let's get one thing straight, little man… I'm in charge. For good or for bad, I'm calling the shots. As for you, Captain, you are to have nothing further to do with it and that's an order. Understood?"

Nick felt himself shaking with emotion. It was all he could do to keep from beating Weller to a pulp. Out of the corner of his eye, he saw Janis from Records peeking out of her office. Had he been shouting? She scurried back in when she caught his glance.

"You saw," Weller shouted after her, "you heard! I'll be calling on you as a witness," he promised the frightened clerk. Skulking backwards, and out of Nick's long reach, the fabric of his jacket made a hissing noise sliding along the wall. "This is the last straw," he promised Nick. "I've stood by long enough and watched you run this department into the ground… no more. I'm taking this to the prosecutor and telling him everything. Just what do you think he's gonna do when he finds out about you having a relationship with the daughter of a prime suspect in three cases?"

Weller had almost reached the stairwell when Nick felt the door give behind and heard Fanny ask in a small voice, "Nick, is everything okay?"

Pointing excitedly at her, Weller exclaimed, "See… in your own office!"

Nick spoke quietly over his shoulder, "Just wait inside, Fanny. I'll be right there." After a moment he heard the snick of the closing door behind him.

"How are you going to explain all that, big man?" Weller wanted to know.

"Keep walking," Nick warned him.

As Weller reached the top of the stairs, he added, "You might think you can blow me off, Nick, but you can't keep all this at bay forever… you can't keep covering up for your new squeeze any more than you can run interference for those priests of yours. You think the county prosecutor will stand by while you cover up for pedophiles?"

Nick began to walk rapidly down the hall towards Weller. "How did you know about that?" he demanded. "It sounds to me like you got an inside track here, Shad. Maybe you're just a little *too* close to the facts—care to explain?" Weller didn't wait for Nick's arrival, but turned and fled down the echoing stairwell.

When Nick got to the landing he shouted down, "Don't bother coming in tomorrow, Captain, you're suspended for insubordination pending a hearing! Be sure and tell that to the prosecutor, too!

"Also, you sneaky sonofabitch, I'm confiscating your fuckin' crayons until further notice!"

Nick heard Weller's footsteps falter at this last, before resuming their former clatter as Nick began to laugh aloud. The sound of it boomed down the stairwell chasing Weller out of the building. When Nick heard the exit door slam he turned once more for his office and Fanny.

He continued to chuckle at his own bravado and the sad image of his captain making crude, hateful drawings of Monsignor Mulcahy, then furtively attaching them to the cars of parishioners. His malice and envy rendered him laughable in the final analysis, he thought—if only it rendered him harmless, as well.

By the time he reached his office the brief moment of levity had evaporated and when he opened the door it was to find Fanny standing and white-faced. She appeared ready to flee as well.

"Fanny," he began, "I'm so sorry you had to hear all that. It's been a long-running thing, I'm afraid…"

She cut him off, "Nick, I really should be going. I had no idea how much trouble I was going to make for you." Brushing past him to the door, she stopped and said, "I don't think it's such a good idea for us to continue seeing one another… not until all this has blown over… if it ever does."

Nick started to speak, but she slipped through the door and was gone. She's probably right, he thought, sitting down at his desk and placing his face in his broad hands. After several minutes of silence, he murmured softly to the empty office, "My God, I'm in deep."

༄

Father Gregory shuttled down the nave of Our Lady's from the altar toward the main entrance, his slightly bulging eyes sweeping the pews. What had once been the shared and rotating duty of securing the church for the evening had, with Monsignor Mulcahy's illness, become his alone. Even so, he approached this task without resentment, as it also allowed him a small time to himself and his devotion to the Eucharist.

Turning off the overhead lamps as he progressed, the church was thrown into shadow by degrees, the dying sun, filtered through the mosaics of stained glass, coloring rather than clarifying the objects within. When he reached the large carved panels that opened into the greeting area, he paused and turned to regard the interior.

At either side of the altar figures clothed in blue, white, and scarlet cloaks raised their hands and eyes to the heavens from their shadowed alcoves. Mary, portrayed as Queen of the Universe, bore a crown of stars, her infant son cradled in her arms. In typical infant fascination of bright baubles, his chubby hands reached for her diadem.

Pulling the doors shut behind him, Father Gregory checked the vestry and the restrooms to ensure that the building was, indeed, empty. Satisfied, he proceeded to the small chapel off the lobby.

He knelt before the Monstrance, a gold cross fashioned to contain the blessed communion wafer, and housed within the open tabernacle. The wafer, paper-thin and white as snow, was incised with a cross and clearly visible behind the crystal oval it was sealed behind.

Grunting as he knelt, the priest cupped his face in his hands for several seconds in order to clear his mind, trying to think of nothing. Finally, he looked up to regard the Eucharist and contemplate its wonder. The cross, captured by several small and cunningly hidden lamps, appeared to hover within the tabernacle—the incised wafer a ghostly white presence at its heart.

Mumbling his prayers in rapid, unbroken succession, the room around him faded into nothingness, and he was unconscious of the rows of empty chairs behind him. A statue of St. Therese of Lisieux guarded his back in the gathering darkness.

Yet, after many minutes of this intense devotion, he began to grow aware of something beyond his absorption with this essential Mystery of the Church—his neck was growing cold. Having come from a land of debilitating tropical heat, his sojourn in America had found him unprepared for actual winter, and even after several years in New Jersey, he felt the approach of the cold with a near physical horror. Rising to his feet with another small grunt, he looked behind him into the spreading gloom. A small window that opened out onto the side yard swung gently on its hinges.

Father Gregory hurried over and shut it once more. Noticing that the latch was not functioning properly, he made a mental note to relay this to the custodian. When he turned back to the room he found a boy kneeling in the spot he had vacated just moments before. Completely caught off his guard, he stood there dumbly regarding the youngster's lean back.

It wasn't just the silence of the boy's appearance that startled him so (though he could not account for how he had missed him while securing the building), but his apparent occupation with the Adoration that he found disconcerting as well—he had never witnessed a mere boy engaged in so esoteric a practice before. He didn't know quite what to do.

Drawing closer, several things became apparent to him at once, the first was the smell—the boy's body odor was a near-palpable presence in the close room, and in spite of his lifetime of experience with the unwashed beggars of India, he found the odor repellant. Next was the child's appearance—his trousers were too short for his extraordinarily long legs and the same applied to the filthy shirt and his attenuated arms. More remarkable yet, his feet were unshod, the soles black as a dog's pads, long and narrow, altogether unnatural looking. His hair was a tousled mop of neglected curls, strewn and littered with stems, dirt, and autumn leaves, the long exposed neck streaked with grime.

Father Gregory leaned down in the dim light. Partially concealed by the tangle of hair, the child's ears peeked out. *Were they pointed?* wondered Father Gregory in a near dream-like state. What kind of child had wandered into his church? He knew without thinking that this was not the son of any parishioner that had crossed the threshold of Our Lady's. Clearly this was a child in need of help. One thing was certain, he thought, never during his time in America had he seen a child such as this.

In spite of the wretched odor, he cleared his throat lightly in order not to startle the boy, before kneeling onto the hard floor beside him. He would not deprive the child of the kneeler when he was so wrapped up in his devotions, but would join him in prayer.

Bowing his head, he strove to return to his previous state of meditation, but the proximity of the odd child floated foremost in his mind's eye and he could not rid himself of the unease he caused. Surrendering to his lively curiosity, Father Gregory cast a glance at his fellow worshipper from the corner of his eye... only to find himself being regarded in the same sly manner—the boy's large, green eyes, blood-flecked and amused. For several long moments this held.

"You are different from the rest," the child spoke at last in a hoarse, sibilant voice, unnaturally loud in the silent chapel.

Flinching at the apparition's address, the priest replied clearly, "What do you mean?" He felt a jolt of adrenalin course through his veins at the sight of the boy's wide mouth, his long jagged teeth.

"I watch," the child explained from his prayerful pose. "I watch when I am able... and you have no woman... or even man."

This casual observation shocked Father Gregory, but he tried not to show it in his expression. After several moments, he managed to say, "Of course not, I am a priest."

"And priests keep no mates, but kneel and watch their gold?" Gabriel asked, pointing a long taloned finger at the Monstrance.

Father Gregory rose to his feet at this, both in shock at the boy's insolence and in terror of the awful hand that stopped just short of touching the cross—a terrible appendage. "I am not watching gold," he protested, "but adoring God Himself made present in the Eucharist."

Turning, Gabriel faced the frightened clergyman. "God," he repeated as if trying the word on for size, rolling it around on his long tongue. "God… he is there?" Again the sinewy arm uncoiled, a cracked brown nail hovering but a millimeter from the object of their discussion.

Father Gregory took a step forward in spite of himself, so great was his concern for the blessed wafer. "Yes," he assured his interrogator, "He is there. Do you know Him?"

Gabriel stretched as if he had not heard the question, sliding bonelessly from the kneeler onto the pew behind him. Draping himself, cat-like, along its length, he appeared to give the question some thought. Father Gregory observed these movements with a growing sense of unreality and horror. His meeting with Professor Howard in the coffee shop rose unbidden to his mind. What had he quoted? "There are more things under heaven…" Unfinished, it slipped away again.

"I listen, too," Gabriel answered at last. "You eat this God… and drink his blood. I would like to drink his blood as well, I think."

Swaying, Father Gregory fought to focus on the boy's words, even as he struggled against his repugnance to his goblin-like features. He could not escape the impression that this face had never been meant for close inspection—could never truly pass for human. "This you may not do unless you have been baptized in the Church," he answered.

The boy, raising the upper half of his body from his supine pose, regarded Father Gregory darkly for several moments. "*You* partake of this God, so if I partake of you, shall I not also drink his blood, by your will or no?"

Father Gregory took a step back, even as the wicked child's eyes, glittering like silica, remained fixed upon him. As if by invisible threads, the feral boy began to rise with each step the little priest took, and Father Gregory groaned with fear.

Turning with almost superhuman effort, he seized the Monstrance protectively, clutching it to his chest and crying, "Who are you… *what* are you?"

Spinning back round to confront his unnatural adversary, he found himself alone in the chapel, the boy having vanished into the darkness. The small, stained glass window swung once more on its hinges. Like a spray of blood, the offering of roses to Saint Therese lay scattered spitefully at her feet.

CHAPTER TEN

Nick Catesby found himself waiting in the lobby of the Prosecutor's office like any other citizen. It was not a good sign. His eyes burned and he noticed his hands shaking slightly. He was already regretting the bottle of bourbon that he had punished the night before and, when he thought of Fanny and how they had parted, his chest felt hollow and tender. A middle-aged woman, glancing up at him from her desk, offered him a timorous smile. He knew by her expression that he was in real trouble.

Outside, in the fields, woods, and salt marshes of Wessex Township, the final day of the search for the children had begun without him. After a week of fruitless activity and a steady dwindling of volunteers as a result, he had determined to bring it to an end. Nothing had been discovered that justified further effort on the ground—the outcome now lay squarely with the police investigators and their counterparts at the county, state, and federal level. The parents had been devastated at the announcement—it was tantamount to admitting that their children would not be seen again… at least, alive. Mrs. Guthrie had slapped his face, and her husband had begun openly weeping.

The summons from the prosecutor had been delivered by Jeff Gilhooly, a kindly man that Nick had known most of his life. He had been the prosecutor's senior investigator for a decade. The fact that it was him was both a courtesy and a signal of the prosecutor's serious concerns.

Having finished his instructions to the captains of his search teams, Nick turned command over to Jack Kimbo once more, before taking a final slurp of his fast-cooling coffee and following the messenger to the prosecutor's office. Now he waited.

A phone rang at the woman's desk and she answered it with a pleasant, "Yes sir?" A moment later she returned the receiver to its cradle, smiling once more at Nick. This time she tried to put more hope into it. "You can go right in," she chirped, her plump cheeks crinkling with effort, "he's ready for you now."

Nodding to her, Nick rose and strode forth with all the confidence he did not feel. "Thank you," he said as he passed her.

The office door opened ahead of him and Jeff, tall, balding, and soft-looking, waved him in with a strained smile. "Nick, I'm sorry about all this." He gestured vaguely at the office in general, and followed him inside.

The county prosecutor, a graying man of medium height, some years older than Nick, sat behind a nameplate that read, "Anthony Calabria." He rose as Jeff closed the door behind Nick, offering his hand. They had met many times before, but only in the most professional of circumstances.

Nick took a seat in one the leather chairs that Calabria indicated. "Thanks for coming in," the prosecutor murmured, settling back into his own seat.

Nick made no comment on the fact that he had been given no choice. "I would have dressed up if I had had more notice," he quipped, indicating the hiking boots, jeans, heavy wool shirt, and canvas jacket he was wearing in preparation for the day's efforts.

The prosecutor's mouth twitched at the edges beneath his thick, untrimmed mustache, never managing to break into an actual smile. Jeff continued to stand near the door. "I understand," Anthony replied, "I wasn't given much notice either." Glancing at his right-hand man, he said, "Jeff, sit down will you, you're making me nervous." Gilhooly hastened to obey. "That's better," he pronounced, tenting his hands beneath his fleshy chin and looking straight into Nick's eyes. "I suspect you know why you're here, Nick."

"Yeah, Pros, I suspect I do—you've had a visit from Shad Weller."

Anthony nodded. "Yes, I did, Nick, and it would be understating it if I said he has a few problems with how you've been handling this case with the missing kids… understating it." He paused and studied Nick for effect. "Sound familiar?"

"It certainly sounds like Weller," Nick answered. "We had a little talk last night and he managed to make himself pretty clear on how he felt about me." Nick felt the low pulse in his skull from the hangover grow stronger. "He may have said more than he intended to though."

"Meaning…?"

Fishing the evidence bag from within his coat, Nick spread it out on the desk of the county's top attorney. Within were the inflammatory drawings from Our Lady's parking lot, dusted graphite coating the edges and revealing several sets of fingerprints.

"He may not have mentioned these to you," Nick said. The prosecutor regarded them without comment, waiting for Nick to continue. "They were placed on the cars of some parishioners of Our Lady of the Visitation a few days ago. As you can see, in the light of the disappearances, they're obviously meant to stir up trouble for the priests there. Weller slipped up last night and said something that made me think he might have had something to do with it." Nick pointed at a pair of clearly discernible prints at the edge of one of the sheets. "Those are his," he announced, "no doubt about it—I had the sheriff's ID unit check them against the card in his personnel file—they're a positive match. He's had nothing to do with this case, absolutely no legitimate reason to have handled these flyers."

The prosecutor stared at the drawings for several moments. "Why?" he asked at last.

"I can't be sure, of course, but I think he found out about the allegations in the Monsignor's past and decided to take advantage of the current situation. Not that there's any chance Monsignor Mulcahy had anything to do with the disappearances of Megan and the boys. I've had that checked out—the monsignor was in the hospital for a chronic lung infection when Megan Guthrie disappeared, and he is far too frail to have taken on two teenage boys... especially those two. Shad wouldn't be the first anti-Catholic bigot to start a smear campaign.

"Lastly, it just muddies the waters, creates a distraction, and makes it harder for me to get to the truth of what's going on around here. I think the bottom line is this—he wants me to fail so that he can crawl over me and get what he's wanted all along—my job."

Nick took a breath before continuing, "But whatever his motivations, Pros, it does speak to one thing—his integrity... of which he has none. So, if I'm being brought here to stand and deliver on his allegations then let's begin with that understanding." Nick found himself leaning forward in his chair.

Raising a finger into the air, the prosecutor answered, "I'll be the determiner of the facts in this particular investigation."

Turning to his own chief, he swept the evidence up from his desk. "Jeff, take charge of these, would you, and run down the sheriff's ID personnel to confirm what Nick's saying here."

Jeff stood, taking the bag from his boss and smiling at Nick. "You know it's not that we doubt you, Nick, but Weller's made serious allegations and we have to treat this just like any other internal—in the long run, it will be to your own benefit... you'll see."

"I know you've got to do what you've got to do, Jeff," Nick answered.

Gilhooly turned and fled the office, bag in hand.

As the door closed behind him, Nick turned back to Calabria. The prosecutor studied him through smeared glasses. "Assuming you're right about your second-in-command, how do you square what he's had to say about you and the Howards? Is it true you're seeing the daughter of a suspect in the case?"

Nick felt himself flushing. "It's true," he admitted.

Folding his hands together, Calabria continued, "That's troubling, Nick. Please tell me it started before her father became a person of interest."

"Not exactly, Pros."

Nick's answer hung in the air between them for several long moments.

"But this..." the prosecutor consulted a pad on his desk "... this Preston Howard is currently in custody?"

Nick nodded once more.

"Thank God for that much."

Pulling himself up a little taller in the soft leather of the chair, Nick stated, "I've never let my personal life interfere with an investigation." It sounded weak even to him.

"Until now," the older man reminded him. "What do you have on him?"

"He was picked up yesterday morning in the Baptist Cemetery... he had blood on his shirtfront. I had samples rushed to the state lab in Ewing."

"Good," Calabria murmured. "That's something, at least."

"He also admitted being in the vicinity at the time of Megan Guthrie's disappearance."

"Better and better…"

"Of course, if the blood matches the DNA of any of the kids' parents, then I'll believe that he's our man."

"You mean you don't right now?"

Nick looked Calabria in the eye. "I mean I've still got an open mind about it." He paused before continuing, "There's something else I should mention."

"Go ahead, Chief… let's hear it."

"He's talked about a boy…"

"Do you mean the Case boy, or the Lacey kid?"

Nick shook his head, running a hand through his hair, ruffling it into a cock's comb. "No, not the victims, Pros, but a kid that he claims has something to do with their going missing. He calls him Gabriel…" Nick clarified, his face grown warmer yet, "…but the truth is, I don't know who this kid is, or even if he really exists."

"A phantom boy…" Calabria repeated quietly.

Nick glanced away again. "I don't know about phantom."

His superior in the criminal justice hierarchy studied him. "How about Preston's daughter, Nick?" he asked, letting the question hang between them.

"She allowed me to search her father's room without him knowing. There was nothing incriminating there and if he *is* involved, I promise you she hasn't got a clue about it."

The other man sat back into his chair, folding his hands across his paunch. "That's excellent, Nick, I'm so glad that you can vouch for her… very helpful." Raising his eyebrows, he asked, "No chance that she signed a 'consent to search' form is there?"

Nick shook his head.

"I see," the prosecutor continued. "No chance you had crime scene technicians respond?"

Remaining mute, Nick awaited the blow.

"Okay," he nodded affably, "all right then…." He looked up at Nick, his eyes turning to grey flints. "You've lost objectivity, Chief, and you stink of whiskey—you can't begin to believe that you've handled this mess professionally." Taking a breath, he continued, "You've left me no choice here, Nick—the Wessex Township Police investigation is now under the direct supervision of my office, and I just hope it's not too late to salvage something useful from this mess."

Nick rose to his feet, but before he could speak, Calabria went on, "Don't even think about fighting me over this, Nick. It would only do you more harm in the end. Go along quietly and we'll keep all this under wraps. Oppose me and I'll leak it to the press. Think about what I'm saying."

Nick managed to ask, "And my particular status?"

"You're off this investigation… period, but you'll continue to run your department's day-to-day operations… understood?"

Head reeling, Nick nodded, turning for the door.

The prosecutor's voice stopped him. "One last thing, Chief… if it turns out you're right about Weller, and I suspect you are, I'm gonna put his balls in a vise."

Nick continued out the door, saying over his shoulder, "That's something then."

⌘

Back in his office, Nick began gathering the pages of the file detailing the department's efforts to locate the missing children. There were hundreds of them, as well as photographs, and he sifted through them mechanically, his mind the blank of a winter landscape. The pages, the notes, the photos all came to nothing, ultimately meant nothing, and he shuffled them like so many playing cards in preparation for sending them over to the prosecutor's office. From outside came bursts of excited laughter as children passed beneath his office windows. Nick heard this without pleasure or recognition.

As he scooped the bulging file into a large manila envelope one of the interview discs slipped out, falling onto his desk. It landed with a tiny clatter to rest next to another official-looking envelope. This one bore the return address of the state forensics lab for the South Jersey Region. Nick stared at it. What did the blood results matter to him now? There was nothing further he could—or would be allowed—to do. Yet, the thought of an answer, any answer, to what was happening to his town began to re-awaken him, stir him to life.

Ripping the envelope open he extracted the single page it contained. With sweaty palms he smoothed out the document, no more than a lab form really, the results carefully typed into the appropriate boxes. Holding it up to the light he read the findings as they had been determined by the forensic scientists.

Afterwards, he set the paper down on his desk, lifting his eyes to a colored print of Saint Michael, the patron saint of police officers, which hung on the far wall. Trampling the devil underfoot, the militant angel's efforts appeared leisurely, accomplished with scant regard for his dangerous opponent, his sword casually withheld from the death blow.

Why, Nick wondered, hadn't the angel destroyed Satan rather than simply casting him into the underworld where he could plot and strike, again and again? There was no answer to this, just as there was no answer to what he had read.

Picking up the sheet, he read it once more. It was both brief and unequivocal; the lab results on the blood taken from Preston Howard's shirt determined that it was not human blood. At the bottom of the form, in the appropriate box, was stamped the technician's name and telephone number. Nick picked up his phone and dialed it.

After being put on hold several times and transferred more than once, the voice of what sounded to Nick like a very young man said, "Yes, Chief? How may I help you?"

Nick was to the point, "In regards to our sample… do you have your findings there?"

"Yes," he answered. "Is there a problem?"

"Maybe," Nick replied. "If it's not human blood, what is it? Can you determine that?"

There was a longer pause than Nick thought necessary, and he barked, "Are you still there?"

"Yes, yes, Chief, I'm here. It's just that, well, we did try to determine what species it might be… we would routinely do that in such a case as this…"

"Yes," Nick prompted. "And…?"

"Well, we couldn't. We couldn't make a definitive determination other than we believe, with almost complete certainty, that it's mammalian." He said this last with some pride, as if this salvaged the lab's unsatisfactory efforts.

"Almost," Nick repeated. "That's it… you're *almost* certain it's from a mammal?"

"Yes… almost."

"Any idea what kind of mammal?" Nick persisted.

"No, I'm afraid not."

"Isn't a human mammal?"

"It's *not* human, I can assure you of that much—we deal with human blood up here every day of the year… trust me on this."

"I see… no chance of a mistake?"

There was a long pause, "We double-blind results here, Chief—if there's a mistake it's not on our end. Is there anything else I can do for you today?"

Nick shook his head before remembering to speak, "No... no thank you. I appreciate your time on this and for rushing us the results."

The other voice softened as he replied, "You're welcome, Chief. I just wish we could have given you better news... I've read about what's happening down there. Good luck." He hung up.

Letting the paper slip from his fingers onto the desktop, Nick rose to stare out the window. In the bright autumnal sunlight, the people of Wessex Township were going about their business with brisk steps, leaves swirling round their feet in the brilliant yellows of elm and plane, the scarlet and wine of maple and oak.

Clutching a section of rope, a file of children was being towed down the sidewalk by their teacher. They were sporting various costumes, some store-bought, others homemade, depicting super-heroes, movie monsters, and even the occasional ghost or witch of traditional All Hallows Eve.

They were probably going to the library, Nick thought, to be read a Halloween story. He thought of going himself, just to catch a glimpse of Fanny, her long, slender neck bent to the task of reading. Picturing her large, dark eyes lively with enthusiasm, her wide, generous mouth open with laughter, he envied the children. Their cries drifted up to him like the language of birds, all trills and excited notes.

He was reminded of the laughter he had only dimly registered earlier—it suddenly dawned on him—it was Halloween.

Turning away, Nick gathered up the bulging file of his failed efforts and carried it down the stairs to the sergeant's office. After arranging for its transfer to the prosecutor, he headed for the exit. It didn't matter to him at the moment where he might go, only that he keep moving.

Bursting out of the door, he collided with Father Gregory.

The little man grunted with the impact taking several steps backwards. Nick managed to grab his sleeve, keeping him upright. "I'm so sorry, Father," he gasped. "I wasn't looking."

"There is no worry, my friend, I am unharmed… just my pride perhaps." Father Gregory's dark face split into a wide smile, his white teeth gleaming. "Everyone is 'super-sized' in your country," he exclaimed, using a phrase he had learned from American television, "while only my stomach is so!" Laughing, he added, "We are well-met… I was just coming to see you, Chief Catesby."

"Do you mind if we walk?" Nick asked. The priest nodded and they turned together in the direction of the rectory. "I have news for you, as well," he told Father Gregory.

"I see… please do go on."

"I think we've gotten to the bottom of the incident in your parking lot, Father. I can't tell you too much right now, but I suspect we'll be charging the suspect under the bias incident statute in the very near future. Until then, I don't think you have to worry about a repeat performance."

"Excellent," Father Gregory smiled once more. "Hopefully, this person will have learned his lesson and will renounce his behavior. A sincere apology will suffice for the Monsignor and me," he assured Nick, adding, "Well, me at least. The Monsignor is very cross about it all and may use his strong language… but in the end, he will forgive as well, have no doubt of that, Chief."

Nick laughed in spite of himself, saying "Oh, I've no doubt, Father… at least about the strong language part."

Laughing too, Father Gregory glanced up at him from the corner of his eye, "You know him too well."

As they walked along, one of the school groups passed them going in the opposite direction, their story hour finished. Recognizing the clergyman, several of the children began to wave and call out to him. Nick smiled as he saw the priest return the greetings of goblins and ghosts with a puzzled expression.

When they had passed, he turned to Nick and asked, "This is a strange custom, I am thinking, dressing up little children as demons and monsters. What is the meaning of this?"

Nick thought of how best to explain, saying, "It's a way of dealing with the coming darkness of winter, I think, about not being afraid of what the darkness—the long night—holds, and learning to laugh at it all. Maybe once, a very long time ago, it meant something else, something less pleasant."

They had reached the rectory, a simple straight up and down white structure from the 1940s with a tiny front lawn. "Can you spare a moment, Chief Catesby?"

"Nick, please, Father."

Father Gregory, who had grown solemn since their meeting with the children, nodded, answering, "Yes, thank you, Nick."

Once inside, the little priest crossed the small room to secure the door to the interior of the house. "The Monsignor is upstairs sleeping, I think—he needs much rest these days."

Returning, he seated himself and Nick did the same. Leaning forward, the smaller man clasped his hands as if he were about to pray. It occurred to Nick that he was about to hear something very important to the priest.

"In my country, Nick, the darkness also holds many frightful things, though we do not approach them with the same levity as Americans. In my own parish witches have been murdered by their victims after being long tormented, men have been known to become tigers in order to satisfy their blood lusts." He raised a hand as if to ward off Nick's objections. "I know… I know what you must be thinking—we are a backward nation… but not so, dear friend. Indeed, we are forward thinking peoples, much interested in modern technology, at the forefront, really." He smiled with ill-concealed pride.

"Now then," he resumed, "having established our credentials, I will admit that there is much yet to fear in the night and it is only wise to think so, to be cautious." Hesitating, he looked up at Nick as if to gauge his reliability before continuing, "Just the other night, in this very town, I was visited by such a creature as roams only in the darkness."

Nick heard the older man's words and felt a sense of unreality creep into the room with them as he spoke.

"He was a profane creature, Nick, in the shape and likeness of a young boy. Yet, only in the shadows would he be convincing in this role. Are you familiar with such a spirit, Nick—is he known here?"

Nick regarded the priest open-mouthed. Was it possible that Preston had been telling the truth all along? How could it be? How could such a creature exist all these years and escape detection… and destruction?

He managed to ask, "Did he have a name… this boy?"

Father Gregory shook his head. "He offered none and I did not think to ask. He accosted me in my own church, and I must admit with some shame that I was much afraid, nearly forgetting God."

"Tell me what happened, Father, exactly."

Taking a deep breath, Father Gregory recounted his meeting in as much detail as he could recall. When he was finished, he added, "It occurred to me that this creature might have something to do with your missing children."

"I need to find this boy, Father. It is very, very important."

Father Gregory raised a long finger to Nick. "This is a child of darkness, my friend. His time here should have ended long ago—he is a throwback to when demons walked abroad in the daylight and he does not belong here any longer.

"As to his current whereabouts," he shook his head sadly, "I, too, am at a loss. But I promise to give the matter great thought."

Nick stood, saying, "I'd appreciate any help you could give me, Father," then hurried out the way he had come. The festive activity in the streets had grown more manic with the lengthening of the day.

❧

Nick's steps led him back to the police station, his pace quickening as he drew near. He blew through the lobby without greeting the surprised dispatcher and on into the building. Bounding up the stairs, he hit the speed-dial on his cell phone, and minutes later, Officer Beckam was knocking politely on the door of his office. Nick waved him in, indicating that he should close the door behind him.

Beckam cast a nervous glance at his boss as he did so. "Am I in trouble?"

Nick shook his head and stood up from behind his desk. This young man was the newest rookie in the department, and the least likely to have been contaminated by Weller's poison, he calculated. He had about him that indefinable quality of an honest man. The bottom line was that Nick needed someone he could trust.

"Beck, I need a volunteer for a special detail. It's confidential in nature and starts right now. Would you be interested?"

Beckam appeared to weigh his chief's words, his lips compressing in thought. Glancing up to meet Nick's gaze with his own mild expression, a slight smile lifted a corner of his mouth. "You're not going to have to kill me after you tell me what it's about, are you?"

Nick laughed, "It's a surveillance detail, Beck, and you'll be answering to me and to me only, and it begins as quickly as you can change into your civies."

Beck nodded his understanding, but waited.

"In a few minutes I'm going to release Preston Howard, our only suspect, and you are going to follow and stick with him, unseen, until further notice. Do you think you can do that?"

Again Beckam nodded. "What am I watching for?"

"A boy," Nick answered.

"The boy he mentioned in our interview?"

"Yes... *that* boy," Nick replied evenly. "But there's more you should know." Then he proceeded to brief Beckam on everything Preston had told him and his daughter about Gabriel, about Fanny's research, the blood-typing results, and lastly about Father Gregory's encounter. When he was done, he waited.

Beckam's bland expression had grown thoughtful during the briefing. After a few moments of silence, he asked, "So you believe Mister Howard then... about this... this Gabriel, is it?"

"I believe there *is* a boy," Nick answered. "As to what exactly his role in all this is... well, that's what we're going to find out, aren't we, Beck?"

Beckam's expression lightened once more. "Yes sir, we are."

Reaching into his desk, Nick pulled out a tiny portable radio with an earpiece and handed it to his subordinate. "It's set to a frequency we only use during surveillance details. Naturally, I'll have one, too. Be sure and plug my cell number into the speed dial on your phone as well, just in case we go out of range of one another on the radios."

The younger officer turned to go. "You've got an off-duty holster?" Nick asked.

"Yes sir, I do."

"Good. In thirty minutes I'm shoving Professor Howard out the door. You'll be waiting. My guess is that the first place he'll head for is the liquor store. After that, it's up to you. Don't lose him, Beck, whatever you do."

"No chance of that, Chief."

The younger man looked content, Nick thought, even happy. He had intentionally not informed him of having been removed from the case—if things went badly, it would allow the young officer an out—he was only obeying what he truly believed were lawful orders. "I'll catch up to you before dark," Nick promised.

"I hope so," Beck replied, pausing at the door, a faint smile playing on his lips. "After all, that's when *he* appears, isn't it, Chief… twixt dusk and dawning?"

"Go to hell, Beck."

"Yes sir," Beck answered, softly closing the door behind him.

❦

Gabriel raced along the sidewalks, his face lifted and nostrils distended, freed by the lowering sun and the costumes of the children he brushed by. Even above the cloyingly sweet scent of candy and the burnt flesh of jack o' lanterns, the salty sweat of the children and the tang of their blood set him to drooling. Yet, he went unnoticed or remarked upon.

Through long watching and experience, he had come to know this night above all others—it was the single night of the year that he dared to walk openly amongst his prey. Yet, even on such an occasion, Gabriel understood that caution was still required.

Coursing along through the tinkling of their laughter, their shouts and cries, he dared not linger. Though his appearance in the growing dusk, amidst the fairies, witches, and savage monsters, allowed him a greater freedom than he normally enjoyed, he understood that he could not stand too close a scrutiny by the guardian adults. And these adults had grown ever more cautious with their young over the years, it seemed to him. Even more so when he had culled the herd in a particular area as he had here. He raced on, careful to avoid meeting the eyes of any he passed.

Halting outside the dwelling of Preston Howard, he watched with narrowed eyes as children trouped up to the door with cries of "Trick or treat!" A passing goblin, with overlarge head and plastic claws, slowed to study him through the eyeholes of his mask, but his adult shoved him on toward the opening door.

Gabriel saw the offspring of Preston Howard framed in the bright lights that blazed from within her home. She was smiling and handing out small paper packets tied with tiny ribbons. Even at a distance, Gabriel could perceive the tension in her posture and lean face. Nonetheless, she laughed aloud at something said by one of the female young at her door, reaching out to cup her chin in her hand.

An adult male waiting nearby for his ward muttered, "Not bad," to his companion, who replied, "Big rack for a skinny girl," both men chuckling as their children charged back up the walk to them.

Turning to leave, the goblin cried in a muffled voice, "You stink" and pelted Gabriel with a piece of hard candy. Gabriel started at being struck and shrank back with a hiss, his eyes blazing.

Seizing his child by the arm, the father began to haul him away. "Knock it off right now or we're going home," he promised. But as soon as they thought they were out of hearing distance, he remarked to his companion, "The boy's right—that kid needs a bath." His friend grimaced in agreement and they risked a look back. The scarecrow boy was no longer to be seen.

Slipping noiselessly along the side of the house as soon as Fanny had closed the door, Gabriel positioned himself to peer through the kitchen window from the backyard. With his long thin limbs he clambered onto the concrete bird bath, perching there like a large, white spider.

This was accomplished so rapidly that Fanny was only just coming down the hallway as he watched. The old man, Preston, also came into his view, exchanging words with his daughter, though Gabriel was unable to hear them distinctly at this distance. Even so, his great ears perceived the angry rattle and hum of their voices.

Clearly, the daughter was fearful for her father. For his part, Preston was frightened for her, as well, but clothed his fear in barks and snarls. The front doorbell rang, and both father and daughter started. Turning, Fanny began walking back to the front of the house and Preston made to follow, but she waved him off.

Preston watched her for a few moments more, then threw open a cabinet, reaching deep within to withdraw a bottle of the substance Gabriel knew him to feed upon. Slipping the liquor inside his shirt front, Preston hurried toward his bedroom. Dropping down from his vantage point, Gabriel followed.

The old man was just entering his room as Gabriel took up his new post, being careful to remain outside the nimbus of light that spilled onto the lawn. Closing the door behind him Preston uncapped the bottle, taking a long pull at the contents, his prominent Adam's apple bobbing up and down. The sight of his unguarded throat made Gabriel thirsty as well and he salivated, panting quietly in the dark.

Preston sat heavily upon his narrow bed, bringing the bottle to his lips once more, this time with less hurry and more savor. Once done, he lay back and stretched his long legs out with a satisfied groan, closing his eyes. Several times he started at the sound of the Halloween revelers outside his home, glancing anxiously at the darkened world beyond his windows. But finally he lay still, and Gabriel could see the even rise and fall of his bony chest, the bottle still clutched and upright over his heart.

Gabriel knew from having tested them before which window to approach. The latch was old and loosely fitted, the rotted screen leaning against the outside of the house. Working one of his long, hard nails into the space between the upper and lower casements, he slid it along until it met with the latch and shifted it. Preston did not stir as Gabriel slid the old window up in its frame, a rush of crisp night air flowing into the room with him.

The doorbell rang once more, and here in the house its sudden alarm caused Gabriel to halt and look towards its source. With a cry, Preston sat bolt upright at the sound, only to find the vampire child within feet of his own bed. Just beyond his door came the delighted cries of children and the low, soft murmur of his daughter's voice. He hurled the bottle at the creature.

Gabriel's oversized hand struck out to snatch the bottle from its flight, holding it far from his face and sensitive nostrils. It appeared dwarfed in his nightmarish fingers and he regarded Preston with fury.

Pushing back against his headboard, Preston had nowhere to go. He eyed the door and the short distance to it. He could never make it, and even if he did... what then?

Looking back to Gabriel he found his expression changed, a cunning having entered into it. The vampire waggled the near empty bottle at him like bait. "Come with me now, old man," he instructed him in his hoarse, sibilant whisper. "I must drink long and fresh once more before I sleep, and you must help me cull the herd."

Preston felt himself shaking, but managed to answer with a calm voice, "I won't go with you... I will not help you."

Gabriel lifted his smeared face, inhaling hungrily. "Your daughter is mere paces away," he assured Preston, "and she may serve, if need be—you must choose."

Preston studied the creature's face, but it contained no hint of mercy or reason. Swinging his long legs off the side of the bed, he searched with his feet for his worn leather loafers, never taking his eyes from Gabriel's. "We are not cattle," he said, "and as far from bovine as you may find to your sorrow." He stood unsteadily and waited.

Gabriel replied, "When first we met you desired my company. Now you wish me dead... What has changed, Preston Howard? Why do you not love me still?"

Preston blinked. "Do you even know what love is?" he asked at last. "Or are you just mimicking the 'cattle' you resemble?"

Gabriel continued to watch him, his broad, idiot face, that of a childish Bacchus. The ferocity and bloodlust rippled just beneath the placid expression like eels in a shallow pond. He said nothing.

"I thought as much," Preston continued, made bold by the boy's silence and the brandy he had consumed. "You can't know love as we 'cattle' do for the simple reason that you are always and forever alone—you have no herd, no pack, no tribe, and exist only to prey on us. You love only your sustenance—our blood, and therefore cannot be human—you are a monster child that grows like a slow cancer in our midst.

"At first, I was mesmerized by your presence, intrigued—you *are* a conundrum, an enigma that harkens back to the dawn of man, and I was fascinated, God help me. Even when you took those awful boys that were going to hurt me, I thought of you as my discovery and my vengeance upon the 'great unwashed.'"

Preston took a shaky breath, the small room blooming with the animal musk that he knew could induce a helpless lassitude. The vampire crouched lower and lower as if preparing to spring.

"You speak too much," he spat at Preston. "You must come now with me."

"I intend to finish what I have to say first," Preston persisted, "in spite of the fact that it is clearly beyond your understanding." He arched an eyebrow at the vampire, continuing, "When I saw what had become of those children that night in the graveyard, the scales fell from my eyes. You paraded their pitiful husks before me like prize sheep, and then I understood how far *I* had fallen. That is why I tried to kill you, as much for me as for them… how I wish I had succeeded!"

"You are too weak to kill me," Gabriel replied evenly. "There is no strength in you."

Preston felt his ballooning confidence burst with this simple observation—for all his grand philosophizing, the vampire child remained his master and was unmoved by his words, if he had even understood them. If he did not obey, his daughter would be slain. He knew Gabriel would be as good as his word on this.

Gabriel held out his filthy, stained hand. After several long moments, Preston placed his own within the boy's sandpaper grasp, and with a shudder of revulsion was led out through the mudroom. Fanny remained occupied with the children coming to the front door. Gabriel returned his bottle and Preston concealed it in his pocket as he might the coin of betrayal. Hand-in-hand they joined the night parade of excited costumed children—a grandfather, with perhaps a "challenged" grandson, out to enjoy the crisp evening air and the timeworn festivities.

Along the way, Gabriel, ever alert to the antics of his prey, snatched a trash bag from a public receptacle, dumping its fetid contents upon the ground. Now the disguise was complete, and he hurried Preston to catch up to a knot of fellow trick-or-treaters that skipped and chattered at the next corner. He was anxious to play this night.

CHAPTER ELEVEN

Preston felt himself dragged along the streets and avenues of Wessex Township as if he were in a nightmare from which he could not awaken. Towing him along as his passport to humanity, the creature tugged and pulled at him as impatiently as any actual child. It was clear to Preston that the vampire had become infected with the excitement of the strange evening, and was enjoying the role he was playing.

After several blocks of simply following the others, Gabriel pointed at a house guarded by a pair of upright plywood coffins set to either side of the doorway. Within lay ghoulish creatures lit by artfully concealed lights that cast a greenish glow. A gaggle of children approached this dread place with both hilarity and sincere trepidation.

"Dead," he smiled, "just as those in the cemetery houses." By this, Preston took him to mean the scattering of mausoleums in the graveyard. It was repulsive to think of this creature squatting there amongst the dead in contented repose.

"But they have no smell," Gabriel added, his broad nose wrinkling in puzzlement.

Just then the ghouls, mere skeletons but for patches of rotting flesh, sprang forth from their coffins, their gaping maws wide, their bony fingers reaching out to grasp and pull down the nearest child. Screams of terror erupted, and the entire group of kids turned as one, fleeing to the arms of their parents. Behind them, ghastly laughter rang out in seeming triumph.

Gabriel leapt free of Preston's hand, recoiling. "They live again," he cried, turning to flee with the others.

The door of the haunted dwelling flew open and a laughing heavyset man with a shock of blonde hair called out to the children, "Wait... wait! It's okay! It's all a trick! Come and get your treats! Don't run away!"

Gabriel hesitated.

The ghouls, picking up plastic cauldrons filled with wrapped candies, began to hand them out to any of the children brave enough to take them. Eventually, the more reticent were emboldened, claiming their prizes as well. Gabriel remained frozen, unwilling to trust the newly risen dead.

Seizing Preston's hand once more, he pulled him on toward another group and less challenging environs. Preston winced at his grasp and felt a trickle of blood run down his ring finger. He could not read the creature's expression.

Soon they found themselves within another earnest tribe of scavengers and Preston felt his hand released. Before he could speak, Gabriel slipped in amongst the children, making so bold as to go to the door of a nearby house with them. Turning, he smiled back at Preston, his previous fear having vanished as he renewed his hunt for a suitable victim.

Preston noticed Gabriel walking closely by the side of a small girl wearing a ballerina costume, complete with tiara. Clutching a glow-in-the-dark wand in one chubby fist, she toted her bag of loot in the other. Her skin beneath the intermittent street lamps was the color of café au lait.

This home, Preston observed, sported nothing more menacing than a giant bat made of black fabric, suspended over the porch by a nearly invisible fishing line. It wobbled in the slight breeze of the evening and Gabriel passed beneath it without alarm.

The group was greeted merrily by a plump older woman with a great pile of grey hair on her head. With a grunt, she bent to cast the required candies into each sack and this she did efficiently until she reached Gabriel. Upon reaching his she recoiled and withheld the proffered gift. Preston watched with growing concern as she appeared to scrutinize the creature and ask it questions. From where he stood, he could see Gabriel's head nod once or twice, but could not tell if he spoke.

The woman took the stinking bag from him and disappeared within the house, leaving Gabriel alone as the other children returned to the street. He turned, watching the young girl with obvious longing, but did not follow or appear overly concerned with her departure. Gabriel caught Preston's eye, pointing at the girl and smiling broadly.

Suddenly the woman returned to hand the creature a black cloth bag decorated with merry flying ghosts. Dumping far more candy into it than she had for the other children; she patted Gabriel's large head. As he turned to follow the others, his expression was as happy as any that he pursued.

Sweeping past to catch up to the departing children, Gabriel commanded, "Follow," and Preston turned, stumbling along in his wake.

He caught up with Gabriel at the next corner where the children regrouped for their next assault. The vampire boy lingered at the edges of the group, away from the light cast by the street lamp. Watchful, but conversing in pleasant tones, the parents strolled behind their little ones.

As they neared the next house, Gabriel raced up to Preston and whispered, "You have seen the one I want, Preston Howard." It was not a question. "She is young and fresh, without disease… I will have her."

The image of the little ballerina stumbling among the headstones of the cemetery, her lovely color and vitality drained, made Preston physically ill.

Before he could protest, Gabriel went on, "Go over to her watchers and speak with them while I make her acquaintance." He stopped, appearing to think something over. "Once they become excited and search for her, come and join me where last we met."

Preston searched the small group of children for Gabriel's next victim, his mind racing for what he should do.

Gabriel interrupted these thoughts. "Do not fail to join me, old man," he instructed, catching Preston's wavering gaze with the intensity of his own, "or your daughter surely will."

Preston felt himself begin to quake with fear, a trembling that started from deep within him and surfaced in small rapid tremors. Robbed of his usual disdainful attitude, his alcoholic suavity, he approached the couple whom he identified as the little dancer's parents.

Sidling up to the father, a healthy looking man in his early thirties with just the beginnings of a paunch, he tried to speak, but his words were hoarse whispers, inaudible. From the corner of his eye he saw the princess dancing her way to the next lit porch amidst the other children.

With a start, he noticed Gabriel moving up to her from the darkness of the lawn, his crisp new trick-or-treat bag swinging in his frightful grip. The creature threw him a quick look to see if Preston was holding up his end of things, and when he registered that Preston stood mute and impotent, his expression darkened.

Preston cleared his throat and both the girl's young parents turned to regard him with ill-concealed distaste. The man gave him the once-over, and Preston understood, as Gabriel could not, that he was a suspicious presence to these parents—to all the parents escorting their children. He was old, disheveled, and none-too-clean, and it was unclear to them as to why he should be amongst them.

"Samhain," he blurted out at last, instantly reverting to his lecturing days in his great stress. "That's what Halloween derives from, you know—a Druidic ritual that was ancient when the Romans first placed a sandaled foot in Britain."

He had succeeded in gaining their attention. In fact, every parent present turned to stare at him. Looking beyond them, he could see Gabriel opening his new bag and transferring candy from it to the ballerina's. She stared solemnly up at Gabriel's face. As the child began to sway, he took her small hand into his unnatural grasp. Preston thought of the creature's stultifying musk.

Preston's gaze swiveled back to the parents, all of whom were regarding him with varying degrees of perplexity and distrust. "It seems harmless enough to us now, of course, but Julius Caesar took exception to the human sacrifice involved—you see, on this very night the Celts would imprison their captives in great wicker cages constructed to resemble a giant man, and set them ablaze, then dance the evening away by the light of their burning victims… a gruesome ritual by any standards. Still, it's hard to imagine Julius Caesar being offended by a little bloodshed," he babbled on. He certainly had their full attention now.

"What the hell…?" the dancer's father murmured.

"So, in due course, the Roman legions stormed the Druid's holy island and slew all their priests, put every man-jack of them to the sword… voila… pax—Roman style!"

The parents looked at him in horror as he watched Gabriel leading the little girl away into the darkness of the side yard.

She walked quietly at his side. "But that was over two thousand years ago, and since then we've drained the barbarity out of the whole mess, have we not…" In a moment they would vanish into the night and she would be no more. "… and so, all we are left is… this." Preston raised his arms to take in the festivities of the night. In two more steps it would be too late.

Leveling an arm to point beyond his captive audience, he shouted, "Stop him," startling everyone and making the mothers scream. "He's got the girl!"

Every head turned to follow where he pointed as Gabriel's swiveled like an owl's to see what was happening behind him. At a glance, he understood that he had been betrayed and exposed. He bared his long yellow teeth and hissed with anger, his grip on the girl's arm tightening. Preston heard her gasp in sudden pain.

"Him," he shouted again, still pointing, "The boy there! Don't let him take her!"

The father, despite his paunch, broke into a sprint, crying, "Hey… you! Let go of her!"

At the same moment, Preston became aware of two other figures charging out of the darkness from opposite directions. They appeared to be closing in on Gabriel with a purpose. "He's gonna break your way," one of them shouted, and Preston recognized the voice of Chief Catesby. The other figure seemed to speed up at this warning as if to cut off the creature's escape.

Gabriel snatched the girl up by her arm, clasping her to his waist in preparation to flee, but hesitated. More of the fathers broke free from the group, racing toward Gabriel and his prize, as if only just awakening to the danger. Catesby's powerful form was closing, as well, but not as rapidly as that of the other man who was within yards of his quarry.

Preston could see from the creature's expression that it apprehended its peril. Flinging the girl to the ground with a thump, Gabriel cried, "I will sup from your only child, old man… and squat in her entrails!" Then, with an impossible bound, he cleared the tackle of Officer Beckam, eluding Catesby's grasp, and vanished with the speed of an optical illusion.

It appeared to Preston as if with the vampire's movement, everything, and everyone, had been slowed to the point of observable detail. The fathers, the policemen, the child herself, all lay before him like a tableau of stupefaction. The young policeman, whom he now recognized from his second interview, drew his gun as if he could think of nothing else to do, uncertain as to what to do with it.

It was the whimpers of the saved girl that reanimated the group, and as one, the mothers charged forth to support the child's own as she lifted her to her breast. Preston stood alone, and only belatedly, lowered his arm.

Catesby trotted up to him, breathless. "Where has he gone, Preston? We have to get him." He bent over to grip his knees and catch his breath.

"My house," Preston managed, "he's going to kill Fanny."

Looking up into Preston's eyes, Nick said, "Not if I kill him first," then began moving again.

"Beck," he shouted over his shoulder. "Get everyone's names and addresses for statements, then follow me to the Professor's house… and bring him!" He hooked a thumb at Preston as he ran for his unmarked car parked nearby. "Hurry," he commanded. Gunning the engine into life, he shot away from the curb, hitting Fanny's number in the speed dial of his cell phone.

❧

Gabriel waited until several children and their parents moved on to the next house before crossing the street. He had narrowly escaped harm just moments before and was now wary of the company of man once more. Keeping to the shadows, he crossed the small patch of lawn that fronted Preston's home, still toting his festive treat bag. Deprived of the child, his instincts told him that time was running out before his next great sleep.

And thanks to Preston, his would be a sleep that would grow hungry and uneasy, his growth slowed as a result. He wished to kill the old man for this, but appreciated that Preston now had strong, fully-matured males protecting him and that it was too risky. Not so the daughter… if he acted quickly he might salvage something from all this—she was not optimal for his needs, but would have to do.

Something crouched in the darkness at the edge of the portico, just beyond the yellow spill of light from the porch lamp. It hissed at his approach and without hesitation Gabriel sprang upon it, seizing it with his taloned hands. When he had done, he raced around to the rear of the house, the sound of children's laughter, and the low murmur of adult voices, at his back. Peering through the same window he had watched Preston and Fanny earlier that evening, he heard the sound of the doorbell, but waited until the female appeared in the hallway before once more slipping through.

Within, Fanny's cell phone buzzed around on the kitchen table in small spurts of mute alarm, its setting still on "vibrate" as required by the library. Walking past it without notice, she continued to the door.

Gabriel felt the autumn air wafting down the hallway as she opened the door, and with it, the scent of the children he had been denied. Even above their excited cries his convoluted ears could hear the thrum of their small hearts, the singing of their blood, and he began to salivate.

As Fanny closed the door once more on the satisfied children, Gabriel glided down the hallway, his treat bag still in tow.

When she turned, he stood before her.

"Trick or treat," Gabriel lisped the time-honored challenge, thrusting his open bag against Fanny's stomach.

A small scream escaped her lips. Though she had only seen him at a distance, and cloaked in the grey drizzle of days before, the awful hand he held up to silence her told all—this was Preston's strange boy—this was Gabriel.

"I…" she gasped, trying to speak while taking in the terrible Pan-like face and edging back toward the door all at once.

"For you," he continued in his odd voice, the rusty voice of throat cancer. "Reach in." Smiling at her with jumbled yellow teeth, his tongue flickered redly within the canyon of his mouth.

Matching her small footsteps with his own, he maintained the narrow distance between them. His odor wafted across her and with it the scent of corpses. A strange, cloying musk lay beneath this and its presence made Fanny grow heavy with the leaden legs of a nightmare.

"For you," he repeated with more authority.

Fanny tilted her head down as he commanded. Within lay something both black and white and her first thought was of a fur boa curled up in the bottom of this awful boy's sack. But why would he insist on showing her such a thing? Something golden glittered within the incomprehensible arrangement and she leaned closer still, a terrible suspicion growing within her.

"What…?" She felt her breath catching in her throat. "Oh my God… that's not…? Oh… my… God!" She tried to seize the bag from the hideous boy, but he was the quicker, dumping its contents onto the floor.

With a soft, awful thump Loki landed at her feet, his fangs bared in an eternal snarl, the one eye visible a golden marble in his smooth skull. His head faced in the wrong direction, left as Gabriel had wrenched it moments before, a thread of blood trickling from his mouth.

Fanny's hands flew to her face, her mouth falling open to scream or wail, but she was not allowed to do either. Leaping upon her, Gabriel rode her to the floor, her skull rebounding with a crack against the floorboards. But rather than feeling any pain, she felt only a sudden tiredness, a growing, paralyzing lethargy. The boy's hands gripped her arms with such strength that it seemed pointless to struggle against him. Like the opening of a grave, his awful, reeking breath flowed over her face. The thought of Loki lying dead at her feet brought warm tears to her eyes, and these ran onto her cheeks.

Gabriel knew that he did not have much time as the others would be searching for him now, the old man having pointed them in this direction. As Fanny's struggles weakened and she became increasingly inert, he released one of her arms to reach up and grasp her chin. Tilting her head back to expose her long throat, he observed with growing excitement the carotid artery throbbing in panic just beneath the paper-thin flesh. His mouth flooded with a saliva that would retard any coagulation of the blood from the wounds he was about to inflict.

Normally, when he had fed his fill, he would reverse this by licking the wounds with his broad furred tongue, sealing them with an exuded paste that ensured his victim might live to feed him again. He had no intention of doing so in this instance.

Through brimming tears, Fanny watched the boy's large face rising above her own, his great eyes flat and merciless as a shark's. She could not raise the hand he had released nor cry out for help. His freakish mouth fell open with an audible click and unhinged to gape bonelessly, as the scarlet tongue curled back to expose the tubes of flesh concealed beneath it. As Gabriel's face drew nearer still, Fanny was able to witness the viper-like fangs slide forth from their protecting muscle, then the creature clamped down upon her throat with its rancid maw.

For just the slightest bit of time nothing happened, then, with only a faint sense of their penetration and a flicker of pain, Gabriel's twin fangs pierced her jugular and he began to feed. She may have gasped, but didn't think so. He drew his sustenance from her with patience and assurance, and Fanny could feel the effect in the form of vertigo—a sense of sinking into a growing and comfortable darkness. He was an incubus squatting on her chest, draining the life from her body, and she no longer cared.

She was only remotely afraid of that moment when her consciousness would wink out, wondering who might take care of her father, and whether Nick would forgive her for her cowardice of the day before. She also thought with sadness of Loki, and the malice shown by the creature in killing him—Gabriel might not be human, but in killing her cat he had demonstrated he was an apt pupil of human behavior. Perhaps he was still evolving. The light that hovered above her was drifting farther and farther away, becoming a dim star, even as the awful slurping and grunting of the creature's feeding grew fainter, less disturbing.

From somewhere far away a roaring, as if from a distant sea, crashed against her fading consciousness, and a tremor ran along her spine. But it was not this titanic, if remote, upheaval that arrested her descent, but the sudden release of pressure at her throat.

With a gasp, she took in a great draught of air and saw the distant star become a flare of light and pain. Her lungs were on fire as if she were drowning.

Crashing through the door, Nick heard his own voice as a hoarse bellow as he beheld the creature feasting. In the milliseconds of his movement, he took in Fanny's stricken face as she lay pinioned beneath the monster, her features already settling into a death mask.

Seizing the unclean child by the back of his neck and the waist of his ragged pants, he flung him into the wall with all his might, even as Gabriel turned to confront the threat that had overtaken him.

His loose mouth spraying crimson, Gabriel recoiled from the impact with a snarl, landing on his long, narrow feet. All in a single motion he leapt over Fanny, racing down the hallway to Preston's sleeping porch and the freedom of the back door.

With a cry Fanny sat bolt upright, grasping her wounded neck slick with the monster's juices, her own hot blood spurting between her fingers in twin jets.

Even as he took in the creature's escape, Nick understood that Fanny was fighting for her life and clamped his large hand over her wounds. The pressure, though growing faint, spewed wetly now between his own fingers, and her face, always pale, was luminous with impending death. "Goddamnit," he cursed, fishing his radio out of his jacket pocket, pressing the send button. "Beck, get an ambulance over here right now!"

After an interminable pause, his radio crackled into life and Beckam answered, "On the way."

"Fanny," Nick whispered, running down the hall to grab a dish towel. Returning, he balled it up, pressing it to the wounds. Within moments, it was heavy with her blood. From what seemed like a great distance arose the wail of an approaching ambulance.

༄

Managing to stanch the flow of blood from Fanny's neck, the EMTs lacked the means to restore her dangerously low blood pressure. They hustled her gaunt form into the back of the waiting ambulance as neighbors came out of their homes to watch. Several passing parents clutched their costumed children to them. Preston made to climb into the back of the rig with his daughter when Nick gripped him by the shoulder.

"Wait," he commanded.

Turning to look at the younger man, his expression hag-ridden and removed, Preston said, "I couldn't tell you about the children... he promised he would kill Fanny, if I did. I'm so sorry... I'm so very..."

"Professor," Nick interrupted him, "I need your help. This creature... this boy... he's real... I can see that now—but what about the children? Are they still alive... where does he keep them? Do you think you know? Did he give you any clues as to where they might be?" He stared hard into the old man's face willing him to know, to answer.

Preston blinked slowly, shaking himself. "They were very weak... they couldn't travel far or fast." He glanced into the interior of the ambulance, at the slender white form that lay waiting there. "I think he keeps them in the cemetery," he continued, the images and memories of the past few days racing through his mind, each scene struggling for primacy. "Yes, that would have to be it, wouldn't it? That's where he wanted me to meet him tonight so that I would be found with them. That's why he wanted me all along—to be his scapegoat for all this." He said this last with a kind of despair.

"Go," Nick whispered, gently shoving Preston toward his daughter. "I'll meet you at the hospital as soon as I can." Slamming the door shut on the miserable old man, he slapped the exterior to signal the driver. The siren rose in answer and the ambulance pulled away, picking up speed, its blue lights painting the houses it passed with fear and uncertainty.

Nick glanced at his watch, his heart aching at sending Fanny off without him. When he thought of the boy at her throat, his grunts and slurping, her ashen, terrified face, he felt a burning, righteous anger. But the children were still out there, perhaps there was a chance yet to save them. Turning, he found Beckam at his elbow.

"I'm gonna kill that sonofabitch," he promised him.

Beckam nodded without expression, as if this kind of statement was to be expected from his superiors.

"The cemetery," Nick said, and they turned to their waiting vehicle.

On the way over, Nick placed a call to Jack Kimbo who promised to join them within minutes. They turned into the cemetery.

Switching off the car's headlamps, Beckam allowed it to coast to a stop beneath a cedar tree that shaded a small family plot. He could read the names on the tombstones by the strong moonlight, but they meant nothing to him—the family had died out a century before and was no longer remembered by the living.

Retrieving flashlights and a tire tool from the trunk, the two men turned to face the sea of upright stones bleached beneath the lunar light. Here and there amongst them arose a compact house, its doors shut to the living world. Some were protected by low iron fences, ornately wrought; most were not. Nick shrugged at the nearest and the two officers started toward it without speaking, their thoughts at what they were about to do private.

From the other direction a car turned onto to the service road and sped toward them, headlights doused. Nick recognized the FBI agent's standard issue car.

Jack threw open the door, announcing, "I'm from the federal government, and I'm here to help." Stepping out with his own flashlight, he held a crow bar up, smiling. "We're all issued these when we graduate the academy; we call them 'search warrants.'"

"Thanks for coming on such short notice, Jack," Nick greeted him. "I needed someone I can trust."

"Didn't I just say that I'm from the government?" Jack quipped, pushing his heavy glasses back up onto the bridge of his thick nose. "Glad to be of service." Glancing around at the quiet panorama of death, he asked, "Split up or stay together?"

"After what I've seen tonight, I think we should stay together." Nick answered. "Beck, you and I will do the heavy lifting," he took the crow bar from the agent; "while Jack here covers our backs—he's the best shot in the county." They started toward the nearest mausoleum.

"Who am I supposed to gun down?"

"It looks like a boy… a teenage boy."

"Looks like?" Jack asked.

"Yeah… looks like. I'll explain later. But for now, take my word for it, Jack, and kill it. I've seen it up close. And I've touched it. You'll know what to do if we find it."

Turning to Beckam, Jack whispered loudly, "Are you taking the same drugs as him, and if so, can I have some?"

Beckam answered, "I'm with the chief on this—he's right—kill it."

They came to a halt before the narrow grey stone building. "He's had more than enough time to get here and kill all three children, God help them," Nick said. "But, I don't think he would chance it. He knows that we're hot on his heels now, and he's got a very developed sense of self-preservation. He couldn't know how quickly we would get here." Then added, "That is, if we're in the right place, if this is where he's keeping them."

Advancing upon the barred gate that covered the door, Nick and Beckam took a deep breath. Nick gave it a yank but it remained fast. Without ceremony, the two men applied their pry bars, popping it open with a screech of metal-on-metal. Then they attacked the bronze-sheeted door within. This too gave way with a shriek and they stepped back, puffing with exertion and nerves, to allow Jack to illuminate the interior. The faint stench of the long dead wafted out to them as they crowded together in the narrow doorway. At the bottom of a short flight of carved stone steps lay the vault. Within, a tier of coffins lined each wall: one to a bier and three high. Dust lay thick and undisturbed on the floor.

Jack laid his flashlight on the floor, rolling it gently from side-to-side, but no footprints revealed themselves—the chamber had not been visited in a very long time.

"The next one," Nick commanded. "It's getting late."

With increasing proficiency the trio assaulted one vault after the next, the results varying only in degree by the horror they inspired. In some, the contents, like the first, were orderly and serene—the coffins unbroken and their occupants confined. In others, chaos had been introduced by the settling of foundations and seepage, through which roots and white tendrils had crept forth over the years to fill the fetid space with sickly growth.

As their flashlight beams penetrated these funereal hot houses, Beckam saw that a number of the coffins had been pried open by the penetrating vegetation, the roots disappearing within and now, presumably, corpse-fed. The stench of rotted flesh had affected him little, but at this sight he struggled not to gag.

Exhausted by their exertions and the prospect of failure, the searchers made their way to the final mausoleum. It lay closest to the edge of the woods that ran northward to join the great Pine Barrens, resting atop a slight knoll. Nick surmised that the small hillock had been the creation of the family that had erected the crypt, as it was the only elevated spot in the cemetery and certainly not natural to the terrain. With a growing sense of despair he urged the others forward.

A great dying oak stretched its bare twisted limbs toward their final goal as if to seize it and uproot it from the earth itself. Its giant roots erupted here and there like petrified serpents. They pushed on, the odor of the dead clinging to their hair and clothes.

Interrupting the exhausted silence that had fallen over them all, Jack said quietly, "I think that door is open a little." He played the beam of his flashlight up and down on the entrance. Slowing, the men strained their eyes, but it was impossible to determine in the sharp black shadows thrown by the waning moon.

"You got it, Jack?" Nick asked.

"I've got it," he responded bringing his pistol into alignment with his light which now remained steady on the door.

Nodding to Beckam, Nick and he circled round to approach from the side.

Drawing nearer, they could see that the door, a heavy-looking, copper-sheeted one with thick, narrow panes of glass in it, was indeed open, but just an inch or so.

Nick and Beckam set their pry bars onto the grass, drawing their own weapons now. With his pocket light in his left hand, Nick edged closer still, bringing his left eye to the tiny aperture. He could detect no movement within the greater darkness that lay inside. The smell of the dead was present, but faint. The open door might account for that, he reasoned. His own ragged breathing interfering, Nick strained to hear any movement within; then risked the light.

The beam flooded the cramped interior with brilliant bluish-white light illuminating the scene within like a flash-photo. Every detail of the death room was revealed with an intensity that burned itself onto his retina, but even so it took him several moments to comprehend what he was looking at: The coffins within had been swept onto the floor of the vault, their occupants tossed from their confines by the impact. These lay in a tangle of rotting bodies whose features had long ago been erased by a black fungus that even now masked the visages of the most recently dead, while the oldest had their faces eaten away by its ravages. The most ancient were little more than skeletons with clots of hair adhering to their skulls. Their tattered clothes showed that both male and female shared the crypt, and these same remnants displayed styles that hearkened back to the 1800s. The most recent sported a dark suit that was popular in the mid-sixties and, but for patches of damp that appeared to have seeped from within it, appeared almost serviceable.

Nick recoiled, his brain momentarily overloaded by the morbid tableau. Why were they thrown to the floor? Who would do such a thing, and why, he wondered. He saw that Beckam was watching his face in some alarm. He had not yet looked in.

Grimacing, Nick returned to the crack in the door, once again flooding the awful room with light. There's a reason for this, he told himself, and that is what he must look for. Even so, it was difficult to tear his eyes away from the horror of the ravaged faces that appeared to seek his own. Those with empty eye sockets were awful, but it was the few that retained their eyes that were worse—the grey jelly reminding him of things that floated in the darkest depths of the sea.

Forcing the beam of the light to move away from the tangled dead, he played it along the perimeter of the room. As the light rose to reveal the emptied biers on which the vandalized caskets had once rested, he saw why they had been displaced—on three of the lower shelves lay the bodies of a young girl and two teenage boys.

Nick felt the breath stop in his chest, and for a moment he could make no sound. Having studied their photographs so closely over the past weeks, he had no doubt at whom he was looking—he had found the stolen children.

The flashlight shook in his hand, its light wavering up and down within the crypt, giving the appearance that Megan's chest rose and fell ever so slightly. With all the will he could muster, Nick steadied his hand and held his breath. In the dank air of the fetid room a tiny, almost invisible vapor arose from her whitened lips.

Turning to the puzzled Beckam who had become trans-fixed by the play of emotion on his chief's normally stoic face, Nick cried, "They're in there, Beck—by God, the children are in there!" He set his shoulder to the door and began straining. Immediately, Beckam followed suit.

With a groan they pushed the door open, Nick shouting in his excitement, "We've found'em, Jack, we've found'em—and I think they're alive!" To his surprise he felt tears rolling down his stubbled cheeks.

Jack jogged toward them, as Beckam stood arrested in the doorway by the awful spectacle within. Nick surged forth, stepping over the bodies to reach the children. Placing a finger to Megan's carotid artery, he felt a rapid, thready pulse. Her face was so desiccated and white that she looked more like an old woman than a child. "Call for three rigs," he commanded Beckam who was already doing exactly that on his cell phone.

"Oh my God," he heard Jack say as he arrived at the entrance and took in the scene.

Nick hurried over to the boys. They too clung to life in bodies impossibly frail. It was clear that none had been given nourishment of any kind, their life or death a matter of indifference to the creature, but for the blood they supplied. There was no sign of Gabriel.

"Let's get them out of here," Nick said his voice hoarse with emotion. Lifting the near-weightless body of Megan into his arms, he carried her out of the crypt and toward the service road. The others followed suit with Jared and Connor.

As the ambulances approached, Nick nodded at Jack, saying, "Do you mind sticking around and dealing with the prosecutor's office on this? They're going to need someone to explain to them what's going on and they will not want it to be me—I've got to get to Fanny."

Jack smiled in agreement, "Always happy to cooperate with local law enforcement. Of course, I don't have any idea at this point what *is* going on, but I'm sure you'll enlighten me in the fullness of time. Meanwhile, I'll just tell them that you were acting under exigent circumstances—that's what I always tell my boss."

"Thanks, Jack. You're the best." He turned now to Beckam. "Beck, I'm going to ride over in the rig with Megan—follow me over in the unmarked... we may need it."

"Sure, Chief."

Nick studied the younger man for a moment before saying, "You're a good man, Beck. I appreciate you sticking with me on this."

"Any reason I shouldn't have, Boss?"

"A few, maybe, but its better if you don't know what they are... you'd lose deniability."

Hefting Jared into a more comfortable position in his arms, Beckam's placid smile returned. "You got the kids back, Boss... that's all anyone will care about in the end. That's what was important."

"Yeah," Nick agreed, adding, "But I still intend to kill the animal that did this."

Still smiling, Beckam replied, "Only if you get to him first, Chief."

CHAPTER TWELVE

Nick stood in the doorway for several moments watching the rise and fall of Fanny's chest in the darkened room. Her breathing appeared regular, if shallow. A white sheet had been pulled up to her chest and her thin arms, pierced by several tubes, lay to either side of her slender form. If it were not for the movements of her chest, he would have thought the presence of Father Gregory at her side was evidence of death. Even so, the sight gave rise to a feeling of panic and near despair.

Preston sat with his back to the door, his chair drawn up to the bed. Stroking Fanny's hand from time to time, he rested his forehead on the edge of the mattress. When Nick thought of the contagion and horror that had nearly taken her, he felt a terrible heat swell up into his heart, his brain.

Father Gregory, his large eyes red and veined with lack of sleep, glanced up to see the policeman in the doorway. Rising to his feet, he cried in a hushed voice, "Chief Catesby, please do come in!" Appearing relieved, he held out his arms in welcome. "Come sit," he indicated his own chair. "You must be exhausted from your efforts this night."

Nick took a few steps toward Fanny as Preston, lifting his head, turned to look at him. He appeared confused, as if he did not recognize Nick, then his exhausted features cleared and reaching out, he seized Nick's wrist with surprising power, "Thank you... thank you for saving her," he whispered.

"The children," Father Gregory ventured. "Were you also successful in this?"

Nick smiled, "Yes... yes, we were. They are here in the hospital now. But I don't know how well things will turn out for them, Father. They've been deprived of blood and oxygen for a very long time—it didn't even bother to feed them—they're in bad shape, and even if they survive they may never be whole again, maybe not even sane. I'm not sure that I've done them any good in the end."

"Leave that to God," the priest directed him, "and do not take too much upon yourself."

Lowering himself into the recently vacated chair, Nick regarded the pale face of his lover. "And Fanny?" he asked.

"She will be well according to the doctors here. They assure us that she has nothing to fear, but will be well once more—you're intercession was most timely, Chief Catesby."

Taking Fanny's thin hand into his, Nick studied the blue veins that threaded their way just beneath the surface of her flesh. He noticed that his own fingers were dirty with the filth of the graveyard.

Nick looked across the bed to Preston, who watched the face of his daughter as if she were someone new and unknown to him. "Preston," Nick murmured, "have you any idea where this boy... this thing might be? Did it tell you anything at all about where it might sleep?"

Preston's gaze shifted to the younger man's face and he said quietly, "I should have killed it as soon as I knew what it was.

"Vanity," he continued after a moment. "It understood me well enough to appeal to my vanity. One of the deadly sins, isn't it, Father?"

"Oh yes," he assured Preston.

Nick said nothing to all this, but waited. Outside the window, he noticed the sky over the Atlantic had begun to redden— a thin crimson line at the far side of the ocean. The unpleasant aroma of institutional food wafted its way into the room mingling with the smell of carbolic cleansers. Nick felt the threat of nausea.

"The only thing I can recall," Preston resumed without inflection, "is something about a house with wings—he said he liked those."

"Wings…" Nick repeated, "… are you sure?"

"Yes, that's what he said, but I think he might have been referring to windmills."

"Windmills…?"

"There used to be a number of them in the county, they were used as grist mills in the days before electricity. You forget," Preston lapsed into his more usual lecturing tone, "there was a lot of Dutch influence in this region during the colonial period, but so far as I know, the last of them collapsed ages ago and it was a ruin even then. I think I read it was in the 1890s."

Sitting back in his chair, Nick replied, "Interesting… but not very helpful."

"May I add my own thoughts here?" Father Gregory asked from his position by the window. Both men turned to look at him. "As Preston instructed us as to windmills, I recalled the vampire's words when kneeling at the Tabernacle. He said," Father Gregory paused for effect, "'I listen… .'" The other men stared at him. "These words had little meaning to me until now. I assumed that he listened at windows like a thief in the night. But when our professor reminded us of the history of this county, I recalled that Our Lady of the Visitation Church began at the site of a derelict mill, just as he described—the original part of the building being constructed on the foundations of the mill itself! This was told to me by none other than Monsignor Mulcahy.

"The miller donated the land to the early church here out of the goodness of his heart, though he was not even Catholic... remarkable, don't you think?"

"Yes, yes," Preston said. "Come to the point, for God's sake!"

"Have I not done so?" Father Gregory appeared perplexed. "I believe he is dwelling somewhere in the church itself—even he is drawn to the worship of God, though he cannot know Him, poor creature! I would imagine that he is hiding somewhere in the cellar—from there he can listen quite well to all that goes on above him."

Nick and Preston looked at one another as a voice at the door said, "I'll bring the car around front." It was Beckam.

"Do that," Nick agreed, then said to Father Gregory and Preston, "You two come with me."

Fanny suddenly gasped in her sedated sleep, startling the men. Outside, the widening red eye of the distant sun cast its first shadows of the day.

๛

Nick knelt to examine the padlock that secured the entrance to the church's cellar. Showing no signs of tampering, it rested undamaged against the twin metal doors that lay almost flush to the ground. He looked up at Father Gregory whose dark face was impassive in the fading grey of the new dawn. The priest shrugged while Preston looked on. The hinges appeared unmolested as well.

Nick saw Beckam approaching them from the rear of the church. As he neared, the young officer announced with quiet urgency, "I think I've found the way he gets in."

Nick stood, feeling the blood rush from his head as he did so. Father Gregory seized his arm in a steadying grip. "You have exhausted yourself, Chief Catesby," he observed.

The senior policeman said nothing in reply, following his subordinate to a small window built into the foundation at the rear of the church. It, like the others that had been installed long ago, was meant to provide light and, if necessary, ventilation to the basement rooms of Our Lady. In a nod to the times, all were screened by metal grates bolted into their concrete casements. Kneeling, Beckam pulled it away from the window, holding it up for his superior's inspection. "The window isn't locked either, boss."

Nick could see at a glance that none of the men present could fit through the small aperture, not even the diminutive Father Gregory. It would only accommodate someone the size of a slender child. The glass was dusty and smeared, but Nick noted that no cobwebs had grown over it. The next nearest lay behind a cloud-like mass of spun quivering fibers, the rising sun captured in dozens of dewdrops trapped within it. Behind the filthy glass the cellar remained obscure, as precious little light penetrated the darkness within. Clearly, someone… or something had made use of the window Beckam had discovered. It was crafty of Gabriel to have left the cellar doors intact, Nick thought—he was a clever creature.

"Beck, stay here and stand guard over this window. If that thing comes out… kill it."

The younger man, even paler than usual in the weak morning light, nodded in agreement while unlimbering his gun with the ease of much practice. He let it rest against his thigh in an easy grip and stood as casually as a man waiting for a bus. "Don't worry, chief," he said.

Hurrying back to the other two men, Nick pointed at the lock. "Father, if you would do the honors."

The priest knelt with a grunt to fumble with the ring of keys he had brought from the rectory, finally succeeding in opening the hasp after several attempts. Nick reached down to pull him away from the doors. "I'll go first, Father." He, too, now produced a .45 semi-auto from its holster.

Scurrying back a few steps, the little priest threw open first one door, then the next, to clang against the cement foundation that supported them. A gust of dank air rose to greet them, bringing with it the smell of damp earth, moisture, and the underlying scent of things that crawl in dirt and darkness.

"If he's in here, he already knows we're around. Right, Professor?" Nick asked. Preston nodded in reply. "So there's no point in pussy-footing around with this thing—you two wait here." He made to descend the slick-looking steps that led into the belly of the church.

"I will accompany you, Chief," Father Gregory announced. "As I am a priest of this parish and responsible for this church, I must insist."

"Me, too," Preston croaked, his throat and mouth gone dry, as much from fear as from nearly twelve hours without a drink. "I discovered this horror and I want to see it destroyed—after what it's shown me, I have to see it die… it's my right."

Nick regarded both men from the corner of his eye while scanning what little of the cellar was revealed in the early morning light. The floor was of packed dirt, dark and oily-looking. Numerous objects appeared to lean into the dim light of the open doors: plaster saints draped in stiff robes, faces chipped and faded, old cabinets long ruined by the damp, and a pensive Saint Joseph clutching a plank of wood and a hatchet, a hole where once he had sported a nose.

"You're certain that there's no way into the church from the cellar, right?" he asked Father Gregory in a quiet voice.

"Absolutely certain," the priest replied.

"Let's go, then," Nick said, descending the stairs. The two older men followed a few steps behind, the old wooden steps creaking with the weight of the three. "There's a light switch?" Nick asked.

"Ah, yes," Father Gregory replied. "It is just to your left, if memory serves. I've only been down here a few times before, I'm afraid... I never liked it."

"Really," Nick chuckled. "I can't see why... it's so cozy." He felt the switch and flicked it up. The length of the cellar was now illuminated by a few bare bulbs smothered with ancient dust. The shadows grew and obtained density with the coming of the weak, yellow light. The farthest from them winked off and on like a beacon... or a warning, Nick thought. Just beyond it was the window behind which Beckam waited like a patient hunter.

Waving the older men behind him, Nick began to advance very slowly along the makeshift corridor created by the ecclesiastical cast-offs: discarded and broken pews, stained, musty furniture, a crucifix bearing a bloody Christ-figure too gruesome to suit the current fashion. As Nick's gaze slid from object to object so went the barrel of the gun. It occurred to him that Gabriel, if he was in the cellar, was awake and watching them from somewhere within the shadowy jumble. He felt beads of sweat forming along his hairline even in the cool dampness.

From amidst a nest of soft moldering materials covered in dust and dotted with mouse droppings, Gabriel did, indeed, watch their approach. He peered through the semi-darkness at ankle level with the intruders, his pupils gone great and black. He felt a rumble deep within his gut, recognizing the fear that wanted to escape in a snarl, but remained silent. He understood the terrible danger of the gun that was clutched in the big man's fist, while behind and above him his pricked ears defined the threat of the human waiting outside—he grasped at once that he was trapped and that the jaws of this trap were quickly closing.

He recognized the largest man as well, remembering their brief violent encounter as Gabriel had tried to sup on Preston Howard's daughter. In all his long life, it had never occurred that a man had been successful in laying hands on him before that night, and the memory of the strength in his grip and the pain it inflicted flooded his senses with terror. Gabriel voided his bladder onto the stinking cloth he crouched upon.

Behind the silhouetted men the doors to the outside world remained thrown open, but this was of little use to him as he could see the strong sunlight that had begun streaming in with the rising sun. Even if he could somehow escape past the hunting men without grievous injury, he would be rushing out into a brilliant world in which he would be virtually blind and helpless, the terrible sun exposing him in its cruel brilliance. He watched the steady approach of the men with the thunder of his own blood sounding in his head.

Preston noticed it first as they neared the sputtering bulb, his long patrician nose wrinkling in disgust. "He's near... I smell his damned musk, its unmistakable!"

Gabriel heard and understood the professor's words just as the humans did, but was powerless to control the reaction that caused them. Like any animal, his instincts governed him, and when he grew frightened or ardent, his musk gland opened to emit the chemical that befuddled both prey and pursuer alike.

Glancing over his shoulder at Fanny's father, Nick asked, "Where is it coming from... can you tell?" To Nick it appeared to emanate from the very air around them. Already he could feel his palm growing sweaty, his vision beginning to blur.

"No... not exactly," Preston hissed. Snatching up a wooden curtain rod that lay propped against a forgotten chair, he began to jab the pole into the debris piled to either side of them. "But he's close, I know that much... the little bastard is watching us!"

"Don't get in front of me," Nick warned.

A stack of children's chairs clattered to the floor as a result of Preston's efforts, and both men lurched back to avoid being struck.

"Goddamnit, Preston," Nick cursed.

"Please, gentlemen… language," Father Gregory admonished in a frightened whisper.

Nick saw a movement in the shadows from the corner of his eye. "Quiet," he commanded, "there's something over there!"

A shadow had detached itself from the rest, but now remained so still and motionless that it was easy to believe that it had been there all along. The stench grew.

The toppling of the classroom chairs had forced Gabriel to move or be struck and injured. Now he waited for what might happen next, his lean body as still as any of the sculpted saints he shared the cellar with. He could see the faces of the men who wished to harm him—frozen masks of fear and terror—they were not sure that he stood before them. Gabriel's breath froze in his throat.

"Is that him?" Nick breathed.

"Shoot it… shoot it for Christ's sake!" Preston demanded.

All Nick's training forbid the use of deadly force without provocation, and this shadow offered none. In fact, was it the creature at all? His thoughts felt blurry and indistinct and the odor was overpowering—the idea of lying down and resting a moment occurred to him.

Suddenly the window that Beckam was guarding was thrown open and the younger man's face appeared, "I heard shouting." Sunlight haloed his head, illuminating that corner of the room.

Gabriel was no longer a shadow, but stood exposed to his pursuers. He remembered the ancient wound to his breast as he stared wild-eyed at Nick's pistol. Catching sight of the black-frocked priest, his mind raced through all he had learned from listening to the humans and their worship.

Falling to his knees, he raised his long hands together above his head, his grappling hook fingers tented in an attitude of prayer. "Do not let them kill me, Man-of-God," he cried out with passion. "Did not the Creator make me as surely as you?"

The creature's words hung in the fetid air—a challenge to their common decency, an unmistakable plea for mercy. His words struck them all dumb, all but Beckam. "Shoot him, Chief, you've got a better angle than me."

Nick felt his aim drifting, his thoughts coming apart like an old cobweb. Beckam had said something, but he couldn't quite grasp the meaning of his words.

Crawling on its hands and knees now, the creature came toward them, pleading for its life. "Is the sheep guilty of eating grass, or the wolf its meat?" he wailed. He reached the little priest, prostrating himself before him. Stroking Father Gregory's shoes with his filthy talons, he cried, "Am I to be crucified for the appetite God gave me, Holy Man?"

Father Gregory gasped at the creature's touch, scuttling backwards. Undeterred, Gabriel resumed crawling, dragging his belly across the dirt and bleating words he did not truly understand, though his fear was genuine enough. Once or twice his eyes flickered toward the big man with the gun, noting his confusion, his hesitancy. "May I not have sanctuary, Father?" he pleaded. "Will you let me be murdered in God's church—at the feet of Christ Himself?" He raised a shaking arm to point at the bloody, torn figure watching from his worm-riddled cross.

"Kill it," Preston mumbled thickly. He, too, was starting to wilt, and he grasped an upright beam to steady himself. "Hurry…"

As if from very far away, Nick heard Beckam's voice, "Boss…?" His words floated dream-like into the damp cellar. "Boss, don't let him get between you and the others." There followed a pause, then, "Do you hear me? He's getting into the middle of you all, Chief. Neither of us will have shot if you let him do that."

His last words seemed urgent and Nick turned to gaze dully at the speaker, but all he could see was Beckam's silhouetted head framed in the small window. He should come in if he's got something important to say, Nick thought tiredly; otherwise, he should stay quiet… it was distracting… annoying, really.

Father Gregory found himself gazing up at the crucified God just as Gabriel had done and the creature once more reached his feet. "*You* drink blood, holy man," he whispered, "don't deny it, for I have watched you drain the chalice and heard your very words day after day." Gabriel tilted his large head in an effort of memory while rising slowly to his knees. "This is my blood which will be given up for you," he lisped, "the blood of the new and everlasting covenant. It will be shed for you, and for all, so that sins may be forgiven—do this in memory of me." He held aloft his own great hands as if gripping the chalice, smiling, his owlish eyes closing in a parody of beatitude.

The priest looked down on his yellowish eyelids in dawning horror, the memory of their encounter at the Eucharistic devotion returning to him in snatches of disgust and loathing. He took one more step back to create some distance between him and the unnatural beast. Gabriel followed on his knees like a medieval penitent. Holding out his filthy hands to the little priest once more, he pleaded, "Is there no mercy for such as me, Priest of Christ?"

"Man was created in God's likeness," Father Gregory managed at last, fighting the mesmerizing effects of Gabriel's presence, "so that we may honor Him. You… your kind," he continued, as his words and thoughts returned to him, "have followed us somehow, acquiring our features and likenesses along the way… even our speech, which you now use wickedly to preserve your own life."

Gabriel shot an angry sideways glance at the man with the gun, gauging his chances… there were mere feet between him and the life-threatening weapon. He could snatch the pistol away and kill the big man within moments in his present state, he thought. The other two he would slaughter at his leisure as they were old and weak. The young one outside troubled him however and caused him to hesitate. The priest raised his voice and Gabriel swung his baleful gaze once more to him.

"You are *not* human," Father Gregory accused Gabriel, attempting to rouse his compatriots as well as himself, "but blasphemous and unnatural! You were never meant to make the same journey as man, but followed nonetheless, skulking in the shadows, a child of darkness!" Placing a foot into the creature's chest, he shoved it onto its back. "Chief Catesby, strike now!" he commanded the policeman.

Gabriel struck the packed dirt floor with an expression of outraged surprise on his pallid face. "You will die first," he hissed, his jaw unhinging even as he spoke. Leaping to his long furred feet in a single blinding motion, he seized the fleshy throat of the priest, his yellow nails drawing blood at every point they touched.

Even as his great mouth fastened over the pulsing throat of the curate, Nick stepped forward in an almost casual fashion, placed the pistol into Gabriel's left armpit and pulled the trigger. The creature's violent movements had, at last, defined the target he had been waiting for in his befuddlement.

Screeching, Gabriel leapt back, clutching the neat hole beneath his arm, his lower jaw snapping back into place. His large eyes surveyed the men arrayed before him, as a tremulous howl erupted from his throat.

Within this echoing cry the men heard and recognized the great aloneness that only such a creature as Gabriel could suffer and give voice to—incapable of mercy and compassion, he expected none from those that walked in the light. With gouts of his own dark blood pumping between his awful fingers, he dropped to his knees with a pitiful whining, then fell over onto his side and, at last, lay still. The silence that followed rang with his cry like a thousand bells.

After several moments of shocked immobility, Father Gregory, touching his unpierced throat, managed to say, "Thank you, Chief Catesby… that was most timely."

Nodding, Nick took a step in the direction of the thing that he had just killed. In spite of all the differences that appeared so glaring at close quarters, he was unable to shake the feeling that what lay at his feet might be human after all. He felt his legs begin to shake.

Gazing down at the slain creature, he saw a face that, up-close, was bestial, and this gave him some comfort. Gabriel's features were large and exaggerated, only meant to be examined at a distance where they might pass for a fellow traveler. Closely scrutinized, the glittering eyes, just visible beneath the lowered lids, were cold and merciless as the space between the stars, the nose too broad, the nostrils distended.

The ears, protruding from the filthy tangle of hair, were overly large as well, obviously adapted for nocturnal hunting, their interiors as convoluted and complex as a dog's. But it was the wide reptilian mouth that branded him undeniably as something other than human. Nick recalled with perfect clarity its terrible loose gape, the jumbled yellow teeth, and the obscenely red, thick, snake-like tongue, that he had glimpsed as the creature fastened onto the priest. With a shudder, he stepped away again.

Preston spoke from the shadows, "He has two hearts… he's forgotten that he told me that." The older man emerged from the darkness still wielding the wooden rod, which he promptly broke over his knee. Hoisting it above his head in the same moment, he poised the jagged end above the creature's right breast.

Gabriel's great eyes flew open as Preston's shadow fell upon him and he threw up his long arms to seize him. But his previous wound had slowed him and the old man was the quicker this time, driving the stake through his rib cage with a sickening crack of bone and deep into his second, and secret, heart. Though his claws raked Preston's shirt into bloody tatters, these were the throes of true death, and with a great shudder he died, his death being followed by a long, final exhalation. His killers stood round him in shocked, bewildered silence, but for Preston's exhausted panting. "There," he gasped, "I've done it… he's dead, by God!"

They witnessed no changing, no sudden dissolution, no crumbling to dust, just the sad, ugly corpse of a misshapen boy spread-eagled in a pool of his own black and stinking blood.

A shadow fell over the three men gathered in the twilight dawn of Our Lady of the Visitation's cellar, and Officer Beckam remarked, surveying their work, "That took some doing."

Panting with exertion, Preston replied, "You have a gift for understatement, young man."

"Listen," Nick turned to Beckam, "give the prosecutor's office a call and get them down here. Tell them they'll want to bring one of the M.E.'s investigators, too."

"You're heading back to the hospital?" Beckam asked.

"The three of us are… she needs us more than they do right now. You can tell them where to find us. Besides, they're going to have enough of a puzzle on their hands with this body before they even think about interviewing us."

Beckam hesitated, "You sure you want to leave them this … this thing? What if they believe it really is a boy… a human, I mean? Do you think they'll understand what's happened here?"

"Why not just bury it and be done with the goddamned thing?" Preston interjected.

Nick threw him a glance, then answered Beckam's question, "The autopsy should settle what it is. In any case, Beck, I've never been a very good liar. We'll just have to let the evidence take us where it will."

Turning toward the sunlight that was now streaming down the distant stairs, he added, "Don't worry, Beck, you have nothing to worry about out of this. You did everything right and I appreciate it."

Beck smiled faintly, saying, "I'm not worried about me, Boss. I just wish you'd think of yourself here… this could get very ugly."

Preston snapped, "Don't be an idiot, there's a shovel right over there!"

"Our chief is a very courageous man," Father Gregory chimed in. "God and Saint Michael will not abandon such a man, I am thinking."

"Oh, no doubt…" Preston agreed.

The priest smiled at Nick, "Come, good man, Fanny is waiting for you."

CHAPTER THIRTEEN

Fanny knelt to retrieve the large turkey from the oven, the mouth-watering aroma filling the room and steaming the windows. She was careful to protect her red velvet dress from possible stains by wearing a full-length apron. This was seasonally festooned with tiny Santa Clauses driving their reindeer pell-mell across a starry sky.

Two strong hands grasped her small waist as she bent to her task, pulling her away. She arose to find Nick, looking very dashing in a blue wool blazer, white starched shirt, and red-patterned tie.

"Sir," she protested, attempting to escape his grip, "I have a dinner to serve and you are becoming a nuisance!"

Leaning down to nibble her neck, Nick tugged her more tightly to him. Only the slightest trace of her wounds remained.

"I'll have dessert first," he murmured while inhaling the perfume of her body. He snugged her rump against him. "I have developed a terrible sweet tooth since I've met you."

Fanny felt the unmistakable evidence of this, but persisted, "You only get dessert *after* dinner in this house… and only if you've been a very good boy!" Freeing herself, she swatted him with an oven mitt. "Now then, take these," she flung the second one at him, "and get that bird out of the oven. And be careful not to spill any of the juices onto my floor!"

Pulling the mitts on with a sigh, Nick bent to his task.

From the dining room her father called out, "Fanny, that damned kitten of yours is shredding my cuffs! Can't anything be done about this beast?"

"No," she answered. "He'll grow out of it, but until then you'll just have to put up with it."

Nick had given her the kitten just the month before, a rescue from the pound that bore an uncanny resemblance to her beloved Loki—even his bad behaviors were reminiscent of his predecessor and she would tolerate no interference with his happiness.

Preston said something more, the words not clearly audible, but the intent plain enough all the same.

"You'll go before he does," Fanny promised her father in return. The complaints ceased.

Nick set the large turkey onto the oven top in preparation for placing it onto a serving dish, being careful of his sleeves. He caught Fanny studying him from the corner of his eye. "What?" he asked. "Did I mess it up?"

She stared at him for a moment longer before saying, "Everything is going to be all right now, isn't it?"

"Yes," he answered. "I think so… In fact, I know so… *now*." Drawing a long envelope from his inside jacket pocket, he extracted a letter from it. Fanny could see the county prosecutor's letterhead at the top of the paper. Nick held the folded corre-spondence out to her, but she just stared at it, shaking her head.

"Please," she asked, "just tell me what they've decided."

"The prosecutor considers the case closed… exceptionally cleared, is the proper term."

"I don't understand, Nick. What does it mean?"

"Officially, it means that the case has been closed and that no further actions will be taken without additional evidence. Unofficially, it means that neither your dad nor I will be facing any charges. In fact, the prosecutor's not even going to call a grand jury to consider them."

Fanny's long thin hands flew to her face, "Oh Nick, that's so wonderful! What a wonderful Christmas present for us all!" She paused to catch her breath, growing thoughtful once more. "But why, Nick? What decided him? At first, I thought he was going to try and hang the entire thing on dad and charge you with the death of that… that… creature. What changed his mind?"

Smiling, Nick answered, "You can't charge someone with homicide if you don't have a dead person… and they didn't. It was just like I thought. The autopsy blew everything out of the water. No matter which way they came at it, the results were al-ways the same… the corpse, or in this case, the carcass, was not human. Even the DNA results were conclusive on that much… if nothing else.

"That's what's taken so long with all this. The M.E.'s Office just couldn't let it go. They even farmed out the remains to Rut-gers's Medical College and still came away no wiser. In fact, the prosecutor told me the whole thing has become an embarrass-ment for all concerned. Add to that Megan and the boys' stories, at least what they could remember, matching our own, and there just wasn't anywhere to go with the case—exceptionally cleared." He snapped his fingers. "I am fully restored as the chief of police and Preston is no longer a suspect. I have it all in writing. And as an added bonus the prosecutor gave Weller the choice of resigning or facing charges over the flyers—guess which he did?"

"Does dad know all this yet?"

"I thought I'd let you tell him at dinner."

Crossing the few steps separating them, Fanny put her arms around Nick's neck, reaching up to kiss him. He returned it with feeling. When their lips separated at last, he said, "You've been a very good girl, I think, so why don't you just whisper in old Saint Nick's ear what you'd like most for Christmas."

Fanny leaned back and thought for just a moment before doing as he asked. Nick's eyes widened as she pulled away. "Well now, that's a tall order little girl, but I'll just see what can be done, and if we don't get it right the first time or two, we'll just keep at it till we do."

Arching an eyebrow at him, she answered with a sly smile, "I'm gonna hold you to that, mister," then flicked him with a dish towel. "Now get that turkey into the dining room and no more tricks! There are hungry men in there!"

Nick hoisted the heavy tray, mumbling, "Yes ma'am," and did as he was told.

Preston sat up from something he had been doing under the table.

"You're not annoying Rastus, are you?" Fanny asked.

Preston answered without meeting her eyes, "It's the other way around, daughter. You're demon cat is making it his life's mission to harass me."

"Good," said Fanny as Nick set the platter down onto the center of the table.

"Marvelous," Father Gregory murmured, folding his hands over his plump belly. "Truly a marvelous bird, is it not, Preston?"

"If you say so," Preston agreed. He tugged at the starched collar and the stricture of the tie that he had grown unaccustomed to wearing. "Of course, anything appears good after you've been kept waiting for hours on end."

The priest laughed at this remark as if it was the best of jokes. Preston cast him a sour look and snapped, "Did I say something funny?"

"You have a wonderfully dry sense of humor, my good friend."

"Oh dear God," Preston cried. "Why don't you make yourself useful by opening the wine... we're perishing for the lack of drink, you know."

"Please do us the honor, Father Gregory," Fanny chimed in. "And disregard the cranky man opposite you—he's a heathen."

"But, God's heathen, I think," the priest smiled as he popped open a bottle of chardonnay and began to fill the glasses. "A man at war with God is a man who acknowledges God."

"Dear Lord," Preston moaned, raising his hands in supplication. "Deliver me from this foreign priest's endless moralizing, I beg you." He turned to glare at Father Gregory, saying, "There, now you should be happy—I've said a prayer at last."

Waggling one of his long fingers at his new friend, Father Gregory replied, "No, no, I must insist, you are good man, Preston Howard, and an instrument of God, as you have so ably demonstrated—it was you that He chose to meet the devil and best him. You cannot refute the truth of this."

"I can and do... it was the *devil* that chose me... so there!"

Fanny interrupted the debate, "Would you please give us a toast, Father? I think daddy will be a little more agreeable once he's had a glass of wine."

"Oh no, thank you," Father Gregory declined. "It is more appropriate that my good friend, Preston Howard, lead us in the Christmas toast. He is the head of the household and its most senior member, is he not?"

Fanny smiled, answering, "I'll agree to the most senior part in any case."

Shoving his chair away from the table, Preston rose to his imposing height, summoning all his previous professorial authority. The glass trembled ever so slightly in his right hand. "Sometimes the priest gets it right," he grunted. "In any event, if I'm ever going to be allowed a drink I guess I must take matters into my own hands."

He paused, appearing to give the subject of his toast some thought, then looking down at the three people who were gathered at his daughter's table, commanded, "Raise your glasses," and seeing this done, continued, "To my daughter, Fanny, who never tires of forgiving, because she cannot stop loving, and to Nick Catesby, valiant police chief and local hero, who has won the heart of the lovely Fanny Howard and the gratitude of her disreputable father." He paused to smile at the couple in a rare show of public affection.

"And speaking of fathers," he went on, "Lift your glasses in praise of Father Gregory Savartha, charlatan of distant lands, whose impractical and improbable faith nonetheless awes while not informing." The priest smiled broadly at Preston's words, nodding in agreement. Preston added, "This little man, against all reason, has become our True North, our own Christmas Star by which we steer."

Father Gregory interjected, "Now you have gone too far… the first part of your speech was the more accurate."

Preston waved him away. "Quiet! I am the toastmaster here, am I not?" He didn't wait for agreement but went on, "To all of us gathered here, not for reason or for gain, but only out of a misguided affection for our fellow man—good on us!"

Bringing the glass to his parched lips, he drained it without further ado. The rest repeated his final words in a lusty chorus, then happily followed suit.

❧

Almost a year after his death, the remains of the creature were returned to the Wessex County Medical Examiner's Office for disposal. As it had been repeatedly opened, and samples of all its tissues and organs obtained, it was of no further use and would in the normal course of things face cremation. Yet, the M.E. hesitated over this very final method.

In spite of her long years of experience, the creature presented an enigma and a challenge that had proved insoluble. And in the back of her mind, in spite of all that had been learned, a fear flickered in the darkness, a terror of misidentification—what if it *was* human after all? Of course it would be a freak of a human… but what if, somehow, it was? A missing link, if you will. What if, someday, someone came to claim the pitiful remains? After a week of mulling this possibility over, she decided against cremation and handed the body over to the undertaker for a pauper's burial.

Having been told nothing of the history of his new charge, the mortician secured the burial site and ensured that the examiner was made aware of its exact location. He stitched the odd-looking boy back together, placing him in a simple wooden casket, and laid him to rest with the other indigent dead in the old cemetery he had once frolicked in.

He was not given a headstone, but an inexpensive plaque set into the earth above his head. As the undertaker had been told neither his surname nor the dates of his birth and death, it read simply, "Gabriel—an unknown boy."

THE END

ABOUT THE AUTHOR

David Dean's short stories have appeared regularly in *EL-LERY QUEEN MYSTERY MAGAZINE,* as well as a number of anthologies, since 1990. His stories have been nominated for the Shamus, Barry, and Derringer Awards and "Ibrahim's Eyes" won the *EQMM* Readers Award for 2007. His story, "Tomorrow's Dead", was a finalist for the Edgar for best short story of 2011. He is a retired Chief of Police in New Jersey and once served as a paratrooper with the 82nd Airborne Division. His ground-breaking horror novel, "The Thirteenth Child," is now available through Amazon, Barnes and Noble, and Kobo Books.

Made in the USA
San Bernardino, CA
26 October 2014